GHOSTS
of
HAVANA

ALSO BY TODD MOSS

FICTION

Minute Zero

The Golden Hour

NONFICTION

*Oil to Cash: Fighting the Resource Curse
through Cash Transfers*

*The Governor's Solution: Alaska's Oil Dividend
and Iraq's Last Window*

African Development: Making Sense of the Issues and Actors

*Adventure Capitalism: Globalization and
the Political Economy of Stock Markets in Africa*

GHOSTS

of

HAVANA

~~~~~~~

TODD MOSS

G. P. PUTNAM'S SONS | NEW YORK

PUTNAM

G. P. Putnam's Sons
Publishers Since 1838
An imprint of Penguin Random House LLC
375 Hudson Street
New York, New York 10014

ISBN 9780399175930

Printed in the United States of America
1 3 5 7 9 10 8 6 4 2

Book design by Gretchen Achilles
Map by Jeffrey L. Ward

AUTHOR'S NOTE

Ghosts of Havana is entirely a work of fiction, but the story draws on true historical episodes and was partly inspired by my real-life experiences working inside the United States government. When I first began conceiving of a thriller about the U.S. and Cuba, I assumed that, after more than half a century of frozen relations, there was little prospect for change. Boy, was I wrong. In December 2014, the White House surprised the world by announcing steps toward normalization with Havana, proving yet again that even the most intractable foreign policy logjams can break at any time. And that what comes next is always unpredictable.

For where your treasure is,
there will your heart be also.

—MATTHEW 6:21

Success is what succeeds.

—McGEORGE BUNDY,
National Security Adviser, secret memo to the President
one week after the Bay of Pigs, April 24, 1961

War is always hell, but Florida seemed worse.

—MICHAEL GRUNWALD
on the Second Seminole War (1835–42) in *The Swamp*

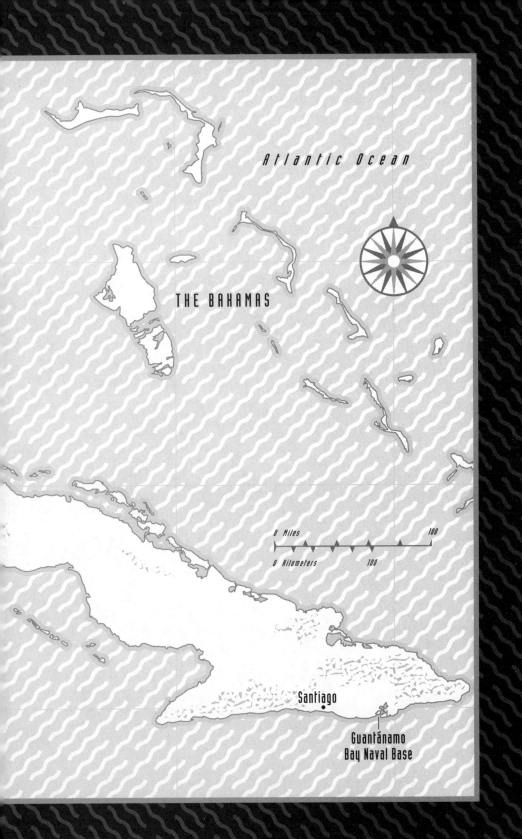

Atlantic Ocean

THE BAHAMAS

0 Miles   100
0 Kilometers   100

Santiago

Guantánamo
Bay Naval Base

GHOSTS

of

HAVANA

PROLOGUE

Pirates don't drive minivans, dammit!"

Alejandro Cabrera was about to reply when he heard the first shot.

Booosh!

"What's that?" Dennis shouted, whipping his head around.

The hollow explosion was followed by an accelerating whistle and, after a momentary pause, a loud splash just off the bow.

The four middle-aged Americans all hit the deck of *The Big Pig*, a white sportfishing boat with a pink stripe along its side.

"*Mierda,*" Alejandro hissed.

"What's happening, Al?" Dennis whined, lying on the floor and covering his head.

"Cubans," Brinkley said matter-of-factly.

"Cubans? Holy cow!" Dennis screamed. "Why, why, why?"

"What the fuck have you gotten us into, Al?" Crawford clenched his teeth.

"Probably MGR," Brinkley offered, his cheek pressed flat against the boat deck.

"MGR? What the fuck is that?"

"Marina de Guerra Revolucionaria," Brinkley replied as calmly as he could. "The Cuban navy."

"I told you we were over the line! I freaking told you we were over the line!" Dennis shrieked.

"Goddamn bonefish," Crawford growled. "We're gonna get killed over a goddamn bonefish."

"We are in international waters, gentlemen. There's nothing to worry about," Brinkley tried to reassure his friends. "Everybody stay calm."

"*Hijo de puta!*" Alejandro spat.

"Holy cow . . . Holy cow . . ." Dennis muttered to himself, his voice quivering.

"Calm down, Deuce," Crawford said. "What do we do now, Brink?"

Brinkley Barrymore III picked himself up and peered cautiously over the side of the boat, which was rocking gently on the ocean swell. He squinted toward the horizon through a pair of high-powered binoculars. The sky was starting to turn a blue-pink in the late sun. "There," he said, pointing off the stern. Brinkley tossed the binoculars to the much larger man next to him. "Craw, give me an assessment and an ETA."

Crawford Jackson caught the binoculars and, in one smooth motion, raised them to his eyes.

"Al, get down below. The radio's in the hold. Call our friends for help. Let them know we've been intercepted."

"*The Big Pig* is my fucking boat, Brink!" Alejandro snapped. "I'm the captain. I say we hit the engine and run for it."

"You want them to shoot at us?"

"I've got more horsepower," Alejandro said. "This baby can outrun anything MGR has on the water."

"Dead astern, naval patrol boat approaching at high speed. Cuban flag," Crawford announced.

"Negative. We're not running from the Cuban navy," Brinkley said. "It's not the prudent move."

"I don't surrender." Alejandro scowled. "Cabreras never surrender."

"Al, who knows what other ships are out there? And planes?" Brinkley said. "We aren't running."

"ETA: three minutes," Crawford said.

"We are just fishing, gentlemen," Brinkley insisted. "There's no need to escalate."

Alejandro removed his Miami Marlins baseball cap and rubbed his goatee.

"This is not the time, Al. Go down below. Call our friends. And take Deuce with you," he said, pointing at Dennis, lying frozen on the deck.

"I don't like it," Al said, putting his cap back on and licking his lips.

"They're still approaching at full speed," said Crawford.

"Now, Al!" Brinkley raised his voice for the first time. "You have to call *now*."

"*Puta!*"

"Two minutes," Crawford announced.

"Deuce, get your ass off the floor and go down below to help Al. Do it now." Brinkley was trying to contain himself. "This is no time for one of your panic attacks."

"This is a perfect time for panic." Dennis looked up, his

face flushed and his eyes already red. "What am I gonna tell Beth?"

"Now, Deuce!"

Alejandro pulled on Dennis's arm. "What does Brink mean by 'intercepted'?" Dennis asked. Al ignored the question, and the two men scampered down the steps to below deck.

The boat's radio erupted with Spanish chatter. *"Barco no identificado! Pare! Ustedes se encuentran en las aguas nacionales Cubanas! Pare!"*

"Ninety seconds," said Crawford, binoculars glued to his eyes. "And they're armed."

"Es La Marina de Guerra Revolucionaria! Pare!" the radio blared.

"This is *The Big Pig*," Brinkley spoke slowly into the radio. "We are American civilians. We are fishing. Just fishing. Over."

"Pare! Prepárense para ser abordados!"

"No Spanish. *No hablo español.* We are just fishing. Over," he repeated.

"One minute," Crawford said. "They aren't slowing down."

Brinkley hollered down to Alejandro. "Have you called yet? You've got one minute!"

"Yes I fucking called them," Alejandro appeared in the companionway, gripping an M16 assault rifle.

"What are you doing, Al?"

"I'm not going back to Cuba," he said, raising the gun barrel toward the approaching boat.

"Are you crazy? Throw that overboard. We can't take on the Cuban navy. Throw them *all* overboard."

"What 'all'?" Crawford lowered the binoculars. "What the fuck is going on here, Brink? Al?"

"I don't surrender." Alejandro bit his lower lip and aimed the rifle. "I told you Cabreras never surrender."

"Lower that weapon now!" Brinkley ordered. "Throw them all overboard. You're giving them a reason to shoot us. *We are just fishing.*"

"Why the hell do you have an M16 on your fishing boat, Al?" Crawford clenched his two fists in anger.

Rat-a-tat-tat-tat-tat! the deck exploded in a line of gunfire. The men hit the deck again.

"Fuck! Fuck! Fuck!" Crawford hissed.

"Stay calm, everybody," Brinkley said.

Dennis appeared in the stairwell with a small arsenal of weapons. Crawford's eyes widened as Dennis began throwing guns into the ocean: another M16, an AR-15, two pistols.

"No!" Alejandro shouted.

"What the fuck is going on here, Brink?" Crawford demanded.

"Deuce, no!" Alejandro lurched toward him too late. Just as Dennis dropped the last pistol over the side of the boat, his body suddenly convulsed, a bright red stain oozing across his back. Dennis Dobson pitched forward and fell into the rolling blue sea.

"Man overboard!" Crawford shouted. Brinkley threw a lifesaver over the side just as Crawford dove headfirst into the ocean.

"Pare! Pare!" bellowed the loudspeaker on the approaching vessel. The fishing boat was raked with more gunfire.

Crawford reached Dennis, floating facedown in the waves, and spun him onto his back. "I've got you," he gasped, trying not to swallow seawater. Crawford tucked his arm under his friend's neck and grabbed the lifesaver's rope with his free hand. "I've got you, Deuce."

"Beth!" Dennis gurgled. "Beth!"

Brinkley pulled in the rope, ignoring the Cubans who had stopped shooting and were now circling the fishing boat like a lion stalking an injured gazelle.

"*Puta,*" Alejandro hissed, flipping his weapon into the sea and raising his hands. He stared ahead with dead eyes as the patrol boat pulled alongside. The deck of the larger ship was lined with Cuban soldiers, all aiming weapons at the now-unarmed Americans. The setting sun bathed the naval ship in a soft, calming pink light.

Brinkley dragged Dennis onto the deck and applied pressure to the wound. Crawford hauled himself back on board, raised his hands, and then collapsed on the deck, panting, out of breath.

Alejandro, his hands still raised high, waved his baseball cap at the soldiers and forced a smile. "Just fishing, *señores.*"

PART ONE

~~~~~~~~

THIRTY-SIX HOURS

EARLIER

1.

Judd Ryker opened one eye and winced at the clock. *Five-thirty.* The good news was that he had slept through the night. And he was home. *My own bed,* he thought, feeling the cool clean sheets as he stretched his legs.

As Judd cleared the jetlag haze from his mind, the conversation of the previous evening flooded back into his brain. *Was it a dream?*

Judd rolled his head and Jessica came into view. His wife was still sound asleep, breathing softly, a slight, satisfied smile on her lips, an expression of gentle relief on her face. He watched the contours of her mouth and listened to her lungs, a comforting rhythm of inhale and exhale. Yes, Jessica was asleep. *And they were both still here.*

The night before, Judd had returned from Zimbabwe, a grueling twenty-two-hour journey that had provided him far too much time alone with nothing but his thoughts. Too much time to think about his latest assignment on behalf of the Secretary of State and how it all had unfolded. It had all come together just a bit too smoothly, a touch too succinctly. Judd's mind ran through the events—the downfall of Zimbabwe's dictator; the election of a new, hopeful democratic leader for that shell-shocked country; a murderous Ethiopian general dead, the victim of a premeditated campaign of revenge—all good results, but . . .

It had required a thick dollop of good luck. *A suspicious amount of good luck.* And so, too, had his previous mission three months earlier to rescue an American ally in the West African nation of Mali.

Judd knew that luck was random. Luck was *always* random. Before he'd arrived at the State Department, he had been a professor at Amherst College, a number cruncher, a leading expert at teasing out patterns in data to uncover what was really going on. And, like any decent scholar of statistics, Judd knew that randomness always—always—washed out in the end.

So, somewhere over the Atlantic Ocean, wedged into a middle seat in row 64 of a South African Airways Airbus A330, Judd Ryker had finally admitted to himself the only possible way it could make any sense at all. The source of his luck could only be . . . *Jessica.*

His wife never conceded what she did, *exactly.* She never spoke the letters *CIA*, never said the word "spy," never mentioned anything about operations or cover. But she didn't have to.

Zimbabwe, Mali. How far back did it go? Was their whole relationship, going back to their very first meeting in the Sahara Desert eleven years ago, *built on a lie?*

Judd should have been furious, he knew. His wife—his most trusted confidante, the mother of his two children—had been deceiving him for years. She had always been private and a bit of a loner. He accepted that. It was one of her attractions. But now he knew that she had been playing him like a puppet master. Worse, if Jessica had manipulated him into an unwitting role in a political assassination in Zimbabwe, then his own wife had tricked him into murder.

As jarring as these realizations were, Judd marveled to find that he wasn't upset. Once he pushed through the confusion, he was, deep down . . . grateful.

Who had ever heard of a college professor running his own special one-man team inside the U.S. government? It was ridiculous, he now knew. Judd's experiment at the State Department, his Crisis Reaction Unit, the baby he had created from scratch, had been *set up* to fail. How could he have expected to succeed without help, without some hidden hand? How could Landon Parker, the Secretary of State's powerful chief of staff, who had created S/CRU and hired Judd, not have known this, too?

Lying in the warm comfort of his bed, Judd realized his world was suddenly turned upside down. But he wasn't angry, because, on the most essential issue, Jessica had been utterly convincing. While he was only now learning her true identity, he still believed that their marriage, their family, their life together, was all real. *Her love was real.*

Jessica's big brown eyes opened.

"Hey," he whispered.

"Hi."

"You sleep?"

She nodded. "You?"

"Yeah. I think so," Judd said.

"Are we still . . . good?" she asked.

Judd paused. "Uh-huh."

"I'm glad we got it all out in the open last night."

"Me too."

"It's better this way," she said.

Judd scooted over in the bed and kissed her softly on the lips.

"Better," she repeated. "I feel . . . free."

"Me too," Judd said.

"But, Judd"—she shook her head—"what are the new rules?"

"Rules? Can't we just be honest with each other?" Judd started to feel sick. "Isn't that what last night was about? Finally coming clean?"

"Not possible, sweetheart," she said. "I think you know that."

"Then let's just promise to stay out of each other's business."

"Also not possible," she said. "We're too good a team. If there's anything to learn from the past few days, it's that."

"Okay," he sat up. "So what are the Ryker family rules of engagement?"

"I think we need three."

"Three? You've already thought a lot about this, Jess."

"Of course I have. Rule one is easy: *Assist*. We help each other. That's been working so far. I think we can achieve a lot by working together. I'll help you with S/CRU and you can help me rebuild my career once I'm active again."

"Rule one is *assist*," Judd nodded. "Fine. Agreed. What's next?"

"Rule two is *avoid*. We can help each other but let's not work the same issue. I can help you on your problem. You help me on my problem. *But we don't play each other on the same problem.* Got it?"

Judd exhaled. "*Avoid*. Okay . . . makes sense. What's your last rule? Does it start with an *a*?"

"Of course it does. Rule three is *admit*. If we find ourselves somehow forced to compromise on rules one and two, we have to be open about that. *We have to tell the other*."

"No more lies?" Judd asked.

"No more lies," Jessica said.

"*Assist. Avoid. Admit* . . . Those are your rules of engagement, Jess?"

"Yes," she nodded. "Do you agree?"

"Do you think rule three is really necessary, Jess? It's a big world. Lots of problems. What are the chances that we both find ourselves working on the same country *again*?"

2.

Not dead yet."

"I know that, goddammit," swore the Deputy Director of Operations. "I don't give a frog's ass about El Comrade Jefe. We know he's staring at the ceiling and drooling all day. He's still eating and shitting through a tube, right?"

"Yes, sir," said the team leader, a tall, muscular man with a flattop brush cut.

"So fuck El Jefe," the Deputy Director scoffed. "If he's out of the game, then we focus squarely on his little brother. El Comrade Presidente controls the security forces, secret intelligence, and the Party. So we aim our sights on ECP. You got that?"

"Yes, sir. ECP, sir." Around the windowless room, a dozen heads, a mix of men and women of different ages, all nodded.

"So what's the latest on his medical prognosis? When's El Comrade Presidente going to start pushing daisies?"

"We have no indications of ECP having any specific health problems, sir."

"How's that possible?"

"He takes Mexican generics of Lipitor and Levitra," one of the analysts offered.

"Christ! He's got cholesterol and can't get his dick up? That's it?" A thick vein, like a lightning bolt, appeared on his forehead, never a good sign for the team in front of him.

"Other than vitamins, yes. That's it, sir."

The Deputy Director aggressively rubbed his bald head. "Don't these Cuban fuckers ever get sick and just die? What the hell do they eat down there? How old is he now?"

"ECP just turned eighty-six, sir."

"Christ!" He wiped his hand on his pants. "Are we sure there aren't any more brothers? Are we sure their mama didn't have some other half-brother spawn hidden in the jungle? Is there some goddamn cousin waiting to come down from the Sierra Maestras to play Jesús when we least expect it?"

"No, sir. No cousins. Not as far as we know."

"Fine," he exhaled. "So, then, who's next on the list?"

"You mean the successor to ECP, sir?"

The Deputy Director's face fell lifeless, his eyes dead and his jowls drooping low. This was a common reaction from the long-time intelligence chief, a sign his staff recognized as a prelude to an explosion of anger. "That's the whole fucking purpose of the Caribbean Special Projects Unit!" he shouted. "That's why you're here and not pumping gas at some strip mall in Leesburg, god-dammit! That's why you're all here!"

"Sir—" The team leader cleared his throat. "Sir, we have no clear successor to ECP identified."

"No one at all?"

"We believe the Communist Party leadership has kept succession deliberately in the dark. It's a tactic to prevent factions and infighting. If no one knows who's next in line, then everyone stays in line."

"I don't care what the fucking Cuban politburo knows or doesn't know. But we are the C-I-fucking-A. We should know. That's our job. That's *your* job."

"Yes, sir."

No one spoke up.

"What about O?" the Deputy Director asked.

"Oswaldo Guerrero?"

"That's what I asked. *What about O?*"

"Oswaldo Guerrero is their military intelligence chief in charge of running counter-destabilization operations. He—"

"I know who O is! He's the fucker who keeps embarrassing *this* goddamn team. He's why all our people keep getting killed. O's the reason Operation Rainmaker failed." The Deputy Director made a fist and ground his teeth.

"Sir, we still don't know much about him." The analyst rifled through a stack of papers. "Oswaldo Guerrero, trained in Moscow, new-generation intelligence officer, we believe he's connected to the Party, the army, the navy—"

"I know all that, goddammit!"

"Here's the only confirmed image we have, sir," the analyst said, holding up a grainy photo of a dark-haired man with a small, gentle face, the sole discernible feature a crooked broken nose.

"He looks innocent," the Deputy Director whispered. "But he's the Devil."

"Yes, sir."

"O is the goddamn *Diablo*!" he said, his voice rising again.

"Yes, sir. That's what we call him in the Caribbean Special Projects Unit. El Diablo de Santiago."

"So that's why I'm asking," the Deputy Director said, trying to calm himself down. "Is O . . . Oswaldo Guerrero . . . El Diablo . . . whatever the fuck we call him"—he jabbed his finger between the eyes of the face in the photograph—"Is this man next in line to run Cuba?"

"We . . . don't know, sir."

"Well, then, is he a recruitment target? If we can't beat him, can we turn him?"

"The HUMINT asset assessment is negative. Human Intelligence sources suggest he's a nationalist. Loyal to ECP. Raised through the commie schools and clubs, recruited early, now a lifer. He's a true believer."

"Pshaw!" the Deputy Director scoffed. "True believers. I don't think there are any pure idealists anymore. Everyone's got a weakness. Even our man O."

The Deputy Director started to pace the room, his staff clearing a path.

"So, what's our leverage?" he asked. "He's got to have something hidden. Everyone does. What're his anxieties? What's his fetish?"

"We haven't found anything. Our past attempts to plant—"

"Fuck me," the Deputy Director interrupted and held up his hand. The room fell silent while he rubbed his head again. After a moment, he stopped, then scanned the room and made eye contact with every member of the Caribbean Special Projects Unit. "Those Girl Scouts over at the State Department may think they can snuggle up to ECP. That Cuba will change if we just play nice and pretend foreign policy is about friendship circles. We can shake their hands, let them hug the Pope, even allow them to host POTUS for goddamn tea and biscuits. We can stick our fucking heads in the sand. But the United States of America hasn't surrendered to that pissy little island yet. In this building, we still know who those communist bastards really are."

"Yes, sir."

"I want a list of all potential successors to ECP, with an assessment of their recruitment potential and some leverage points on each one. I want to know who they are, what they dream about, where they shit, and what they think about when they jerk off. And I want this by the end of the day!"

"Today, sir?"

"That's what I said! You think I called you all to the office before dawn by accident?"

"Is there some special urgency we should know about, sir?"

"Cuba is going to blow up. It could be any day. It could be any minute. Things are heating up in Havana. They are ready to explode in Santiago."

"Explode, sir?"

"I can feel it. Everything looks calm, but underneath the surface Cuba is a tinderbox. The only thing missing is the spark."

3.

Full boat. Jacks over sixes." Brinkley Barrymore III gently laid down his fan of cards. The total lack of satisfaction on his face aggravated the other three men even more.

"*Hijo de puta!*" hissed Alejandro Cabrera as he threw down his cards and took a healthy swig of his rum and Coke.

"Captain Barrymore, you are one lucky motherfucker," Crawford Jackson said. "Was your ass born in butter?"

"Yes, it was!" Al said. "His mother gave birth to him right into a big silver bowl of *mantequilla*. He's been swimming in that shit ever since."

"Jealousy is an ugly sentiment, gentlemen," Brinkley said, sweeping up the poker chips. "Thou shalt not covet." He plucked a Cheez Doodle from a bowl in front of Al and popped it into his mouth. "That's God's word."

"The Bible says you're not supposed to covet your neighbor's house," Dennis Dobson said. He scanned his friend Brinkley's newly renovated basement, outfitted with a sixty-five-inch high-definition television, stainless steel fridge, full bar, billiards, and the centerpiece: a bright-green-felt-topped professional poker table. "But I sure as heck would rather live here in your man cave than my place."

"Thank you, Deuce," Brink said, holding up his cocktail. "I can always give you my contractor's phone number."

"Fuck you, Brink," Al snorted.

"I can't believe we played poker all night again. Beth is gonna kill me. I've gotta go home," Dennis whined, looking at his watch. "Heck, I've gotta go to work."

"Too late," Alejandro said. "You can sleep tomorrow. We're playing another hand. Deuce, go get Craw one more beer."

Dennis dropped his shoulders. "I'm too old for this."

"Michelob Ultra," Crawford said, flashing a thumbs-up.

"How do you drink that piss?" Al sneered. "Deuce, make me another Bacardi and Coke. And none of that diet shit. Give me the real thing."

"Got to watch my weight. I'm running the Marine Corps marathon at the end of this month," Crawford said, standing up and flexing both biceps. "Navy SEALs got to represent." He kissed each of his muscles and sat back down.

"Cheers to that, Commander." Brinkley raised an empty tumbler.

"Brink, what are you having?" Dennis asked.

"Gin and tonic, please. With a slice of lime. Thank you, Deuce. So kind."

Dennis Dobson disappeared behind the bar.

"Well, I don't covet your house, Brink," Al said.

"Good for you, Alejandro."

"I do covet your wife, though." A wide grin was smeared across Al's face. "She's one fine piece of ass."

"I'll be sure to tell Pippa you said that, Alejandro. I'm sure she'll be honored that her daughter's soccer coach is dreaming about her."

"Oh, Brink, I'm not asleep when I'm thinking about her," Al said. "I'm usually wide awake and I'm—"

"All right, Al, enough," Crawford interrupted. "I don't want to hear any more about your jerking off."

"Are you saying you've never rubbed one out while thinking about the honorable Mrs. Pippa Barrymore?" Alejandro flopped an arm around Brinkley's shoulder. "Come on, Commander Jackson. Haven't you seen Pippa in that yellow sundress?"

"I'll be sure the dress is ritually burned in the morning," Brinkley said, deadpan.

"Can we get back to playing poker?" Crawford said, shuffling the deck. "Deuce! Where are those drinks?"

Al kissed Brink on the cheek. "I'll burn her dress for you."

"Yes, I'm sure she'd appreciate that."

"U8 championship coach," Alejandro said, flopping back into his chair with a grunt.

"Excuse me?" Brinkley tilted his head.

"You said I was your daughter's soccer coach. I'm clarifying that I'm the under-eight girls' *championship* soccer coach. I know that's what you meant to say."

"Deuce! Where are those goddamn drinks?" Crawford shouted.

Dennis arrived with the tray of beverages.

"Good Lord! Just in time," Crawford snatched his Michelob.

"Why do you let him talk to you that way, Brink?" Dennis asked. "I mean, geez, doesn't it get to you?"

"At Annapolis, Brink never got worked up," Crawford said,

dealing the cards. "He was unflappable. Even the cadet hazing never bothered him."

"No, sir," Brinkley said with a mock salute.

"One time, senior midshipmen burst into our room in the middle of the night," Crawford recounted. "And they stuffed us into duffel bags up to our necks and held us out the third-story window. I was screaming my head off. One of the guys pissed himself. But you know what Brinkley did?"

"What?" Dennis leaned forward in his seat.

"Just dead in the face. No emotion. No expression. No fear."

"No kidding?" Dennis said.

"Total zombie face," Crawford said.

"Zombie face—I like that," Dennis said. "You ever use that move in court, Brink?"

"All the time," Brinkley said, peeking at his cards.

Alejandro glanced quickly at his cards and announced, "I'm all in."

Brinkley cocked his head, studying Al.

"I'll bet you used your zombie face to buy this house," Dennis said.

"No wonder people hate lawyers," Al said. "Fucking zombie-McMansion, little-dick lawyers."

"I'm in," Brinkley said. "Call."

"I'm out," Dennis conceded, flipping his cards into the middle of the table.

"Me too," Crawford said. ". . . Al, why're you such an asshole?"

"It's what makes me such a good real estate agent," Al smiled. "Don't blame me that Brink has to compensate for his little pecker with a trophy wife and this bullshit trophy house."

"Didn't you sell him this house, Al?" Dennis asked.

"Let's just play poker, gentlemen," Brinkley said.

"Yeah, I made a big fucking commission on this dump. How else could I afford my fishing boat?" Al smirked.

Crawford flipped over five cards.

"Flush," Brinkley whispered.

"*Puta!*" Alejandro erupted. He threw down his cards and drained his drink.

"Darn, you're lucky, Lord Brinkley Barrymore the Third," Dennis shook his head. "Why does the rich guy always win?"

"I'm not the rich guy," Brinkley said, "Al is."

"Shut the fuck up!" Alejandro barked, lowering his eyes.

"Come on, Al," Dennis pleaded, "how many houses can you sell?"

"Oh, he's not rich from selling houses," Brinkley said. "Don't believe that for a second."

"I don't want to talk about it," Alejandro said.

"Go on, Al," Brinkley insisted, "tell them. Tell them about the diamonds."

"Diamonds?" Crawford sat up.

"Fuck you, Brink," Alejandro said.

"Come on, Al! I'll make you another Bacardi," Dennis offered. "Really, how on earth are you rich? How do you have diamonds?"

"I don't," Al said. "My family has money. Or, my family *had* money. That's true. But I can't touch any of it. I've never even seen it."

"Never seen it?" Dennis scowled.

"Not one dime."

"How's that?" Crawford asked.

"Commies."

"What?" Dennis and Crawford exchanged looks of confusion.

"Nineteen fifty-nine," Al said. "My grandfather had a diamond-trading business in Cuba when Fulgencio Batista's government collapsed and everyone had to flee before the commies took over Havana. My family had to leave everything behind to get to Miami. They buried the diamonds underneath the house."

"Holy cow, Al!" Dennis said.

"That's unbelievable!" Crawford said.

"Tell them the rest." Brinkley poked Alejandro in the ribs.

"*Mi abuelo* is dead now. *Mi padre,* too. But the diamonds are still there. In a lockbox beneath the house."

"How many?" Dennis asked.

"Plenty."

"You know where it is?" Dennis was leaning all the way forward.

"Sure."

"You have a map? You have a *treasure* map?" Dennis's eyes widened.

"No," Alejandro said, tapping his temple, "it's all in here."

"So, why can't you just go get it?" Crawford asked.

"It's now a fire station. Goddamn commie firefighters walking around every day on top of my family fortune. They have no idea."

"Wow. A real-life treasure chest full of jewels. Just sitting there in Cuba," Dennis said. "I'm impressed."

"And you know where it is," Crawford said, shaking his head.

"Yep, I know exactly where it is."

"Let's go get it!" Dennis said. "I'm up for a treasure hunt."

"Yeah, me too," said Crawford. "Let's go."

"We can't get it." Al shook his head. "Not yet. Maybe one day."

"Tomorrow we can wave at your family jewels from a safe distance," Brinkley offered.

"Tomorrow?" Crawford and Dennis asked in unison.

"Yeah, we're flying down to the Florida Keys tonight after work," Alejandro said. "*Mi asere* Ricky's got *The Big Pig* moored at Marathon."

"What the fuck is *asere*? Is he your bitch?" Crawford and Dennis clinked their beers.

"Oye!" Alejandro scowled. "*Asere* is Cuban for 'amigo.' What are you, stupid?"

"Relax, *asere*."

"Fuck you. Brink and I are going marlin fishing at first light tomorrow. *The Big Pig* is down in the Keys. Ricky's got it all ready for us. You two should come."

"Tonight?" Crawford shook his head. "I've got work."

"Me too," Dennis said.

"Work?" Alejandro laughed. "Craw, whatever bullshit you are up to at Carderock can wait. Take a few days off and come down with us. It's *marlin*, brother!"

"The Naval Surface Warfare Center might disagree with you, Señor Cabrera."

"I thought you're retired. You're not even real Navy anymore." Alejandro threw a pretzel at Crawford's head. "You're a goddamn consultant."

Crawford ignored the taunting.

"And I know that Deuce can come," Alejandro said. "All you techie start-up boys love to play hooky. Sit around on beanbags and drink coffee and shit. You're in for marlin fishing, Deuce."

"I can't," Dennis said. "I've got a deadline."

"You're telling me that some app you're writing for kids to watch porn on their iPhones can't wait until Monday?" Al jeered.

"It's not porn. It's not even an app," Dennis said. "You don't know anything about what I do."

"I know that tomorrow you're fishing for *marlin*, Deuce." Alejandro held out his hands as wide as he could. "They're bigger than this! And they fight like hell!"

"It's cybersecurity. I've told you, like, a hundred times," Dennis huffed. "I design software for unbreakable scrambled communications."

"We don't care," Al replied. "You're going marlin fishing."

Crawford and Dennis shook their heads.

"You really should come," Brinkley said. "It's good fun. And you should see Al's fishing boat."

"*The Big Pig*," Crawford chuckled. "Is that you or your boat, Al?"

"I've got to go shower for work," Dennis said, standing up. "Cash me out."

"Fuck that, Deuce." Alejandro laughed to himself. "It's barely six o'clock. I'm buying back in and it's your deal." He pushed the cards toward Dennis. "You don't need to go home. Play one more hand, then call in sick and go take a nap. You're going marlin fishing, *asere*."

4.

Nice work, Ryker."

Judd looked up from his desk, which was covered with a mess of intelligence reports and diplomatic cables. "Thank you." Landon Parker was standing in his doorway. Judd pushed the papers into piles. "I wasn't expecting you, sir."

"Sorry to surprise you, Ryker."

"It's your building."

"Yes, it is, Ryker," Parker said with a satisfied smile. "I came to congratulate you. Good outcome on Zimbabwe. The old man is gone, and I'm hearing positive things about this new Gugu . . . something."

"Gugu Mutonga."

"Yes, that's her. I don't know how you pulled it off, but good work."

"Thank you, sir. I had a lot of help. Ambassador—"

"Don't be so damn gracious, Ryker. I know Tallyberger had nothing to do with it. You got it done. S/CRU got it done. I'm glad to see my confidence in you is starting to pay off. I think people are finally seeing that S/CRU gets results."

"Thank you, sir."

"We still have work to do, Ryker."

"You have a new crisis assignment?" Judd raised a sheet of paper scrawled with bubbles and arrows. "I'm still working on breakthrough scenarios for Egypt and Angola—"

"Whoa, Ryker! Slow down."

Judd dropped his diagram.

"Egypt is being run by the White House. No space for you to get involved there," Parker said. "Why are you bothering with Angola? That's not a country on my radar. Is there an opportunity coming?"

"I don't know. That's what I'm trying to figure out," Judd said, holding up his paper again. "Angola is a closed oil state. Same president in power since 1979. It looks calm, but I think there's instability under the surface."

"Are they approaching"—Parker grinned and leaned forward—"*Minute Zero?*"

Minute Zero was what had just happened in Zimbabwe. It was Judd's concept, his label for the moment of great uncertainty after a shock hits a country. It could be a hurricane or a surprise invasion or the death of the president, anything big and unexpected that causes a seemingly stable political system suddenly to collapse. Minute Zero was when anything could happen next— and so it was the time to act, to shape events the way *you* wanted them to go.

In the past few days, Parker had become a big fan of Minute Zero, which thrilled Judd, but he had to admit, "Angola already had their Minute Zero and we blew it."

"*We* blew it?"

"In '75. After the Portuguese pulled out, anything could have happened. But we backed the wrong guy. He talked a good game about killing communists and even drove an old Cadillac around the battlefield. But our man was quickly wiped out with the help of the Cubans. And the same Marxist party has been in control ever since." Judd waved his paper, "I'm trying to figure out our options today. If Minute Zero arrives once again in Angola, how do we avoid losing a second time?"

Parker grunted. "I don't want you wasting time on Cold War history, Ryker. It's a new age. Hell, we're even making friends with the Cubans."

"Yes, I know that, sir."

"That's what I've come to talk to you about, Ryker. I'm going to need your help with Cuba."

5.

This hearing shall come to order," announced the chair, banging down the gavel to quiet the room.

The dark wood paneling, the high vaulted ceiling, and the elevated seating for the members of Congress gave the appearance of a royal court. But the audience suggested something far less majestic. The seats were swarming with anxious bureaucrats in dark suits, pock-faced interns in ill-fitting button-downs, tourists in tacky, bright-colored T-shirts, and a small band of exhausted journalists.

In the middle of the hearing room, the epicenter for the action, was the committee chair's seat, which was now occupied by a short woman in her early sixties, well-tanned, dark hair cut in a classic Washington, D.C. bob. Her face was leathery and a little too taut for her age, but the scars were professionally hidden behind her ears. Just behind the nameplate that read MS. ADELMAN-ZAMORA, the chairwoman loudly hammered her gavel again.

"This is a special open hearing of the House Permanent Select

Committee on Intelligence. I have called this hearing so the United States Congress and the American people can learn more about intelligence failings that have continued to hamper the global march of freedom and democracy."

Brenda Adelman-Zamora scanned the room over the rims of her reading glasses before continuing to read her opening statement. "The Founding Fathers of this great nation wrote in our Declaration of Independence that 'all Men are created equal, that they are endowed by their Creator with certain unalienable Rights, that among these are Life, Liberty, and the Pursuit of Happiness. That to secure these rights, Governments are instituted among Men, deriving their just powers from the consent of the governed.'"

She placed her paper down and looked straight into the television cameras. The nine-term congresswoman from Florida's 22nd District was a political pro. Brenda Adelman had grown up on Long Island on the fringes of the powerful political machine of Rockland County. Witnessing the mass migration of her elderly Jewish relatives from New York to the Southern states, she, too, moved with her political ambitions—and built an impressive congressional career on the magic formula of the South Florida triple defense: Social Security, sugar subsidies, and Israel.

Brenda had been less successful in romance, however. She'd hastily married an ophthalmologist of Cuban descent. They quietly divorced after only a few months and the episode appeared to have had little impact on her life. The political benefit of a hyphenated last name was, however, substantial. Becoming a champion of democracy in the Caribbean bolstered her hawkish foreign policy credentials—and turbocharged her fund-raising capabilities across South Florida.

"Consent of the governed," Adelman-Zamora lectured. "Those words have meaning. We as a nation believe in democracy and freedom. We defend these values at home and we promote these values abroad. This means we must fight against dictatorship and repression, wherever it may rear its ugly head. That is the destiny of the United States. Freedom and democracy are interwoven into our values and ultimately into our national security. And that brings us to our topic of this hearing this morning.

"A principal task of our intelligence services is to monitor and analyze the political forces of tyranny. We cannot defeat an enemy that we do not understand. We rely on the capabilities of the great men and women who serve our country in the intelligence services to look underneath every rock, to listen in the dark corners, to unearth the secrets of our enemies so that the march of freedom can resume. However, too often we have failed to foresee change coming."

The chairwoman returned to her written text and continued, "We did not predict the Iranian revolution coming in 1979 and we continue to fly blind on political change in Tehran. We did not foresee the collapse of the Soviet Union and we have been unable to foresee new Russian aggression. We have repeatedly missed the signs of new threats to the state of Israel, our most important democratic ally in the Middle East."

Chairwoman Adelman-Zamora removed her reading glasses and sighed deeply for the cameras. "And most obvious of all, our neighbor to the south has been imprisoned by tyranny since 1959. That once-proud nation should be a close American ally. It should be an engine for prosperity in our hemisphere. Instead, our long history of failure to bring liberty to a country just ninety miles from our own shores is an affront to free people everywhere. Our missteps are a lingering embarrassment for these great United States. Today, we are continuing to fail freedom-loving people around the world by the misguided policy of our own administration. Despite the ill-advised steps by the State Department to embrace dictatorship and apologize for oppression, our neighbors remain locked in chains. I have called this special hearing today to ask a simple but vital question: *How are we still losing Cuba?*"

6.

The red file taunted the Deputy Director. He snatched the folder labeled OPERATION RAINMAKER and threw it across the room. It flew like a Frisbee for a second before the papers scattered everywhere and floated down around his office like snowflakes.

"Dammit," he swore to himself. He grimaced at the tall pile of files on his desk, a catalog of every covert operation by the Central Intelligence Agency against Cuba since the revolution in 1959. OPERATION TASMANIAN DEVIL, OPERATION PANDORA, OPERATION DEMON BARBER, OPERATION PIT BOSS, OPERATION BANANA SUNRISE. *This mountain is a pathetic collection of history,* he thought. *A graveyard of bad ideas.*

On the very bottom was a file much fatter than the others. He extracted OPERATION ZAPATA, tipping over the rest of the folders into a fan on his desk. As he opened the thick ZAPATA file, he winced as his chest tightened. The first document was a memo summarizing the Agency's most embarrassing fiasco, the April 17, 1961, botched invasion by CIA-supported Cuban exiles at the

Bay of Pigs. The memo to the CIA Director had been by Randolph Nye, the Deputy Director of Operations during the height of the Cold War. Nye was the man who had occupied this precise office, this seat. *His seat.*

Nye had accomplished many things that the world would never know about, but he had died a year ago, unredeemed. Quiet victories in Egypt, in the Congo, in Mexico, and in the Philippines. But the world would always remember the black eye of the Bay of Pigs. The air cover wasn't approved. The ammunition ran out. The weather turned. The cash never arrived. Everything had gone wrong on that day.

Randolph Nye was now gone, but his ghost lived on in these walls, thought the Deputy Director. He wouldn't allow that to happen to him. He wouldn't allow that to happen *again.*

The intelligence game had changed so much. After the failings of 9/11, the United States' multiple intelligence services had been reorganized. Instead of the clarity of a CIA Director leading America's secret information-gathering and covert operations, a new super Director for National Intelligence was created to advise the President on all intelligence matters and to oversee all sixteen U.S. intelligence agencies, including the CIA. The DNI was suddenly above the CIA Director, a new player in town and a new layer between the CIA and the White House. To compensate for this slight, the boxes were shuffled and renamed in Langley, too. The Deputy Director of Operations, the person responsible for global covert operations, was renamed the Director of the National Clandestine Service.

In a classic Washington move, the elevation in title was actually a demotion. He believed this was political theater and text-book ass-covering, the kind of bureaucratic crap that he had grown to despise about Washington, D.C. Just like the incessant meddling from Congress, the politics of management was a growing distraction from the real work of fighting America's enemies. And a further erosion of the CIA's preeminence.

So when he was eventually promoted to run covert operations, he insisted that they call him by the old name, the Deputy Director of Operations. That was the great Cold Warrior Allen Dulles's title, too, before he became CIA Director. A lesser title on paper, but a symbolic nod to better times and older ways of doing things. And he had made a bargain with himself to make it all worthwhile.

The Deputy Director closed the Operation Zapata file and randomly opened another. This outlined an aborted attempt in the 1960s to poison El Jefe's cigars. The next file detailed a bungled attempt to add an undetectable toxin to the Cuban leader's aftershave. Another plot had planned to induce paranoia and psychosis by lacing his coffee with LSD via a tainted sugar cube. A fourth scheme made covert payments to bribe his security guards into turning their guns on their leader. They had accepted the cash but never pulled the trigger.

None of these operations had worked. His predecessor Randolph Nye had let America down. And let down the brave Cuban people.

The Deputy Director sighed to himself, knowing that, decades later, he was still letting them down. All nineteen successors between Nye and the current occupier of this office had let them down, he thought. The Deputy Director knew he now had access to more money and more technology than anything Nye could have ever imagined. Yet the same old men, the same ragtag rebels who had seized Havana in 1959, still ran Cuba. The island was in a prison and part of the blame lay squarely on him.

It wasn't for lack of trying. The Deputy Director had green-lit operations to spark street riots by creating false bread shortages, to disrupt the banking system by implanting a virus in the central bank's computers, and to plant misinformation in the local newspapers about luxury homes in the Spanish Costa del Sol owned by top Cuban politicians. He had provided seed capital to Cuban exiles in Costa Rica to create a SMS text network about the Miami Marlins baseball team that was a cover for organizing social protests on the island.

His boldest PsyOps gamble was to launch *AeroLibre*, a high-altitude plane to beam television broadcasts into Cuban homes. The Deputy Director had even signed off on a Top Secret plan to create BesoPeso, a new electronic currency that could be used to evade the control of the Cuban authorities and, if necessary, pay off potential friends in Havana without drawing the notice of the U.S. Treasury.

None of these plots had had the desired effect. None had even made a dent in the Cuban armor. Cuban intelligence had countermoved each scheme. They jammed *AeroLibre*'s signal. They uncovered and blocked his phantom BesoPeso. Oswaldo Guerrero had found a way to choke his every move. The Devil of Santiago had to be the luckiest bastard on earth, he thought. Or, perhaps, the man known as O was actually the smartest.

The Deputy Director collected the files again into a neat pile and carefully aligned the corners. He plucked every page from

OPERATION RAINMAKER off the floor and returned it to the top of the pile. Then he sat back in his chair to clear his head. The long list of Agency failures was an embarrassment. He didn't want to end up like Randolph Nye. He didn't want the next man sitting in this chair to muse over *his failings*.

Most Americans had long forgotten about the fight for Cuba. Hell, most Cuban exiles in Florida had given up, too. Inside the Agency, there were only a few Cold Warriors left, only a few old men like him that even remembered the competition with the Soviets and what it really meant to wage war for freedom. The chess games they played in Poland, Romania, Chile, Angola, Vietnam, Nicaragua. The current generation didn't even think about communism. They studied Arabic and Pashtun and Mandarin. They wrote computer algorithms and tracked terrorist bank accounts and flew satellites and built biometric databases.

Worse, the civilians at the White House and over in the State Department were going soft. They were surrendering our goals in the Western Hemisphere for the sake of taking the easy path on Cuba. No one worried about old communists on a tropical island anymore. They were only too happy to ignore history for the sake of expediency. To just roll over and pretend history didn't matter. That freedom didn't matter. The administration he served, like most of the country, was willing to just give up on Cuba. Open the embassy, exchange ambassadors, do the POTUS whitewash tour. Close our eyes and take a victory lap. Pretend everything was just normal. Nothing to see here, amigos. It made him sick. But he wouldn't abandon the Cuban people.

The Deputy Director just needed a fresh idea. He needed to spark something. To break the regime. To rally the crowds. The Cubans just had to want more than what brain-dead El Comrade

Jefe and his little brother El Comrade Presidente could offer. This could be redemption for Randolph Nye and for the Central Intelligence Agency. This could be *our* historical triumph. The Deputy Director cracked his knuckles as he thought of how, after so many decades of American failure and humiliation, he could be the man finally to break Cuba free.

But how to ensure that Operation Triggerfish wouldn't merely join the other flops sitting on his desk? How would he outflank Oswaldo Guerrero this time? The CIA's Caribbean Special Projects Unit was no match for O. He knew that wouldn't do. He would need his best people to make Operation Triggerfish succeed. To free Cuba and to redeem history, he would need no one less than his very best.

He knew exactly who to call.

7.

Cuba will be the Secretary's legacy," Landon Parker declared. "That's why I'm worried."

Across the coffee table from Judd Ryker sat the Assistant Secretary for Western Hemisphere Affairs Melanie Eisenberg. As the top U.S. diplomat for Latin America, she was known as a determined, sharp-elbowed veteran of Washington, D.C. elite circles.

Parker had asked Judd to join this meeting with Eisenberg in his private seventh-floor office to talk about the State Department's unfolding Cuba strategy. Judd knew from turf battles past that Eisenberg wouldn't welcome his presence this morning. But since the topic was Cuba, her top policy priority, she would humor the chief of staff. Moreover, she wouldn't want any disasters derailing her ambitions—or her next Senate confirmation hearing.

"We've looked like blind, bumbling fools in Cuba," Parker continued. "For my entire life we've been embarrassed by Havana thumbing its nose at us from across the Straits of Florida. But this administration has committed to fixing U.S.-Cuba relations once and for all." Parker began counting on his fingers. "We've removed most of our sanctions. We've taken Cuba off the blacklist of state sponsors of terrorism. We've restored diplomatic relations and cut ribbons on shiny new reopened embassies. The president's visit was a tremendous success. After so many years of failure, it's all finally happening." Parker opened his arms wide. "That's why I'm worried."

"Landon, relax," Eisenberg said, with a casual familiarity that Judd found out of place for the State Department headquarters. "My next round of talks is supposed to set a timetable for free and fair elections and resolve the status of our naval base at Guantánamo Bay. Our Cuba legacy plan is right on track. It's going better than we even could have ever hoped."

Parker frowned and shook his head.

"Are you saying the Secretary isn't happy?" Eisenberg asked. "I just had breakfast with her this morning and she didn't say a thing."

"It's not the Secretary."

"The White House?" Eisenberg's face flushed. "Is the NSC meddling on Cuba again? Do I need to call Tony and rip him a new one?"

"No, it's not them. It's me. I've been in this job too long, I've seen too much, to believe it could be going so well. It's unsettling, Mel."

"You're upset that Cuba's too clean?" Eisenberg scoffed.

"Not upset. Wary. And that's why I've asked Ryker here from S/CRU to join us. He's been doing some fascinating work on big-data analytics for the department. He's crunching numbers to try to anticipate problems before they happen. I thought Ryker could help us today to problem-solve on Cuba."

"What problems, Landon?" Eisenberg ignored Judd. "We're following the reengagement playbook that we all agreed on. You signed off on it. You just said it's all going according to plan."

"Our side is moving quickly. But Cuba's not changing fast enough, Mel. I don't see any signs of real democracy inside the country. Do you? The same geezers are still in charge. The police are still arresting activists. The intelligence services are still suppressing the opposition. The government isn't even allowing American business to operate freely."

"This all takes time, Landon. You knew that," she said.

"Capitol Hill is getting impatient," Parker said. "They're complaining that we gave away the embassy exchange without any assurances of democratic change. Did you see Adelman-Zamora's hearing this morning?"

"Of course I did," Eisenberg said. "The Miami lobby is never going to be happy. You can't get cold feet on me now, Landon."

"Well, let me play devil's advocate for a second, Mel. What if Adelman-Zamora . . . is right? What if we're giving benefits to the Cubans and not getting much in return? Now that we're locked in to normalization, what's our leverage?"

"Now you sound like the Cold War dinosaurs we had to fight just to get where we are. Don't tell me you're working some other angle, Landon. Is there a Track Two strategy going on here that I need to know about?"

"No, Mel. There's no second track. I'm just trying to help," Parker said.

"We just need more time, Landon. We're building trust with Havana, brick by brick."

"I don't know if we have much time. There are still too many people here in Washington and in Havana that want us to fail.

And every day that it takes is another opportunity for something to go drastically wrong."

"What are you saying, Landon?"

"I'm saying that we've bet the Secretary's whole legacy on Cuba's transition to democracy. I know it all looks smooth on the surface, but I worry there's trouble brewing. Isn't that right, Ryker?"

"There are definite signs of economic strain," Judd said. "I was just looking at the data this morning. Without support from Venezuela and Iran, Cuba's hard currency reserves are at their lowest level since the fall of the Soviet Union. There are shortages of fuel and cooking oil in some parts of the country. We are even seeing wheat scarcities."

"Wheat?" Eisenberg winced.

"Yes, prices for staple starches like wheat, corn, and rice are a leading indicator of political distress," Judd explained. "And Cuban wheat stocks are at an all-time low."

"That makes no sense. Why would wheat stocks be low?"

"No one knows," Judd said. "It's a puzzle."

"See, Mel," Parker said, "this is what I'm talking about. How are we securing a Cuba legacy for the Secretary if we don't have a clue what's going on inside the country? Are they really ready for normalization? Or are we walking into a trap?"

"Look, Landon," Eisenberg said, taking a deep breath. "The Cubans are nervous about letting go. It's understandable. Their system's been stuck in a time warp for half a century. This was never going to be all smooth sailing. You knew that."

"They still don't trust us," Parker said.

"Of course not," she said. "That's the whole point of our new strategy. To build confidence."

"Mel, do we have any signs—I mean, actual evidence—that our carrots are encouraging Havana to move toward open markets and a free democracy?"

"It's still a socialist country, Landon," Eisenberg said. "The government provides free housing, free education, free health care. It's taking time for them to open up to private enterprise."

"I thought they agreed to allow private business in exchange for a reduction in our travel and trade sanctions. Wasn't that the deal?"

"On paper, yes. But the government still owns all property and controls all wages. It's one of the issues we're working on."

"Cuba still has a maximum wage," Judd offered.

"A *maximum* wage?" Parker grimaced.

"Socialist." Judd shrugged. "Just like Assistant Secretary Eisenberg said."

"Christ," Parker huffed. "What about the recent arrests? What's the story with these police sweeps, Mel?"

"It's to be expected. The diplomatic thaw with America has created high expectations among the Cuban public. They are expecting to see money pour into the country, to see life get better right away. It's almost inevitable that progress would generate some backlash. The opposition is stirring people up, too. That probably explains the uptick in dissident chatter and the surge in police arrests. But most of the trouble has been in Santiago in the east. That part of the country has always been hostile to authority in Havana. That's where El Jefe started his rebellion. And eastern Cuba is where the opposition is strongest."

"When will we have a timetable for elections?"

"Soon."

"What about clear succession for when El Comrade Presidente eventually dies?"

"Not yet." She shook her head. "That's all part of the next round of negotiations."

"Is ECP even in control?" Parker asked.

"Yes," she insisted. "We don't see any credible challengers to him. Not from within the Party and not from the opposition."

"What about military intelligence?"

"There are some hard-liners. But we believe they will stay loyal to ECP as long as progress continues," she said.

"As long as progress continues," Parker repeated. "That's why I want Ryker here with us. His idea about Minute Zero just worked wonders in Zimbabwe. So, what about Cuba, Ryker? What do you think—"

"Excuse me," Eisenberg interrupted. "Minute *what*?"

Judd sat up straight and quickly explained the idea. "The moment of chaos after a shock. That's Minute Zero. That's our window," he said.

Parker winked at Eisenberg.

"I don't understand," she said, frowning. "We're trying to make history by thawing relations with Cuba. We're trying to keep things on track. You're talking about disruption? About *creating chaos*?"

"Minute Zero is a theory of crisis response," Judd said.

"Well, we don't have time for ivory-tower academic theories here," Eisenberg said. "We have to be practical."

"Cool your jets, Mel," Parker interjected. "Ryker knows all about the drivers of crises. And he's applied his ideas to help us in Mali last year and just recently in Zimbabwe. I'm hoping he can work his magic again and help us identify problems. To head off anything that could interfere with our Cuba policy."

"So you'd like S/CRU to identify potential risks to our relations with Cuba?" Judd asked.

"The longer Melanie's negotiations drag out, the more chances for something to go drastically wrong. What should we be most worried about? And how could we respond to the most likely problems? If the economy gets worse . . . If they get slammed by a hurricane . . . If El Comrade Presidente suddenly dies . . . I want to know how we can control events if things get crazy. Can you do that, Ryker?"

"Of course, Mr. Parker. I'll get right on it."

"How about *right now*? What do you think?"

"Right now?" Judd wriggled in his chair.

Parker nodded. "Start with the economy. What should we do?"

"Well . . . if the Cuban government is bankrupt and economic collapse is a possibility, why don't we give them a large aid package? Or an emergency loan? That would calm the markets," Judd suggested.

"No," Eisenberg replied. "Congress has our Cuba budget on a tight leash and there's no way we'd get approval to pay the government directly. What else you got?"

"What about injecting money directly into the economy?" Judd offered. "We wouldn't need the government. We could stimulate the economy through the banks."

"The Cubans still aren't allowing American banks," she said, shaking her head again. "Everything's still done through the government or in cash."

"Cash?"

"After the BesoPeso debacle, the Cubans are wary of opening up the financial sector," Eisenberg said. "That's a dead end, too."

"Ryker," Parker turned to Judd. "BesoPeso was a secret CIA program to create an electronic currency to pay off opposition groups. Cuban military intelligence uncovered and blocked it. They've got a counter-destabilization team in Havana that's still very powerful. They've beaten our guys across the river for years. Isn't that right, Mel?"

"Yes, Landon. Cuban intelligence has been one step ahead of us. That's why we are pushing the diplomatic solution. But injecting cash through the banks is out. Unless you want to drop dollar bills by helicopter, we'd need something else."

Judd stared at the ceiling for a moment while he thought. Then he pulled a sheet of paper out of his briefcase and held up a chart displaying lines rising and falling in waves. "I've been analyzing Cuban price data. The black line is the black-market exchange rate for the Cuban peso on the streets in Santiago. It's the true value of the local currency. The green line is an index of social media activity on the island that's been coded as supportive of the underground opposition. Neither measure is perfect, but they are reasonable indicators of financial stress and political sentiment. What's interesting is that they are highly correlated. When one moves, so does the other."

"See why I invited him, Mel?" Parker smirked.

"This little chart tells us . . . what, exactly?" Eisenberg asked with a wince.

"The correlation suggests that even very small amounts of hard currency, deployed in the right places, could have large effects," Judd explained. "It means that if we're smart about it, we don't need much cash to influence people in Cuba."

"U.S. dollars equal political influence," Parker said.

"In a place like Cuba, anyone controlling foreign currency is highly powerful," Judd said. "We just need to use this leverage."

"Money is power." Eisenberg wasn't impressed. "Big deal. Where isn't that true?"

"But wait." Parker paused for a moment. "I thought you just said we couldn't send money to Cuba through the banks?"

"That's right," Eisenberg agreed.

"That actually *helps* us," Judd said. "The Cuban government's restrictions on banks and their control over foreign currency make U.S. dollars even scarcer. *Even more valuable.*"

"So cash can be a powerful weapon." Parker nodded. Then he narrowed his eyes. "But how do we exploit this? What's the *plan*, Ryker?"

"I don't know yet, I've got to figure that out," Judd said. "But if Cuba has a crisis, if the economy tanks or there's a leadership vacuum, strategically deployed cash could be one of our strongest levers."

"You're suggesting we prepare for a massive campaign of bribery?" Eisenberg scowled.

"Not exactly," Judd said. "You can't just pay people off and then expect them to do your bidding. You'd need to sequence payments so your targets are always anticipating the next payout. Otherwise, they take the money and run. You pay, but you lose leverage."

"That's what we've been doing already," Parker said. "Giving away concessions and not getting much in return."

"Right. Immediate cash is never as powerful as the *next* payment. Any decent strategy must align these incentives."

"Align incentives?" Melanie Eisenberg stood up to leave. "Are we still talking about Cuba policy, Landon?"

"We need to harness greed," Judd said. "Individual greed can promote the common good. You see—"

"Is this another one of your theories, Dr. Ryker?" Eisenberg stood by the door, hands on her hips.

"It's not my theory. It's Adam Smith's."

"Adam Smith? The British economist who's been dead for, what, two centuries?"

"Smith was more of a philosopher," Judd said. "And Scottish. But, yes, him. He popularized the notion that individual motivations lead to collective good. It's the foundation for capitalism."

"In Cuba?" she growled, and turned to leave.

"Even communists respond to incentives," Judd said.

"Melanie, wait," Parker interrupted. "What are you saying, Ryker? How do these ideas help the United States in Cuba?"

"He's saying that our Cuba plan should be to hope for a hurricane and then start handing out cash." Eisenberg shook her head. "Hell of an idea, Landon, but I've got real work to do."

"How about this." Judd rubbed his hands together. "Imagine the Cuban leader died and in that same moment, when no one knows who or what comes next, we deployed suitcases of cash to the right people at the right time. We would control events. If we're smart about it, we might even be able to pick the next leader of Cuba."

"Now, *that* would be a legacy for the Secretary," Parker said, nodding.

"I don't understand why we're even talking about this," Eisenberg said. "ECP is healthy. We don't kill foreign leaders, as far as I know. And we don't have suitcases of cash to drop across Cuba. I thought Dr. Ryker was here to help us prevent problems, not invent fantasies. I've got a lunch meeting," she said, and stormed out of the office.

Judd and Parker sat in silence for a moment.

"That went well," Parker finally said, "I think."

"You do?"

"Mel's just trying to keep me out of her hair. She doesn't want anyone getting in the way of her negotiations. Me, you, the White House. But I think you're onto something, Ryker."

"Thank you, sir."

"It's not implausible that something could throw our plans way off track. ECP could die or there could be a riot that turns Cuba upside down. Something big that we don't expect that derails Mel's negotiations. That's why I want you thinking ahead about what could go wrong. And what we could do to respond."

"I'll get right on it, sir."

"Great. I knew I could count on you, Ryker." Parker stood up, indicating that their meeting was over.

Judd tilted his head to one side. "If you're really worried about the formal talks breaking down, you might want to try an old Henry Kissinger trick."

"Kissinger?"

"He always had a second communication track just in case things went wrong."

"A backchannel?" Parker sat down again in his chair.

"He wanted always to be able to reach the right people at the right time. So he could drive events and keep negotiations moving ahead."

"Ryker, let me get this straight," Parker leaned forward and narrowed his eyes. "You're saying that if things went haywire in Cuba—I mean, if our negotiations really fell apart—that your Minute Zero formula for political change in Cuba is . . . seize uncertainty, harness greed, create a backchannel? Have I got that right?"

"Yes, sir. And you'd need a replacement candidate ready to run. If things really come down to Minute Zero, you should have already bet on your horse. After the crisis hits is too late."

Landon Parker sat back in his chair and thought in silence. After a moment, he extracted a small black leather notebook from his breast pocket, scribbled a few notes, then replaced it.

"It's a hell of an idea, Ryker. Of course, I don't know how we'd produce uncertainty, we don't have suitcases of untraceable cash, and the United States government has never been able to keep secret diplomatic talks out of the newspapers. And I sure as hell don't have an off-the-shelf candidate ready to lead Cuba. With apologies to you and Adam Smith, I think we are zero for four." He smiled. "But it definitely is one hell of an idea."

8.

Aren't you going to invite your boss into the house?" the CIA's Deputy Director of Operations asked. He almost looked offended. *Almost.*

"Why are you here?" Jessica asked, holding the door tight in case she needed to slam it in his face.

"Is that any way to treat your mentor?"

"Mentor? I don't even know your real name."

"Neither does my wife," said the Deputy Director. "What does it matter?"

"You didn't answer my question," she said.

"Yes, I am your mentor. You were nothing when BJ van Hollen brought you to me. What were you going to do, run around the world and dig wells for the rest of your life? Waste all your talent on small, meaningless bullshit?"

Jessica held his gaze and didn't flinch.

He continued his rant, "I'm the reason you are where you are. I'm the reason you are running Purple Cell. I'm the whole goddamn reason that Purple Cell even exists. You can surely remember that."

"What I remember, sir, is that you suspended me," she said.

"You gave me no choice after the shit you pulled in Zimbabwe. You should be grateful I didn't fire you for going rogue."

"The question you didn't answer was, why are you here?"

His face softened. "I'm worried about you," he said.

She narrowed her eyes and gripped the door tighter. "That's funny, sir. Why are you *really* here?"

"Am I not allowed to check on my people?"

"I'm not some asset you're running. You don't need to flatter me."

"I'm here because I've got a big operation in the pipeline and I'm going to need you."

"You're reactivating Purple Cell?" She loosened her grip on the door and stifled a smile.

"Not yet. I need to let things cool off first. The building has a buzz that I haven't seen since 9/11. I know I'm going to need my best team."

"So, then, I'm still asking why are you here *now*?"

"I'm going to need you *fresh*. Your last mission, authorized or not, took something out of you. I can see it in your face, Jessica. I can hear it in your voice. In the way you're standing. You're not yourself. You're stressed-out. You're tired."

"You drove to my house all by yourself to tell me to take a rest?"

"Not a rest." He dangled a set of keys in front of his face. "A vacation."

"What are those?"

"My Florida house. In Fort Lauderdale. I want you to use it. Take a few days down there to relax. Take the kids, take your husband, go to the beach, use my boat. Nothing fancy, just a little Cobalt bowrider. You can handle it, no problem. The kids will love it." She eyed him suspiciously. "Go take a little vacation and I'll be in touch after you get back. We can talk then about reactivating your team and your next assignment."

"A vacation?"

"It's eighty degrees and sunny today in South Florida."

"What else?" she asked.

"What else *what*?"

She narrowed her eyes. "What are the strings that come with the house?"

"Can't I do something nice for my people without an agenda?" Jessica raised her eyebrows. "Okay, okay, of course there's something in it for me. I need you, Jessica. I need you to clear your head, to get right, and to come back ready to work. And if you're at my Florida house, then I'll not only know that you *are* relaxing, I'll know where to get ahold of you if something comes up. I'll know that you're not off the grid on some beach in some hellhole thousands of miles away. *That's* my agenda."

"I don't need a break, sir."

"Yes you do. Take the whole family. From what I hear, I'll bet your husband could use a vacation, too."

"Judd knows."

The Deputy Director stepped back. "He knows *what*, exactly?"

"Not everything"—she shook her head—"but enough."

"I see . . . That's too bad . . . Maybe it's for the best."

"I promised I wouldn't run him."

The Deputy Director rubbed his head for a moment and then nodded. "Seems fair. You shouldn't run operations on your own family members. I wouldn't advise it. Too complicated. Too messy."

She nodded. "I promised Judd I wouldn't lie to him either."

"Well, that was stupid. Lying is your job."

"Well, I won't do it to Judd. That's the only way I can make this work."

He looked her up and down and then stared into her eyes. "That's even more of a reason for you to accept my offer." He shook the keys again. "Come on, Jessica. *You need this.*"

She held his gaze until the Deputy Director of the CIA blinked. Then she held out her hand. He smiled ever so slightly as the keys dropped into her palm.

9.

Where the heck are we going, Al?" Dennis Dobson asked from the backseat of Alejandro Cabrera's Honda Odyssey mini-van.

"The airport is that way," Crawford Jackson said, pointing back toward the exit off Highway 66. "You just missed it."

"We aren't flying out of Dulles, gentlemen," Brinkley Barrymore III replied from the front passenger seat.

"Shit, brothers, we're not flying commercial," Alejandro crowed, punching the accelerator. "You'll see, *aseres*."

"We've made special arrangements. We've got a lot of gear for the trip," Brinkley explained, gesturing toward the back of the van, which was loaded high with heavy-duty cases. The Odyssey was an older model of faded burgundy, highlighted by a bright pink soccer ball sticker boasting KILLER LADYBUGS! on the rear bumper. The interior was worn and emitted a subtle aroma of peanut butter. Its engine growled under the weight of the four men and all the cargo.

"What's all that shit?" Crawford asked.

"Fishing gear. Supplies. And some parts for the boat," Alejandro said. "You'll see."

They rode listening to the Nationals baseball game on the radio for the next ten minutes. Alejandro then turned the minivan off the highway, and Brinkley reached over and shut off the radio.

"Where are we?" Dennis asked.

"Almost there," Brinkley replied just as Alejandro turned again, down an unmarked road cut through a thick-wooded area. Dennis elbowed Crawford in the ribs and scrunched his face. Crawford shrugged back.

"Seriously, guys, where the heck are we? What kind of airport is on a dirt road?"

"You'll see, boys," Alejandro said. "You're gonna love it."

"This is the kind of place where they hide dead bodies," Dennis said. "Are you taking us down this track to cut our throats and leave us for dead?"

"I'll never leave you for dead, Deuce," Crawford said.

"Don't get your balls in a twist," Alejandro said. "If I wanted to kill you, I would have done it years ago."

"It's nineteen-thirty," Brinkley announced. "Right on time."

"The only one who's gonna kill you is Beth," Al said. "You tell her you were going fishing or did you make something else up?"

"I told her," Dennis said. "She always knows when I'm lying."

"Good man," Crawford said. "Vanessa can tell with me, too."

"I still can't believe I blew off my project to go fishing." Dennis shook his head. "The office knew I wasn't sick."

"Here we are, gentlemen," Brinkley announced just as the van arrived at a clearing in the woods with a long asphalt airstrip hidden in a remote valley of rural northern Virginia. Parked at the very end of the runway was a sleek white corporate jet, the setting sun giving it a sparkling aura.

"Holy cow!" shrieked Dennis. "Is that for us?" He hopped up and down in his seat.

"What the fuck?" Crawford gasped. "A G5? You fucking with us?"

"It's a Gulfstream 650ER," Dennis chirped. "It's the latest in long-distance corporate jets. That plane could take us to Rio. Or Hong Kong."

"What the fuck's going on here, Brink?" Crawford asked.

"Don't worry, amigo," Alejandro said. "Brink knows a guy."

"I have a client," Brinkley said.

"A client lent you his private plane? So you could take us fishing?"

"He owes me a favor."

"Is your client Warren Buffett?" Dennis asked. "Or Bill Gates?"

"Shit, Brink," Crawford said, "is your client the CIA?"

"Who gives a fuck?" Alejandro said. "We'll be at the Key West Airport in three hours and then on *The Big Pig* at first light tomorrow morning. Who gives two shits which white-collar criminal our boy Brink is defending. The motherfucker is lending us his plane. So stop asking questions."

"Cool," Dennis muttered to himself.

"I told you to come on this trip, boys," Alejandro crowed. "You're gonna love Florida! Marlin fishing. And who knows what else we'll find."

10.

Florida?" Judd was surprised.

"Fort Lauderdale. It'll be great. For *all* of us. We could use a break, sweetie," Jessica said.

Judd opened the fridge, searching for a beer behind jugs of milk and boxes of low-sugar apple juice. "I can't leave tomorrow. I've got work." He pulled a brown bottle from the back of the fridge, popped the cap, and took a swig. "Impossible."

"I knew it would be tough. But we could use some quality time together. We could clear our heads. Come back refreshed."

Judd took another gulp of beer and mulled over Jessica's offer.

"After what we've been through, Judd, we could all use a few days to decompress."

"Whose house is it again?" he asked.

This was the question that Jessica didn't want to answer. How could she really tell him without opening the door to a long list of more questions? What did she even know about the Deputy Director? *Maybe just a small lie to escape having to answer the big ones?*

"I told you already. Sharon borrowed the house from her boss, but now her son is sick and she can't go." Her stomach churned as she realized she had already broken her promise. It wasn't even a full day since their agreement and she was already lying again to her husband. "The vacation house is just sitting there empty. That's why she's giving it to us." *And there it was: Lie Number One.*

"Sharon?"

"My friend from grad school. From Madison. She was *at our wedding.*"

"Oh, right," Judd said. "Since when have you been talking to her?"

"I talk to Sharon all the time."

Judd shrugged.

"It doesn't matter, Judd," she said. "I've got a free house in Fort Lauderdale and I want to go. I'm going to take Noah and Toby. They love the beach. I could use some sun. The only question is whether you're going to join us."

Judd dropped his shoulders. "I can't. Work is blowing up again. Landon Parker keeps pulling me onto special projects. I'm in the middle of a memo for him now. The timing is just terrible."

"I get it," she said. Jessica took the bottle from Judd's hand and gave him a kiss on the lips. "I get it," she repeated. Jessica tipped back a drink and then handed the beer back to him.

"I'm sorry, Jess."

"Stop apologizing. I need to clear *my* head. I'm taking the boys."

"Maybe if things at the office ease up, I'll come down. Maybe . . . if nothing new blows up . . . I'll come meet you in a few days. In Florida."

11.

The CIA's Deputy Director of Operations slowed down his car as he pulled into the turnout where the sign read SCENIC OVERLOOK. He scanned the empty parking lot and then eased his wife's black Audi A6 into a spot where the tree cover was low and he could see the lights of the city down the Potomac River.

He cut the engine and reached over to his briefcase, sitting on the passenger seat. He extracted all three of his cell phones and carefully removed the battery from each, then placed the batteries and dead devices in the glove compartment. He checked his watch. She wasn't late yet.

Traffic on the parkway was light at that late hour. A trickle of cars headed south along the river, past Georgetown University, the Watergate Apartments, the Kennedy Center, the Lincoln Memorial. Then the road skirted the Pentagon before ending near Ronald Reagan National Airport. *Can't count the number of times I've made that drive,* the Deputy Director thought.

More often, nearly every day as far back as he could remember, he had driven north on the George Washington Memorial

Parkway to the exclusive entrance to the headquarters of the Central Intelligence Agency. The epicenter of his life's work. *Thirty-five fucking years.*

Beyond the CIA was the highway ringing the nation's capital, the artery that fed the city's sprawling suburbs. The Beltway was the barrier, physically and psychologically, between Washington, D.C. and the rest of the world, he thought. *The bubble.*

Twenty excruciating minutes later, a white Cadillac Escalade pulled into the parking spot next to him. The Deputy Director impatiently stepped out of his car, double-checked to be certain that no one else had entered the overlook lot, and then slid into the passenger seat of the SUV.

"Sorry I'm late," said the driver.

"No need to apologize."

"Damn fund-raisers. They always run late." She checked her hair in the rearview mirror. "Donors always have to tell you one more story. Some favor they need. Or some boohoo about their successful daughter looking for a job."

"I wouldn't know," the Deputy Director said.

"I don't think this town used to be like this," she said. "It's still beautiful." To the east, across the river, they could see the top of the steeples of the old buildings at Georgetown University. Farther down the river, off in the distance, they could just make out the peak of the brightly lit Washington Monument. "I love Washington. I really do. But the money has made it dirty."

The Deputy Director grunted noncommittally.

"This town used to be about principles. About American values. When I first ran for office, I could talk about ideas and what we wanted to achieve. How we were going to stand up for what we believe. For freedom. Now . . . it's all about money."

This topic made the Deputy Director uncomfortable, so he changed the subject. "Madam Chairwoman, I saw your hearing this morning."

"Don't call me madam, dammit," Brenda Adelman-Zamora hissed. "It makes me sound like an old woman. And don't blow smoke up my ass about the hearing. I don't have much time. Where are we?"

He cleared his throat. "We're proceeding."

"How're you going to do it?" She leaned toward him.

"I believe we agreed that it was better that I not share any operational details."

"I'm the goddamn chair of the House Intelligence Committee. I have constitutional oversight of your agency. I think I can handle a few details."

"I promised to update you on progress. That's why I'm here now," he said with as much patience as he could muster. "But we also agreed that it was best if specifics be kept to a minimum. If there's anything you need to know, I will tell you."

She sat back and frowned. "I've heard that need-to-know shit before. I won't stand for another screwup."

"We won't have another failure. I'm personally taking charge of this operation," the Deputy Director said.

The congresswoman harrumphed.

"I'm sticking my neck out," he said, hiding his irritation.

"I am fully aware of our deal. You make this happen and I will ensure that you are the next Director of the Central Intelligence Agency."

He winced at her words, their arrangement laid out so crudely. So *quid pro quo*.

"You just make sure you hold up your end," she said.

He grunted again.

"What else do you need from me?" she asked.

"The less you're involved, the less you know, the better. I don't think we should meet again. Not until the operation is over."

"I've heard that all before. You think I can just trust the CIA to get this done for good? How many times have we been down this road?"

"This time is different. I told you. This is *my* operation."

"I hope so," she said. "No excuses. So I'm asking you again: What do you need?"

"Nothing, ma'am."

"Nothing? I've never heard that one before. You don't need money?"

"No."

"How's that possible? How are you running a major covert operation and you don't need cash?"

"Your committee oversees the intelligence budget. You know we have resources."

"You buy that constitutional bullshit I just threw at you? You think we have oversight?" She laughed. "I don't know shit. That budget is a long list of black accounts."

"I have all the resources I need. We agreed it's in both our interests that the sources of any financing remain undisclosed. For operational security."

She eyed him. "For deniability, you mean. In case it all goes wrong again."

He didn't reply.

"Fine," she huffed. "I don't want to hear later that this thing flopped because you were short of cash." She narrowed her eyes. "I don't want any excuses this time."

"There won't be."

"Christ, it's almost midnight," she said, checking her watch and turning the ignition back on. "I've got to go. I'm on the first flight tomorrow morning down to my constituency for another fund-raiser. You may not need cash, but I do."

12.

Judd nudged the steering wheel to ease off the George Washington Memorial Parkway at the exit for the airport.

"You really didn't have to drive us," Jessica said. "We could've taken a cab."

Judd patted the dashboard of his car, an aging silver Honda Accord that he'd bought off one of his Amherst College students. Jessica hated the car and had been urging him to replace it for months. But Judd liked this small piece of his old life back in New England. His grandmother had driven a silver Honda until she died in her farmhouse in Vermont. Every time he drove this car, which wasn't often, he thought of her.

"It's really no problem. I have plenty of time to drop you and then get to the office. And I get to see my family off," Judd said with a forced smile.

"Plane!" shouted Noah, their three-year-old son, strapped in his car seat.

"Is that our plane?" asked his older brother, Toby, pointing at a low-flying Boeing 737 making its final approach for landing at Reagan National Airport, just across the Potomac River from downtown Washington, D.C.

"It could be, baby," Jessica said. "Are you excited?"

"Yes, Mommy," Toby said. Noah, sucking on the remains of what was once a raisin bagel, nodded in agreement.

Judd weaved through the heavy early-morning airport traffic and squeezed his car into a tight space at the departure zone between two black Lincoln Town Cars. Jessica busily helped the two boys and their Ninja Turtle backpacks out of the car while Judd extracted a small orange wheelie suitcase from the trunk. Once the whole Ryker family was assembled on the sidewalk, Judd hugged and kissed his children.

"Be good . . . for Mom." Then, turning to his wife, he gave her a long kiss, "Have a great time, Jess."

"Who's that, Mommy?" Toby interrupted, pointing at a woman getting out of one of the Town Cars. She was in her early sixties, with heavy makeup, a golden tan, and wearing a red designer pantsuit. An aide unloaded several matching Valextra leather suitcases and carried a tiny Yorkshire terrier. "Is she a movie star?" asked the six-year-old boy.

Noah was staring, too. "Is she a princess?"

"Congresswoman," Judd said. "You remember the big white building shaped like a snow cone? She works there."

Jessica nudged Judd in the ribs. "Is that Adelman-Zamora?"

"Yep. Brenda Adelman-Zamora. House intel committee chair."

"I've seen her on TV."

"Maybe she's on your flight," Judd offered, raising his eyebrows.

Jessica scowled and then gave him another kiss.

"Don't do any work when you're down in Florida, Jess. Just try to enjoy yourself. Try to relax."

"That's the idea," she said.

"I got you this," he said, handing her a dog-eared copy of Robert Louis Stevenson's *Treasure Island*.

"Awww," she purred. "You remembered."

"I know it was your favorite." Judd shrugged.

"It is," she said, touching her chest. "I still don't know how mine got lost when we moved from Massachusetts."

"I thought it might help you forget about work. You know, for the beach."

She accepted the gift and slid it into her handbag, already stuffed with children's books and small baggies of corn snacks and pretzels. "Enjoy the quiet while we're away." Then she paused for a moment. "Scratch that." Jessica leaned forward and whispered, "Kick some ass."

13.

A soft pink glow on the horizon hinted at the imminent sunrise. The predawn water was calm, barely a hint of a cool breeze off the Caribbean Sea. The only sounds were seagulls and a gentle sloshing of waves against the pier at the Marathon Marina and Boat Yard.

"Motherfucker!" bellowed Alejandro Cabrera, bear-hugging a thin man with sunken cheeks, long greasy black hair, and skin that was dark from a mix of sun and motor oil. He was wearing flip-flops and a dirty T-shirt with the sleeves cut off, exposing tattoos on both arms. "*Que bolá, asere?* You're so skinny! Don't you eat down here? You're wasting away!"

"You're *gordo, asere,*" said the man.

They hugged again and slapped each other aggressively on the back.

"We all good?" Alejandro asked.

The beach bum nodded.

"You staying out of trouble, brother?"

"Doing my best to stay off the grid and outta trouble," the man replied.

The two men fist-bumped and then turned to face the others.

"Boys, this is Ricky. We go way back," Alejandro said. "Ricky, you know Brink already. And this is Craw and Deuce." The men all exchanged firm handshakes and head nods. "These are all guys from the neighborhood up north."

Then with a dramatic flourish, Alejandro opened his arms wide and announced, "And this is *The Big Pig*."

"It's fabulous, Al," Dennis said, gawking at the sparkling-white sportfishing boat docked beside them. "But what's with the pink stripe?"

"Fuck you, Deuce!" Al said. "You don't know style when you see it."

"Florida, baby," Crawford said.

"Fuck you, too."

"She's impressive," Crawford said, running his hand along the bow of the boat. "What can she do? Thirty, thirty-five knots?"

"Forty-two," Ricky said. "She's fully loaded."

"How's that possible?" Crawford asked.

"Custom-built," Brinkley explained. "Alejandro made some modifications to the standard engine package."

"Ricky juiced it for me," Alejandro said, his face again beaming with pride.

"*The Big Pig* flies," Ricky said, hands on his hips. "But if you boys want to catch some marlin today, you need to get going. *Vamanos*."

Ricky started unloading cases from a huge red Ford pickup truck on oversized tires.

Al whistled. "When'd you get this?"

"New F-150 Raptor SuperCrew. A 6.2-liter V-8 under the hood." Ricky strained with the weight of a large steel case, his muscles flexing and showing off his tattoos. "And *las chicas*, they love it."

"I'll bet." Al raised his eyebrows. "It's fucking beautiful, *asere*."

"Geez, Al," Dennis said. "A private plane, this fishing boat, monster trucks. What the heck is going on down here?"

"What can I say? We Latinos are lovers. And we love the toys. Same goes for the brothers. Isn't that right, Craw?"

"Am I your *only* black friend?" Crawford joked.

"Nah. We Cubans are all black. Don't you know that—"

"I don't want to interrupt your discourse on contemporary race relations," Brinkley interrupted. "But we've got marlin to catch. Can we get the boat loaded, gentlemen?"

"I've got this one," Ricky said as he hauled a large case onto the boat and then disappeared down the hold.

A few seconds later, Ricky's head reappeared. "Let's get the rest of these down below and then I'll run an engine check for you, Al."

"*Bueno*, Ricky. Where's the new GPS?"

"In the secure case in hold four. It's with the backup satellite phone. I'll leave you with a spare battery, too."

"You're not coming with us?" Dennis asked.

"Not today."

"I'm the fucking captain of *The Big Pig*," Al said. "Plus I've got two Navy boys with me. You can be my radio officer, Deuce. Not a bad crew for a little fishing expedition."

Crawford set down a crate. "This is a shitload of gear for a fishing trip, Al. What the hell are we loading?" he asked.

"Provisions," Al said. "You never know what you'll need hunting out in the open ocean. And we can't run out of beer and Cuban sandwiches." Al winked, then lifted a red cooler.

"All this for marlin fishing?" Dennis asked.

"Marlin." Brinkley nodded. "Maybe some bonefish."

14.

Judd had arrived in the office early that morning to continue working on his memo for Landon Parker. He was trying to anticipate scenarios that might go wrong in Cuba and outline responses for the State Department. It was precisely why his Crisis Reaction Unit had been created.

This morning, however, Judd was stuck. *What causes revolts?* It was a question that politicians had been mulling for centuries. *What final straw causes people finally to rise up and overthrow their own government?* Analysts had been trying to unlock that puzzle for decades. It had been an academic interest of Judd's when he was a graduate student and then a professor at Amherst College. Databases had been compiled with every variable possible: population, demographics, ethnic composition, corruption, and financial data. Complex statistics attempted to tease out the factors that were associated either with a rebellion or with prolonged periods of stability.

Judd had used this exact approach of building large databases and quantitative analysis to come up with his Golden Hour theory about the need for speed when responding to an international crisis. He had discovered that slow reaction time was statistically correlated with failure. He then made a slight—and he thought defensible—leap to claim, therefore, that waiting too long to react to a coup or outbreak of civil war meant a steep decline in the chance of U.S. policy success. It was the kind of conclusion that would be scorned in the academic community. But they gobbled it up in Washington. The Golden Hour was the basis for S/CRU. His job was built on a data model. And on Landon Parker's enthusiastic support.

Quick response by the United States government made intuitive sense to Judd, even if he didn't quite fully believe the numbers himself. *Correlation does not equal causation.* That was the very first lesson he taught his students. But inside the American government, quantitative evidence was seen as *proof*, and thus was a powerful weapon in the policy trenches. Whether the numbers were right or not was entirely beside the point. That was the very first lesson he had learned from Landon Parker.

Now he was tasked with helping Parker foresee problems in Cuba. However, this morning Judd wasn't finding much. He looked at his two computer screens. The one on the left was unclassified, connected to the Internet. The monitor on the right was connected to SIPRNet, the government's computer system cleared up to level Secret.

On his unclassified computer, he opened an online window to access the Amherst College library and searched the political science journals for determinants of popular mass revolts. One study from Stanford pointed to ratios of ethnic composition of cabinet ministers. Another from the University of Texas suggested that the concentration of land and livestock ownership was a factor. A third study from Tufts University found correlations between political unrest and changes in the prices of an index of rice, cooking oil, and fuel. Nothing particularly helpful.

"Dr. Ryker?" Judd looked up from his computer to see the familiar face of his assistant, Serena. "I'm sorry to interrupt, but I thought this might be useful," she said, brandishing a bright red folder. "I compiled all the cables from Havana and highlighted the most critical sections."

"Thank you, Serena. I don't pay you enough."

"No comment, Dr. Ryker. I've also forwarded to you the latest intel assessments on SIPRNet. Will you be needing a SCIF today?" she asked. For really squirrely information, anything classified as Top Secret, Judd would have to go down the hall to a special room called a Sensitive Compartmented Information Facility—a SCIF, in government shorthand.

"No, thank you, Serena."

"I also printed you a copy of Assistant Secretary Eisenberg's speech that she gave last month at the Miami Chamber of Commerce. I think you'll find it useful."

"Melanie Eisenberg . . ." Judd muttered to himself. "Have you found out anything that . . . I should know?"

"The Assistant Secretary is a shark."

"A shark?" Judd eyed his assistant. "I heard that she's close with Bill Rogerson over in African Affairs. Is that what you mean?"

"She's bigger than Rogerson. Eisenberg has the ear of the Secretary. A direct line."

"What's her relationship with Landon Parker?"

"She knows to give him his due respect," Serena said. "I heard she rolled him on Cuba."

"Eisenberg did an end run around Landon Parker on Cuba policy?"

"Yes. And that's not all. Word on the seventh floor says the Deputies Committee is considering her for P."

"P? Melanie Eisenberg is going to be the next Undersecretary? Number three in the building?"

"I told you she's a shark."

15.

Ten hours later, the fishermen were getting cranky.

After a whole morning of fishing and no sign of any marlin, Brinkley had suggested they head farther offshore to the
Seminole Flats to try their luck catching bonefish. "Per pound,
bonefish are the strongest fish in the world," Brink had told them
proudly. "And the Seminole Flats in the Florida Straits is the best
place in the whole world to catch them." Alejandro had navi-
gated *The Big Pig* due south.

But it was now early evening and they still had no sign of
any fish.

"I think we're over the line," Dennis muttered. He glared
down at the GPS unit in his hand. "Brink, you gotta take a look
at this."

Brinkley set down his fishing rod and walked over.

"Right here, this looks like we are over the line," Dennis said,
pointing to the little screen. "I think we are . . . in Cuban waters."

"No way. I don't think that's accurate. We may be close,

but we're still in international waters, don't worry. Where's your gear?"

"Close? I don't want to be *close* to Cuba."

Brinkley took the GPS unit from Dennis and examined the map again. "Alejandro, what time is sunset?"

"Seven o'clock sharp," he called from the cockpit.

Brinkley checked his watch. "Ninety minutes . . ." he mumbled, scanning the horizon with a pair of high-tech binoculars.

"What are you doing, Brink?" Dennis fidgeted with his fingers.

"I think we could make it." Brinkley nodded to himself.

"What're you talking about?"

Alejandro put the engine in neutral and joined the conversation.

"That firehouse, where your family used to live, it's in what town again?" Brinkley asked.

"Outside Santa Cruz del Norte. East of Havana," Alejandro said.

"You know where it is?"

"Of course." He tapped his skull with a forefinger.

"We aren't far." Brinkley pointed at the GPS unit. "We could wait for a few hours, kill the lights, go in dark. We've got the gear. We could be in and out before sunrise."

"Sunrise?" Crawford threw down his fishing rod. "What the fuck are you talking about, Brink?"

"Alejandro's diamonds. We're nearly there already. Maybe we could go get it. Tonight."

"Are you fucking crazy?" Crawford said. Dennis's fidgeting accelerated.

"It's not *that* crazy," Alejandro said. "We've got all the gear we need. I've got wet suits, shovels, even night vision goggles, down in the hold."

"You are seriously suggesting that we land *in* Cuba?" Crawford's eyes were wide.

"We'd need one of us to set a fire," Brink said. "To draw the firemen away from the station. Then—"

"Set a fire? Are you fucking crazy? No way."

"Yesterday, you both said you were in," Alejandro said. "You were up for it, Deuce. You said, 'I'm up for a treasure hunt.'"

"That's true," Brinkley nodded. "Those were your exact words."

"I was drunk. I thought you were kidding!" Dennis said, his eyes fluttering.

"Well, I'm not kidding," Alejandro said. "We can go get my family treasure right now."

"Is this why you fucking brought us down here?" Crawford growled. "For fucking diamonds?"

"You were joking!" Dennis squealed. "I thought you were joking!"

"Let's do it," Brinkley said, making a fist. "Dennis, you're our communications expert. You stay on the boat and monitor the radios. Crawford, we need our Navy SEAL to land on the beach undetected and then set the diversion fire. Once they are all clear, Al and I will go to the firehouse to get the diamonds."

"Treasure hunting. Just like pirates." Alejandro grinned.

"Pirates hunting for treasure? Are you out of your fucking mind?" Crawford put both hands on his head in frustration. "You think we're pirates?"

"We're so close," Brinkley said, tapping the GPS.

"We'll all be rich. We can do it," Alejandro agreed.

"No we can't!" Crawford's eyes were wide. "We aren't fucking pirates. We live in the suburbs. I'm retired. Brink's retired. You're a goddamn real estate agent, Al. Deuce isn't a comms officer. He writes software code!"

"Take it easy, Craw," Brinkley said, holding his palms up.

"We can go in and out," Alejandro said. "We can do it. Just like pirates."

"Pirates don't drive minivans, dammit!"

Alejandro was about to reply when he heard the first shot.

Booosh!

PART TWO

〜〜〜〜〜

THURSDAY

16.

I don't think we've had a crisis like this since the 1980 Mariel boatlift!" The commentator sitting next to the studio anchor adjusted his round tortoiseshell glasses and made a face of feigned exasperation.

"Well, I think it's worse than that, Wolf," interrupted a voice from a box in the corner of the screen. "I think we've got to go back to the Cuban Missile Crisis in 1962 and the Bay of Pigs in 1961. I mean, to have innocent American citizens captured in international waters—kidnapped, really—and then to have them paraded on television like that, it's really shocking. It's an act of unprecedented hostility from the regime in Havana."

"Is this unprecedented?" asked the anchor.

"We have to remember that, despite the diplomatic thaw and the reopening of embassies, Cuba is still a one-party communist state," said the commentator in the studio. "I just don't see how our negotiations with Cuba can continue now. The State Department is in a real bind. The Secretary had staked a lot on continuing to negotiate with Cuba. But that's all coming to a screeching halt."

Landon Parker paced around his office as the television blared.

"The Secretary of State really looks weak," said another voice on the screen. "Melanie Eisenberg has been leading the negotiations. Critics have attacked her for making too many concessions to the Cubans. And now this. I just don't know what the administration is thinking."

"If you are just joining us now, we are covering the unfolding crisis in Cuba," the anchor announced. At the bottom of the screen CAPTURED IN CUBA! was flashing in bold red letters behind black bars. "We'll be covering this unfolding drama out of Havana as it happens. This is a special early-morning edition of *The Situation Room*. Only on CNN."

Parker pushed the intercom button on his desk. "Call the Ops Center and get me the Chief of Mission in Havana."

"If you're just joining us now," Wolf Blitzer continued. "Here's what we know. Around five-thirty last night, a distress signal was sent out to the U.S. Coast Guard by a private American fishing boat reporting they were under attack by a Cuban naval vessel. Contact was lost with the fishing boat several minutes later. This morning, four men who appear to be American citizens were shown on Cuban state television. We have this brief clip."

On the screen, four middle-aged men, in handcuffs and orange jumpsuits, were shown being led by a uniformed soldier from a gray concrete-block building and hustled into a van with blacked-out windows. They marched in order: a tall Caucasian with wispy blond hair, a muscular black man with a shaved head, and a pudgy Hispanic with a goatee. The fourth man, pale white, was shorter and skinnier than the others, his arm in a sling and his shoulder heavily bandaged.

"The missing vessel is *The Big Pig*, a fishing boat registered in the state of Florida to one Alejandro Cabrera of Rockville, Maryland. CNN is still confirming if Cabrera is one of the detained men. We are also seeking confirmation of the identities of the other men shown in the video, but we believe they are all from the suburbs of Washington, D.C. and were on a fishing trip. Their last-known location in the Florida Straits is an area popular for bonefishing. I'm turning now to our correspondent in Miami. Christina, what else do we know?"

"Thank you, Wolf. At this time, we don't have much more on the exact timeline of events or the identities of the men. We don't have any information about their condition either. However, from the clip broadcast this morning on Cuban state television, it is clear that one of the men has been injured."

"CNN's chief medical correspondent Dr. Sanjay Gupta has examined the video and told our producers that the bandages visible on the fourth man are consistent with a gunshot wound. Do we know if there were shots fired, Christina?"

"We don't have any information about that, Wolf. The U.S. Coast Guard spokesman at Miami Beach Station did not release any details to me beyond confirming that an SOS message was received by the Coast Guard in Key West from a private fishing boat in the Florida Straits at approximately five-thirty p.m. last night. The Cuban government has not responded to CNN's requests for further information about the incident or the detainees. We are also waiting for a statement from the State Department."

"Fuck!" Parker hissed to himself.

"Do we know why the Cuban government would do this now, just as relations with the United States seem to be going so well? Why would they capture Americans and parade them on TV? What would they have to gain?"

"We don't know what the Cuban government is thinking, Wolf . . ."

Parker snatched the remote control off his desk and flipped the channel to Fox News.

SOCCER DADS DETAINED IN COMMUNIST CUBA scrolled across the bottom of the screen, with a shot of the same four men.

"Fuck!" he shouted again, and threw the remote control across the room. "Where is the goddamn mission chief?"

His secretary opened the office door. "Ops is still tracking him down. Is there anyone else you want me to call? Assistant Secretary Eisenberg, perhaps?"

Parker glanced back at the screen. The announcer was urging viewers to follow events via #soccerdad4 on Twitter.

"What the fuck is bonefishing?"

"I have no idea, sir. Do you want me to call someone to find out?"

Parker sat down heavily into his chair and swiveled in a circle. After two spins, he stopped abruptly. "Get me Judd Ryker."

17.

The beach along the Fort Lauderdale strip was still quiet. The boardwalk was slowly filling up with runners in tight exercise clothes and neon-colored running shoes, darting between steady streams of elderly walkers in all whites and nursing-home shoes.

The sand was mostly abandoned. Jessica established camp as far from other beachgoers as she could, laid out two large white towels, a small red plastic cooler of drinks and bagel sandwiches, and set up a low-slung chair for herself. A few feet away, Toby and Noah, generously slathered in sunscreen, played noisily with buckets and shovels in the wet sand on the water's edge. They dug a moat and built a high wall to try to protect their sand castle from the incoming waves.

Jessica watched her sons for a moment, then adjusted her peach-colored bikini top and settled into her chair. She dug her toes deep into the sugarlike warm white sand and stared up into the cloudless blue sky. She felt the light breeze through her hair.

This was just what she needed. A relaxing day on the beach

with her sons. She tried to push any thoughts of the past few days, the past years, from her mind. No stress, no work. Just relax.

Jessica pulled *Treasure Island* out of her bag and opened to chapter one.

> *Squire Trelawney, Dr. Livesey, and the rest of these gentlemen having asked me to write down the whole particulars about Treasure Island, from the beginning to the end, keeping nothing back but the bearings of the island, and that only because there is still treasure not yet lifted . . .*

Her phone buzzed. She groaned but decided she had to check it. On the screen flashed DANIEL DOLLAR, her code name for the Deputy Director. *What could he want?* Against her better judgment, she pushed ANSWER.

"Hel-lo?"

"How's the house? Everything all right?" the Deputy Director asked.

"Yes, thank you. It's lovely," she said. "We just got in yesterday morning."

"Have you gotten to the beach yet?"

"Yes, we're here now."

"Wonderful. Did you find the towels?"

"Yes, thank you."

"The white towels are for the house. The big blue ones are for the beach."

She glanced up just in time to watch Noah drop a bucket of wet sand on one of the white towels. "Yes, got it. Thanks again. I really needed this break."

"You're very welcome. I'm glad you could use the house. It's been in my family for years, but I rarely have time to get down to Florida."

"Okay . . ." she said. "Is there anything else?"

He didn't reply.

"Sir?" she said.

"I know you need a break, Jessica."

"Yes, I do. You were right."

"And . . ." He paused. "I need you to run a small errand for me."

"Sir?" She gritted her teeth.

"I know you're on vacation. I want you to relax. But, I need your help, too. It's a small thing. Very small, I promise."

"What kind of help?"

"Is this your secure phone?"

"Yes, sir," she sighed.

"Good girl. I'm going to need you to clean up a mess. A sensitive mess."

"You're reactivating me already? Right now? While I'm at the beach with my children?"

"I didn't want to ask you, but it's time-sensitive. And delicate. You're the only one I can trust with this."

"The *only* one?"

"This is why we created Purple Cell. To go anywhere. To do what's needed. When it's needed. No bureaucracy. No bullshit."

She didn't say anything. She was steaming inside. Mad at herself for not seeing this coming.

"Don't worry about your kids," he continued. "I've got someone on the way already. Her name is Aunt Lulu. I've now got your location, so she'll be there in thirteen, maybe fourteen, minutes."

"Where am I going?"

"Lulu will tell you the rest of the details. It's a quick one. You'll be back on the beach before you know it."

"What am I really doing in Florida, sir?"

"Excuse me?"

"Why did you really send me down here? What kind of urgent cleanup could I have in *South Florida*?"

"Lulu will explain. If you need me, you know how to reach me on the pizza line."

"You didn't lend me your beach house as a favor, did you? You sent me to Florida for a *mission*."

"Jessica, you needed a break. That was obvious."

"But?"

"But good case officers always think ahead. You know that. I taught you that. The best case officers always pre-position assets."

18.

Judd was checking the cost of last-minute flights to Fort Lauderdale when Serena burst into his office.

"I'm sorry, Dr. Ryker. I know you asked not to be disturbed, but I have to interrupt."

"It's fine, Serena. I was about to call you. Can you clear my schedule for the rest of the week? I'm going to join my family in Florida since I'm done. I've just sent my memo to Landon Parker."

"That's why I'm here, Dr. Ryker," she said, out of breath, "Mr. Parker is on his way down."

"He's coming here? What for?"

"I don't know, but his assistant just called to give me a heads-up that he's on his way *right now.*"

"Now?"

She nodded and left to stand guard in the outer lobby. Judd tidied his desk and groaned to himself. *So much for Florida.*

"Ryker!" Parker barked from the next room.

"Hello, Mr. Parker," Serena said as she escorted him in.

"Love your ideas on Cuba, Ryker. Adam Smith didn't go over too well with Melanie Eisenberg." Parker smirked. "But I like how you think. That's why we have S/CRU in the first place. To throw out new ideas. To shake things up."

"Thank you, sir," Judd said, offering the chief of staff a seat, which Parker declined with a wave. "I've just sent you the memo on potential problems in Cuba and a menu of responses. The first—"

"Oh, right," Parker interrupted. "That's OBE now. Overtaken by events, I'm afraid. I need you on a special project that's just come up. I need creative thinking and fast. You'll need to drop everything and help me on this. *Now.*"

"On . . . what, sir?"

"We don't negotiate with hostage takers. That's a redline, of course. But I need someone who understands the subtleties. Someone not stuck in the bureaucracy. Someone not worried about the media. Or covering his ass. I like how you don't care about sticking your neck out. No matter how crazy your idea, you don't care what people think."

"Okay . . ." Judd furrowed his brow.

"That's what I need, Ryker."

Judd nodded—to what, exactly, he wasn't sure.

"We'll let Melanie Eisenberg run the front channel." Parker flicked his hand dismissively. "Let WHA be visible. Let her handle the press and the interagency. Let Mel run the show. She'll insist on that anyway." Parker placed both hands on Judd's desk and leaned in. "You told me I need a backchannel. Well, that's *you.*"

"Me?"

"I need S/CRU to be my backchannel. This will be delicate.

I need someone I can trust. Someone discreet. Someone to operate in the shadows."

"Thank you, sir. But what are we talking about?"

"The AMCITs, of course." Parker stood up straight. "I need
you to come up with a way to get them back. You'll be helping
me. You'll be helping the Secretary. And you'll be helping to prove
S/CRU. It's a win-win-win, Ryker. Are you in?"

"Yes, sir, of course."

"Good. Figure out what the hell those bastards are up to. Why
now? What are they getting out of this? What are they thinking?"

"Who, sir?"

"The Cubans, Ryker! Who the hell else could I mean?"

Judd nodded.

"And, Ryker, you have to figure out how we're going to get the
AMCITs back without giving anything away. Who do we even
talk to? I want some creative ideas! No more oldthink!" Parker
turned to leave.

"I'm in, Mr. Parker. I'm in one hundred percent," Judd said.
"But I've been on lockdown all morning with this memo. What
citizens are you talking about?"

Parker didn't turn around as he walked out of Judd's office.
From the outer lobby, he called out, "Turn on your TV."

19.

The television camera zoomed in on the chairwoman's face as she approached the podium. A bouquet of microphones clustered at the front. A large American flag hung in the background, perfectly positioned by her press secretary to frame the screenshot.

Brenda Adelman-Zamora wore her most serious business pantsuit and an even sterner expression. Her personal makeup artist had used extra eyeliner that morning, adding subtle black lines to suggest intense ferocity.

The congresswoman stared into the camera for a moment, ensuring that all the networks had time to catch her opening statement. Satisfied the assembled media was ready, she inhaled deeply.

"I have called this press conference on short notice to express my deep outrage at the actions of the Cuban government. Last night, the Cuban navy illegally detained four innocent American citizens. My office has learned that these four men were on a fishing trip. These men are husbands. These men are fathers. Their young daughters play on the same soccer team in the great state of Maryland, just a few miles from where we stand this morning. One of the detained Americans is the coach. A hardworking businessman and a girls' soccer coach. These soccer dads were together on a fishing trip out of the Florida Keys, enjoying the bounty of my own beautiful state, when they were illegally captured by the communist regime."

Adelman-Zamora took another deep breath and hung her head in grief. "My thoughts and prayers are with the families of these innocent men. These fathers have been torn from their wives and children. These men and their families are suffering needlessly from the actions of a ruthless dictatorship."

She lifted her chin. "We have not yet had any official statement from Cuba, but they have shamelessly released a video clip to their state-controlled media of the men in detention. Contrary to what the Cuban propaganda machine is reporting, there is no evidence whatsoever that these Americans were engaged in anything other than recreation. There is no evidence whatsoever that these Americans strayed into Cuban waters. My office has now confirmed that their last communication sent to the U.S. Coast Guard came from a location well within international waters. It is thus clear that any claims by the scurrilous regime in Havana that these men penetrated Cuban waters are patently false. There is no excuse for this gross violation of international law."

Then she gripped the lectern with both hands and looked directly into the camera. "I am calling on the regime in Havana to immediately and unconditionally release these innocent men. Anything less is unacceptable."

She shook her head in disbelief, her hair remaining firmly in place. "This is further evidence of the immoral brutality of the

Cuban regime. This act of barbarism is evidence that despite recent steps taken by the United States to extend the hand of friendship, the Cuban regime has nothing but disdain for basic human
rights. It is evidence of their utter disregard for international
norms. The United States must never waver in the face of tyranny."

She paused for a moment and pursed her lips.

"I am calling on our own government to denounce in no
uncertain terms this illegal action by Cuba. I am calling for the
White House and the State Department to spare no effort to gain
their release."

She narrowed her eyes and looked down at her notes. "Even
as we seek the freedom of these innocent husbands and fathers,
we must also remember that the United States can never reward
such acts of aggression. We cannot engage in direct talks with
a regime that behaves in this manner. We cannot appease tyranny. We can never negotiate with terrorists."

She looked directly into the camera. "I am therefore calling on
the White House and State Department to immediately suspend
any diplomatic negotiations until further notice. If necessary,
we will reimpose sanctions on Cuba. If necessary, we will place
them back on the list of state sponsors of terrorism. As the record
shows, I strongly opposed the administration's lifting of sanctions and the reestablishment of diplomatic relations. I take no
pleasure in seeing my warnings come to pass. Our olive branches
have only been interpreted by Havana as a sign of surrender. It
can be no coincidence that just as the Cuban government believes
we are weak, they undertake this latest escalation by kidnapping
these innocent Americans. They are testing our resolve.

"But make no mistake, America is stronger than ever before.
We will show Havana that we are unwavering in our pursuit of

liberty. That there can be no compromise with democracy. No compromise with freedom. We will show the dictator in Cuba that his aggression will result in serious consequences."

The chairwoman banged her fist on the podium. "There will be no direct talks with the Cuban government until these innocent men are released unconditionally and full democracy is restored. We will give the communists nothing in return for their safe release."

Adelman-Zamora softened her scowl. "I am calling on all Americans to let our own government know that they stand with the Soccer Dad Four. That they stand with their families. And that they stand with the Cuban people who seek nothing less than their own freedom."

An aide off camera handed her a white poster board. "The Free Cuba Congressional Caucus is calling on Americans to stand with us today by contacting your representatives, calling the State Department, and by expressing yourself on social media." Adelman-Zamora flipped the sign and held it up to the camera: #freesoccerdad4.

20.

Jessica Ryker drove the rented white convertible Ford Mustang over the bridge, departing Long Key. The waters of the Florida Keys reminded her of Jamaica, the lonely palm trees hanging precariously over the clear blue seas and sugar-white sand. It was a warm, cloudless day. She should have been enjoying this drive through paradise. Instead, she was pissed off.

Jessica had been in the car for the past two and a half hours, driving south from Fort Lauderdale, then taking Route 1, a series of two-lane bridges connecting the archipelago of the Florida Keys. The bridges began just south of Homestead on the mainland and then ran for more than a hundred miles. Route 1 eventually reached a dead end at Key West, the southernmost point on the continental United States. Just ninety miles from Cuba. But Jessica wasn't going all the way to Key West today.

She had been yanked off the Fort Lauderdale beach that

morning by the Deputy Director of the Central Intelligence Agency. She was ordered to drive to Marathon, about halfway along the Keys, to find out what she could about what had happened to a fishing boat seized by the Cubans. Her first thought had been *Cuba?*

few minutes after she had hung up the phone with the Deputy Director, an elderly lady in a white housecoat and a long leopard-print sun visor had arrived at the beach.

"Hello, Jessica my dear," she had said warmly.

"Aunt Lulu? Is that you?" Jessica replied to a face she had never seen before.

"Yes, dear. How lovely to see you and the boys. Noah and Toby have gotten so big."

Jessica had coughed as her two sons had stared with quizzical looks at the strange old woman who had suddenly invaded their space. "Toby, Noah," she said slowly, "this is your Auntie Lulu. You haven't seen her for a very long time."

Both boys had stared up emotionlessly at the old woman.

"She's going to help you make a sand castle while mommy runs an errand. Auntie Lulu will then take you to lunch and I'll meet you all back at the house later today. Okay?"

Toby shrugged and returned to digging holes in the sand. Noah's eyes watered.

"Oh, baby, be brave. Auntie Lulu will take good care of you. And I'll be back before you know it. She'll take you for pizza."

"That's right, dear," Lulu had said with a broad smile.

"Pizza," Noah had said, choking back tears.

---

astard," Jessica hissed to herself as she punched the accelerator to pass a gigantic Winnebago covered with destination stickers: SOUTH OF THE BORDER, THIS CAR CLIMBED MT. WASHINGTON, VIRGINIA IS FOR LOVERS.

She should have known that the Deputy Director wouldn't have given her his vacation house without some hidden agenda. She cursed herself for not knowing better. A rookie mistake. Of course he had sent her to Florida on purpose. For a purpose. For some kind of *mission*.

Lulu hadn't provided many details, but Jessica hadn't wanted to argue in front of her children. She was leaving them with a total stranger and the last thing she wanted was to appear anxious. *But Cuba?*

Cuba seemed like a relic of the Cold War. What could possibly be so important about a lost fishing boat that the Deputy Director would have sent her down to Florida and then ordered her to drive all the way to the Keys? To find some deckhand and see what he knows? She decided she'd go, do her job quickly, and get back to her children as soon as possible.

The bridge was a single lane in either direction over the water. A green sign announced that Marathon was four miles away. *Almost there,* she thought just as her phone buzzed with a call from Judd.

"Hi, sweets!" she answered.

"How's the beach?"

"Great. We all miss you."

"Wow, it sounds windy," Judd said.

Jessica took her foot off the accelerator and regretted not pulling over to take the call. "Yeah, it's breezy. It's . . . Florida."

"How are my boys?"

"They're playing in the sand. They love it."

"Do they want to say hello to their dad?"

"Um . . ." Jessica stalled as she decided how to play this. "They're busy with their buckets. And they're all wet and sandy." *Lie Number Two,* she thought with a pang of guilt.

"Okay, I guess," Judd tried to hide his disappointment.

"We're going to visit with my Aunt Lulu later today. I want the boys to meet her," she said.

"You have an Aunt Lulu?"

"Yes, I'm sure I told you about her. She's not really an aunt, more of a distant cousin." *Lie Number Three.* Jessica changed the subject. "So how's work?"

"Fine, I guess. It's going fine."

"That doesn't sound good."

"I pitched my idea about cash incentives to Landon Parker."

"Incentives? You didn't talk about aligned incentives and Adam Smith, did you, sweets?"

"Yeah. That was a mistake, Jess."

"So, what did Parker say?"

"I mean, he liked my ideas, but they're going in another direction."

"I'm sorry, honey," she said. "You'll get another shot."

"Sure."

"The good news is that you're free, right?" Jessica brightened up. "Maybe you want to come down to join us? Maybe tomorrow?"

"That's what I was thinking, too. But Parker has pulled me onto a special assignment. Something different. Actually, that's . . . what I'm calling about."

"What kind of special assignment?"

"Have you seen the news? Have you seen the story about these soccer dads down in Florida on a fishing trip who were captured by the Cubans?"

"Cuba? Really?" Jessica gripped the steering wheel tightly. "Judd, you're working on *Cuba*?"

"Sort of. I'm helping Parker out. I'm not supposed to talk about it. But I'm helping the State Department get the hostages released. I probably shouldn't say any more on the phone."

"Judd, why didn't you tell me you're working on Cuba?"

"I am. That's why I called you. Why"—Judd paused—"Why does it matter?"

"It matters"—she calmed herself—"because . . . maybe I can help you? Assist. That was one of our rules, remember?"

"Right, I remember. Assist, avoid, admit."

Jessica knew it was already too late to avoid. They were now both working on Cuba. On the very same case. This was Jessica's chance to admit. To avoid *Lie Number Four*.

"So how can you help me?" Judd asked.

"Um, I don't know yet," she said as she passed a shiny red replica lighthouse announcing WELCOME TO MARATHON. "But I am down here in Florida . . ."

Her mind spun. Should she admit that she was also now working on the Cuba detainees? Or could she get away with it one more time? Maybe her Cuba assignment would be short-lived? Maybe it would be over this afternoon?

"Oh, I don't know, Judd." *Lie Number Four.* "You'll think of something. Maybe if you get stuck, there's someone I can call?" Jessica offered.

Yes, Jessica thought, *I know exactly who to call.*

21.

The cubicle, in a drab room labeled AFRICA ISSUE on the third floor of the old CIA headquarters building, was unusually neat for an analyst work space. Most of the cramped desks were littered with papers, the half walls covered with worn maps, stolen street signs, pilfered campaign posters, and other detritus from undercover field visits.

The analysts, the academic teams working for the Agency's Directorate of Intelligence, always lived slightly in the shadow of the other side of the CIA house, the operatives working for the National Clandestine Service. Most of the newer analysts, some barely out of college, competed with bravado to acquire unique souvenirs—a sword bought off the streets of Khartoum, a battlefield talisman used by a Congolese rebel, a hand-painted barber's sign snatched from the inner slums of Kumasi—to prove their mettle. It was a game, mainly for the rookies, dismissed by the older salty CIA professionals as the youthful follies of intelligence community tourism.

This analyst's cubicle, however, was different. It was spotless.

The papers and maps perfectly stacked and aligned with the edge of the desk, any coffee stains immediately wiped clean. The occupant of this particular cubicle, a man named Sunday, was also immaculate. His Afro cut tight, his wide face carefully clean-shaven except for a perfectly trimmed short goatee. The only concession to his personal life, a small formal photo of his parents, first-generation immigrants from Nigeria.

Sunday had no time for childish contests. Not that he wasn't fiercely competitive. He had inherited from his father an intense drive to adapt to his surroundings and find unconventional ways to get ahead. His father had been a northern Nigerian working in the southeast, a Muslim working in a zone dominated by Christians. When the secessionist Biafran War exploded, Sunday's father knew trouble was coming and fled by boat to neighboring Cameroon. He had then managed, by ways that Sunday was never told, to get to Chad, then Tunisia, Paris, London, and eventually he joined a distant cousin in southern California.

When Sunday was born, he inherited his father's instinct for adaptation and survival, hidden among his genes. Only later, as a young man, did he exhibit his dad's patriotic passion for their family's adopted nation.

From his mother, Sunday received two birthrights: a tight emotional bond with Nigerian culture and an obsession with cleanliness. His mother cooked traditional Hausa foods—goat stew or okra-and-pumpkin soup were his favorites—at least once a week. She also graciously hosted an unending parade of Nigerian visitors in their suburban Los Angeles home, an occasion that often was accompanied by a feast of a whole roasted lamb.

This combination of cunning, patriotism, and meticulousness, paired with links to a foreign culture, made Sunday an ideal recruit for the Central Intelligence Agency. It was only natural that he became a scholar of politics and the motivations of organized violence. In hindsight, it was almost inevitable that one day Sunday would fall under the wing of Professor BJ van Hollen. That eventually he would use his gifts to help the United States of America better understand what was happening in a faraway corner of the globe. That was what had brought him to this tidy cubicle.

But unlike his Africa Issue colleagues, Sunday had little time for silly competitions over weapons or street signs. Like many Americans working undercover, Sunday really had two jobs. His day job was as a Directorate of Intelligence analyst, currently assigned to a special task force on piracy in Somalia. Yet Sunday was also working covertly for the supersecret Purple Cell, an autonomous operational unit within the National Clandestine Service run by Jessica Ryker. That, too, was thanks to BJ van Hollen.

Someone on an upper floor of the CIA was convinced that Iran was using criminal gangs in Somalia to fund violent extremist cells, and Sunday's current assignment was to hunt for financial fingerprints. He scanned the screen on his classified computer, running an algorithm that was trying to discern a pattern in banking transactions between Tehran and the informal *hawala* banks in Somalia. It was looking like another all-nighter.

"Hey, S-Man, who's this?" a voice shouted from behind Sunday. He spun around to find an overweight colleague, holding a stuffed moose head with a wide-brimmed safari hat. Before Sunday could reply, Glen answered, "Moose-eveny . . . Get it?"

Glen roared with laughter.

Sunday smiled politely, "President Museveni from Uganda. Ay. I get it."

"Museveni, Moose-eveny!"

"Did you steal the president's hat?"

"I bought it off a coffee farmer in Kampala. Moose-eveny! I love it! I'm going to hang him up by the front door. Hey, Sunday, you want half my muffin?"

"No thanks," said Sunday, turning back to his computer.

Glen occupied a faraway cubicle, but he always seemed to be hanging around this side of the office with his snacks. This morning he was brandishing an extra-large dark-chocolate muffin. "Okay, more for me," Glen said.

He ripped off the muffin top and shoved it into his mouth. "So . . . you find anything yet?" Glen asked while still chewing.

"Not yet," Sunday replied, his back still turned to his colleague.

"Nothing?" he mumbled through a mouthful of muffin. "I've got SIGINT on more than a dozen pirate gangs. And I'm mapping their scouting routes correlated with the tides in the Gulf of Aden. Cutting edge analytics. The task force team chief is gonna love it. And you've got nothing, S-Man?"

"No, Glen," Sunday said. "And if I did, I wouldn't tell you. We are compartmentalized on this. Everything goes through the team chief, remember?"

"I know," he said, choking down the last of the muffin top and taking another bite. "But I thought you were supposed to be some kind of expert at tracking financial data?"

"I'm not going to tell you that either."

"Hall chatter says the DNI is waiting on this one." Glen nodded to himself. "Iran is the big leagues."

"I wouldn't know, Glen."

Just then, Sunday's desk phone rang. The screen showed an external line with a code he recognized. "Sorry, Glen, I've got to take this. Can you scarf your muffin somewhere else?"

Glen snorted. "I've got pirates to catch," he said, tucking the moose under one arm. "See you later, S-Man!"

Once Glen was safely out of earshot, Sunday picked up the receiver. "Sunday," he whispered.

"You still chasing pirates?" Jessica asked.

"Yes, ma'am."

"Have you seen the news?"

"No time for TV, ma'am. Neck-deep in Somalia."

"Turn on CNN. Last night, Cubans seized an American fishing boat. Four civilians on board," she said. "I need everything. Background, motives, anything you can find."

"Roger."

"Both sides. I want to know what the Cubans are up to. *And us.*"

"Got it," Sunday said.

"Story doesn't make sense. Go deep."

"Yes, ma'am. Cuba. I'm on it."

"Do you need help with access or an alibi?"

"No, ma'am."

"I thought you were neck-deep in Somali pirates?"

"Yes, ma'am. This sounds like pirates to me. Ship attacked and robbed at sea, right? Pirates of the Caribbean."

"Treasure Island."

22.

The parking lot of the Marathon Marina and Boat Yard was packed with television news vans, their satellite dishes sprouting like weeds reaching for the sun. A gaggle of well-coifed South Florida reporters were jostling for the same picturesque backdrop of a palm tree and the dock bar. The Monroe County Sheriff's Office had set up a yellow police tape perimeter to keep back a crowd of onlookers.

Jessica Ryker drove slowly past the scene and parked her Mustang down the road, under a coconut tree at Castaways Bar & Grill. She slid on sunglasses, a sun hat, and walked inside.

"What's all the fuss?" Jessica asked the bartender, a blonde in her late forties with leathery skin, name tag: BECKY.

"Fishin' boat gone missin'." The walls were covered in fishnets, dented street signs, starfish, and old wine bottles. A twelve-foot stuffed blue marlin, with a sharp dorsal fin and long bill like a sword, was mounted behind the bar.

"Oh my." Jessica put her fingers to her lips. "Is that the boat on the TV?" she asked, pointing at the silent television above the bar where an overly tan brunette reporter was speaking into a microphone. "That broadcast is from . . . here?"

"Uh-huh. Right outside," Becky said, jerking her thumb toward the front door.

"What happened?"

"Don't know. They musta strayed too close to Cuba. That's what the TV says."

"Oh dear, that's too awful."

"Who knows what happens out there on the high seas. You wanna drink, girl?"

"It's not too early?" Jessica shrugged.

"It's Florida," she said, nodding toward an armless clock that announced IT'S MARGARITA TIME!

"Okay." Jessica slid onto a stool at the bar. "What's your specialty?"

"Margarita, rocks, salt."

"Perfect."

A few minutes later, the barwoman delivered a lime green cocktail, chunky ice cubes, and the rim covered in white specks. "Here you go. Becky's Marathon Special."

Jessica took a sip, the sour lime juice mixing with the tequila and rock salt. She winced as she swallowed. "Yum. Thanks."

"Uh-huh."

"I'm Alexandra. From New York," Jessica said.

"Nice ta' meet you. Weather way too cold up there for me."

"You get used to it," Jessica said. "I wish I could live down here. Near the ocean."

"Uh-huh," said the barwoman. "It takes some gettin' used to as well."

"How long you been down here in Marathon?"

"Too long."

"Oh, I think it's lovely."

"Uh-huh. Too quiet."

"Not today!" Jessica said. "Kinda crazy out there with all those TV cameras, don't you think?"

"Been like that all mornin'. They'll be gone by tomorrow unless somethin' happens to them boys."

"Which boys? Did you know them?"

"Nah."

"Not locals?"

"From up north. Tourists out for some fishin'."

"My goodness, how terrible," Jessica said, touching her chest. "You go out on a fishing charter and wind up in a Cuban jail."

Becky clicked her tongue and shook her head.

"They weren't on a charter. It was a private boat. *The Big Pig.*"

"What's that?"

"That's the boat that's gone missing."

"Wow, *The Big Pig*," Jessica said, widening her eyes. "If it wasn't a charter, whose boat was it?"

"Eh, who knows?" The bartender shrugged. "No one ever knows who really owns what around here."

"I didn't know," Jessica said. "I was hoping to rent a boat, actually. For me and my boyfriend."

"Uh-huh. Where's he?"

"He's still sleeping at the hotel. It's our one-year dating anniversary," Jessica smiled cheerily at the woman.

"A whole year. Good for you."

"I was hoping to surprise him with a day out on the ocean. Maybe some fishing. Or a private booze cruise."

"Uh-huh."

"But it looks like the marina is all tied up with TV people today."

"Uh-huh."

"So, Becky"—Jessica leaned on the bar—"if I wanted to hire a boat and go somewhere special, who's the best person to talk to?" Jessica took a gulp of her cocktail. "Who knows what's *really* going on around here in Marathon?"

Becky eyed Jessica, who gave the barwoman her most innocent smile.

"You should ask . . . Ricky. He knows what's what."

"Ricky, huh?"

"Yeah, Ricky helps out on some of the boats and watches houses for them rich people when they aren't here. Which is almost always," she winked. "If anyone knows what's goin' on around here, it'll be Ricky."

"Where'll I find this Ricky?"

"Probably hiding from them TV people."

"Where should I look?"

"He's usually out by the charters. Cute, but too skinny for me. Look for his red Ford pickup. It's a beauty."

Jessica drained her drink and left a twenty-dollar bill on the bar with a wave. "Thanks, Becky. My boyfriend thanks you, too."

23.

You want a Cuban or reuben?"

"What?" Judd asked, looking up confused from his desk.

Serena put both hands on her hips. "You asked me to get you a sandwich, Dr. Ryker. The specials today are Cubans and reubens. Or do you want your boring old turkey on rye again?"

"Oh, thanks, Serena. Right. I forgot," Judd said, turning back to his papers. "I don't care. You choose."

Judd glared down at the page in front of him, a list Serena had tracked down from the State Department's Operations Center.

```
DENNIS DOBSON, US Citizen, DOB September 28, 1969
    Address: Rockville, MD
    Education: BSc, Massachusetts Institute of
        Technology
    Employer: Engineer, CommScramble Software Inc,
        Reston, VA
    Military record: none
    Criminal record: none
```

BRINKLEY BARRYMORE III, US Citizen,
DOB January 4, 1970
  Address: Bethesda, MD
  Education: BSc, US Naval Academy; JD,
    Georgetown University Law Center
  Employer: Partner, Prince Hatton Horowitz,
    Washington, DC
  Military record: Captain (CAPT), Judge
    Advocate General's Corps (JAG); Retired.
  Criminal record: none

CRAWFORD JACKSON, US Citizen, DOB May 11, 1970
  Address: Bethesda, MD
  Education: BSc, US Naval Academy
  Employer: Consultant, Naval Surface Warfare
    Center, Carderock, MD
  Military record: Commander (CDR), Special
    Operations (SEAL); Retired.
  Criminal record: none

ALEJANDRO CABRERA, US Citizen, DOB April 17,
1968
  Address: Rockville, MD
  Education: BA, Florida State University
  Employer: Owner, Premier Real Estate,
    Rockville, MD
  Military record: none
  Criminal record: Driving under the influence,
    2005; Disturbing the peace, 2007; Open
    container violation, 2007; Public indecency,

```
2007; Disorderly conduct, 2008; Resisting
arrest, 2008; Driving under the influence,
2009; Disturbing the peace, 2011;
Disorderly conduct, 2013; Disorderly
conduct, 2015.
```

Judd read the details on the page twice, then set it down. The State Department didn't have anything more than what was on the news. Less even. At least CNN had figured out the four men were fathers with daughters on the same soccer team. Or had that come from the congresswoman and her twitter campaign? Didn't matter. Judd had nothing. Other than this Alejandro Cabrera, whose criminal record suggested he was rough around the edges, this didn't seem like much. Bunch of guys, two Annapolis grads, out for some fishing.

"Anything else you need, Dr. Ryker?" Serena asked.

"Anything more on these AMCITs?" Judd waved the page at her.

"That's all they gave me at Ops."

"What am I supposed to do with this list? There's nothing in it."

"I couldn't say, Dr. Ryker."

Judd thought for a moment. "Serena, how long would it take me to drive out to Bethesda and Rockville? To talk with the families?"

"I could get you a car from motor pool. The drive is only twenty minutes if you go before rush hour."

"I might need that."

"Of course. But Consular Affairs already sent someone out there to talk with the spouses. They've now got the FBI, Mont-

gomery County PD, and the local TV news crews all parked outside their homes. So I wouldn't expect to just walk in there and
start asking questions. You'll have to be more discreet."

"How do you know all that, Serena?"

"When you're on the job, so am I."

Discreet. That was what Parker said. *What could I even ask
them? What the hell do I know about hostage negotiations?*

Judd huffed and punched the desk with his fist.

"Sir?"

"Sorry, Serena. I'm just thinking . . ." *Parker has me on an
unsolvable mission to negotiate for four suburban dads who got
lost on a fishing trip? Is this another setup to fail? Or is Cuba an
opportunity?*

"Dr. Ryker, sir?" she said.

"Make it a Cuban."

24.

'm here in Marathon, in the heart of the Florida Keys," a tall Hispanic woman with bright red lips read into the camera. "Behind me is where the fishing boat set sail yesterday morning with four American soccer dads on their fateful trip into the Seminole Flats. They sailed straight into the grasp of the Cuban navy . . ."

"That's right, Tammy," said another reporter, touching his earpiece with one finger and holding a CNN microphone with the other hand. "The authorities aren't releasing any further information about the men . . ."

Jessica had left Castaways Bar & Grill and skirted the media circus in the main parking lot. On the far side was a small boardwalk where fishing charter boats docked: Capt'n Bill's Charters, Florida Frank, Mad Marlin Max, Sun 'n' Sport 'n' Fish. At the far end, across from an empty slip, sat a massive cherry-red Ford pickup truck on oversized tires.

Jessica strolled past the truck. In the bed were ropes, buckets, and fishing gear. Glare on the tinted windows blocked her from being able to see what was inside the cab. No one appeared to be around, so she quickly took a photo of the truck and license plate with her phone. She then raised a hand to her forehead and leaned against the window to peer inside. The cab, too, was filled with boating gear and cardboard boxes.

"Hey!" shouted a gruff voice from behind her.

Jessica spun around to find a lean man with olive skin and long dark hair. He was wearing torn jeans and a cutoff T-shirt that exposed tattoos on both arms. His face was gaunt and unshaven. Jessica could see that he'd once been handsome, but something in this man's life had taken a toll.

His eyes narrowed in anger.

"Oh my," she gasped, flashing her friendliest smile and touching her chest with her fingers. "I'm so sorry."

"That's my truck," he said, relaxing once he saw Jessica's face. He took a step forward, and Jessica was overwhelmed by the smell of stale cigarettes.

"It's beautiful," she said, running her fingers across the roof. "I was just admiring it. So . . . red!"

"Yes, it is," he said, looking Jessica up and down. "I didn't mean to scare you, *chiquita*."

"It's my fault." She pouted. "I shouldn't have been looking inside your truck. It's not right." Jessica could see one of the man's arms was inked with tattoos of a buxom mermaid and ¡EN LA GLORIA DE DIOS!

"Well, don't you worry. We've just had some trouble around here, that's all." He shrugged and held up his hands. On the other arm was a tattoo of a naval ship, a cross, and the numbers 2506.

"I can see that," she said, gesturing toward the camera crews.

The man grunted. "You just here to admire trucks, *chiquita*, or can I help you?"

"I hope so," she said, cocking her head to the side. "I want to hire a boat."

"This is the place." He grinned. "Take your pick."

"I'm looking for Ricky." His smile disappeared.

"Don't know any Ricky." He shook his head.

"You're . . . not Ricky?"

"I just said I don't know any Ricky," he said through pursed lips.

"Becky over at Castaways said I could find Ricky around here."

"I don't know any Becky either." He pointed at the charter boats. "You should ask Bill or Frank. They'll take you out on a boat for the right price. Now, if you'll excuse me, I've got to go."

The man ducked his head and slipped into the truck, started the engine, and reversed out. Jessica waved good-bye to the man, who acknowledged her with a slight nod, before he quickly drove off, heading southwest.

Once the pickup truck was out of sight, Jessica ran back to the Mustang and peeled out of the parking lot in the same direction.

With only one road out of town, it wasn't long before Jessica caught up with the bright red truck just as it accelerated onto the Seven Mile Bridge, a low, flat, two-lane highway suspended over the ocean. She settled behind at a safe distance and forwarded the photo of the Ford to Sunday back at Langley.

A few minutes later, she received a reply text:

Richard Green, Everglades City, Florida.

"Ricky!" she tsked to herself. "You little liar."

Jessica trailed the truck for twenty more minutes and several more bridges before the Ford finally turned off the main road and headed north on one of the islands, then slowed again and veered down a dirt path cut through a mangrove stand.

Jessica crawled along slowly behind the truck and then parked behind a thicket to hide the Mustang. She stashed her hat, grabbed her phone, binoculars, and a bottle of water and pursued the truck on foot.

On the other side of the mangroves, she found a clearing and crouched in the tall grasses at the tree line to get a clear view. Through her binoculars, she watched the Ford pickup drive over another bridge, which led to a small private island with a single structure. The truck parked in front of the house, an enormous Spanish-style villa of whitewashed walls and a red tile roof. At the front were immaculately trimmed gardens, a tropical blend of elephant's ear plants, bougainvillea, banana trees, and pineapple bushes. Orchid vines of flourescent pink and purple flowers covered a trellis at the main door.

Ricky exited the Ford with a bucket and walked right into the house without knocking. Jessica scanned the windows, unable to see where he had gone. She aimed her binoculars at the back of the house, where she could see a vast deck with a pool overlooking a small private beach. A ring of orange bouys in the sea marked a swimming area.

With no sign of any activity, Jessica set down her binoculars and took out her phone. She marked her location with GPS and sent the coordinates to Sunday, along with a short note:

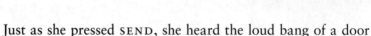

ID on this house?

Just as she pressed SEND, she heard the loud bang of a door slamming and a man yelling, "Sunshine! *Compadre guapo!*"

Through the binoculars, she watched Ricky lumber out to the edge of the deck by the beach, carrying the bucket. He pulled a bloody fish from the bucket by its tail and dangled it for a moment before tossing it into the swimming area, igniting an eruption of white water. The shiny black skin of a shark leapt out of the water and then disappeared again. After a few seconds, the shark's fin reappeared, cutting through the surface. Ricky threw another fish, which was immediately attacked by the shark.

"Sunshine! *Compadre guapo!*" he shouted again, a huge smile plastered across his face.

It wasn't a swimming area, Jessica realized with alarm. It was a shark pen. *What kind of lunatic keeps a shark for a pet?*

Her phone vibrated with a reply from Sunday to both her questions:

Ruben Sandoval.

25.

Ruben Sandoval was bored. *Dead bored.* He'd been at the George P. Shultz National Foreign Affairs Training Center all week. Stuck in dull seminar rooms, under fluorescent lights, and now on his fifth straight hour sitting in an uncomfortable plastic chair.

His stomach rumbled with hunger. He'd paid fourteen dollars cash for a squished ham-and-cheese sandwich wrapped in plastic and crammed into a small cardboard box along with a bag of salty potato chips and a bruised apple. He had picked up the lunch, examined each item with mounting disgust, and then had thrown the whole thing in the trash. Even the coffee was unbearable. He licked his lips at the thought of a proper thick, black café cubano, with a twist of lemon, sipping it while relaxing on a chaise longue in the Florida sun.

The woman sitting next to him coughed loudly, a wet, mucousy bellow that jolted Ruben back to the seminar. At the front of the room, a plump man in an ill-fitting suit with a bad comb-over was tediously explaining how to handle classified documents.

"Standard procedures for determining the level of classifi-cation are based on Executive Order 13526 . . ."

This wasn't how it was meant to be. An ambassadorship was supposed to be *glamorous*. This was to be the pinnacle of his professional life, coming from nothing to be the official represen-tative of the President of the United States of America. His mind drifted again, marveling at what he had done to get here.

Ruben had been just six years old when he had arrived in Amer-ica alone. His family had tried to flee, hustled onto a plane in the middle of the night, carrying only what they could stash in their pockets. But they were stopped, yanked right out of their seats on the plane by armed men. Ruben remembered his mother screaming, his baby brother wailing, as they dragged away his father. It was the last time he would see his *papi*.

Ruben's father had been one of six children raised in a poor village in eastern Cuba. He had moved to the capital at six-teen and worked his way up through Havana's casinos. His *papi* started by sweeping floors on the overnight shift, then became a bartender, a blackjack dealer, a pit boss. When American inves-tors opened the grand Hotel Habana Riviera, the same year that Ruben was born, his father was named head of casino security. Links to powerful gringos had been the reason his family had seats on a plane to Miami after the communist guerrillas closed in on the capital.

But those connections were also why they dragged his father away, leaving a single mother with young Ruben and his infant brother, Ernesto.

"There are three levels of document classification. 'Confidential' is the lowest level, where release of such information to the public would cause damage . . ."

Without his *papi*, Ruben's mother was heartbroken and alone. Their family home was then seized by the government and turned into a headquarters for the local chapter of the communist Rebel Youth Association. So Ruben's mother, through an inconspicuous friend at the Catholic church, made the most difficult choice for a parent: She sent her eldest son away to safety. Ruben, along with fourteen thousand other unaccompanied Cuban minors, was flown to America in a secret effort dubbed Operation Peter Pan. It was the last time Ruben would see his mother or his baby brother Ernesto.

Unlike the fictional Peter Pan, Ruben was forced to grow up immediately. He was sent to an orphanage in Buffalo, New York, and then on to a boarding school in Oklahoma. Once he turned sixteen, he quit school, like his father, and made his way to the big city. Ruben hitchhiked to Miami, where he took odd jobs running errands up and down Calle Ocho for the old men of Little Havana. At eighteen he worked as a hotel cabana boy, bringing clean towels and cold tropical drinks to middle-class tourists on Miami Beach.

As he ran along the pool deck in the sun, young Ruben remembered something valuable he had learned from his father: There was big money to be made in selling effortless leisure. The tourists in Havana's casinos didn't know that the bright lights and shiny hotels were a façade for a crumbling system. And they didn't care. They paid handsomely to escape their regular lives, to have fun, and to look fabulous. Pretending to have it all was *good enough.*

Miami in the 1980s was so similar to Havana of the 1950s.

The notion of effortless leisure was the inspiration for Ruben's first Sunshine Yoga Studio & Juice Bar, opened in Coral Gables. The upscale neighborhood, known as "The City Beautiful" and home to the University of Miami, was the training ground for South Florida's attractive elite. Within a few years, Ruben had Sunshine Yoga Studio & Juice Bar branches in Fort Lauderdale, Boca Raton, and Palm Beach. After a decade, he had a studio in every wealthy zip code in the state of Florida. Then he cashed out.

"SBU is a special designation which stands for 'sensitive but unclassified.' This is used for personnel records and other information that is not technically . . ."

Getting rich wasn't enough for Ruben. He had learned that, too, from his father and the pain of his exile. Sure, he had grown to appreciate fine wine and Italian sports cars. He owned luxurious vacation homes in the Bahamas, the Florida Keys, and in Puerto Banús on the Spanish Costa del Sol. But Ruben also knew that to protect his fortune and his family, he needed to be politically connected. To get what he really wanted, he would use his wealth to buy power.

Ruben learned quickly that hosting fund-raisers for American politicians was easy. For a catered cocktail party and fifty grand in cash, passed through a network of straw donors, you could buy a congressman every other November. It was almost too easy.

"The distinction between Secret and Top Secret information is based on a determination of whether revelation of that information might cause extreme damage . . ."

Ruben was always thinking of a grander plan. If he could own a congressman for a pittance, then what about a President? Campaign donations paid his way into the inner circle of the White House. He had stayed with his wife in the Lincoln Bedroom and then with a girlfriend at Blair House, the President's official guesthouse just off Lafayette Park normally reserved for visiting heads of state.

Why not bigger? What about an ambassadorship? It didn't matter which one, really. Just a title and an entrée into the upper echelons of the American political game. Which he could leverage to expand his network and plot his ultimate goal.

"Top Secret information that is designed to be sensitive compartmented information is handled only in specially designated areas . . ."

Sitting in the dreary seminar room, that final dream, the inner motivation that drove everything Ruben Sandoval did, seemed so very far away.

Ruben wasn't even supposed to be here. Officially, he *wasn't* here. The President had not yet formally announced his nomination to be the next U.S. Ambassador to Egypt. And then he'd need a Senate confirmation hearing and a full Senate vote before he could go to Cairo. He could be weeks, if not months, away.

But Egypt was important. The State Department was especially anxious to have that post filled quickly, so someone in the Secretary of State's office had arranged for Ruben Sandoval, the presumptive nominee, to spend an inconspicuous—and, technically, unofficial—week at the Schultz Center to get an early start on ambassadorial training and to begin Arabic-language lessons. He had also been fast-tracked for his security clearance. Filling out all those pages of disclosure forms had been painful. This all seemed so unnecessary, a distraction from what he was hoping to achieve. Rather than sitting in this pointless seminar, he should be ensuring that his plan was in motion. He needed to get out of this room.

"For Top Secret information we use a Sensitive Compartmented Information Facility, which we usually call a SCIF, pronounced 'skiff.' Inside a SCIF, communications are protected from external listening devices and swept regularly . . ."

Ruben snapped out of his daydreaming and interrupted the speaker. "Excuse me. You're saying that discussions and phone calls in a SCIF are entirely private? They can't be bugged or decoded?"

"Yes, sir. That's where any information that has been classified as TS/SCI can be handled and discussed."

"And phone calls from a SCIF are undetectable?"

"Yes, sir. All communication in and out of a SCIF is encrypted and untraceable. It's fully secure."

"Where are these SCIFs?" Ruben asked.

"Everywhere. In the State Department. Inside our embassies. Anywhere that a cleared USG official needs to handle Top Secret information."

"Is there a SCIF here?"

"Yes, sir. We have a SCIF on campus. Would you like to see it?"

26.

Sunday had never heard of Ruben Sandoval, but there was plenty of information on him.

The immigration and naturalization database listed Ruben Sandoval as arriving in the United States from Cuba in 1962 at the age of six. He had arrived unaccompanied and in the custody of the Catholic Church of western New York. In the church records shared with the government, his father was recorded as Fulgencio Sandoval, age thirty-eight, and his mother as Yanitse Sandoval, age twenty-nine, along with one sibling, Ernesto, three years old. But Ruben is the only one in the family who appeared to have ever entered the country.

From tax records at the Internal Revenue Service, Sunday learned that Ruben Sandoval had moved around to different addresses in South Florida for years with little income. He had started a string of failed ventures until the Sunshine Yoga Studio & Juice Bar, Inc., made a small profit. The real money flowed once the business expanded. Then, three years ago, he sold out. Sandoval's income shifted from the yoga and juice business to a portfolio of investments, an erratic mix of real estate in Nevada and Arizona, a chain of check-cashing outlets in Texas, and a hotel complex in Naples, Florida. Sandoval's most recent financial statements showed that he had abruptly disposed of a significant minority shareholding in a defense contractor Kinetic Xelaron Systems in Tampa and paid tax on $78 million in capital gains.

Sunday sat back. What he could do with $78 million! He would buy his parents a big house, maybe in the Hollywood Hills or out in the desert near Palm Springs. Ay, would the cousins come from Nigeria in droves! Everyone expecting their share of the payout. And the goats! And lambs! He'd probably have to buy a ranch to keep all the livestock for feasts! Ay! Sunday laughed to himself at the thought and returned to his research.

For such a successful and wealthy self-made businessman, the newspapers didn't have much on Ruben Sandoval. Sunday found a grainy *Miami Herald* photo of him at a charity gala for marine wildlife protection. In the picture, Sandoval wore a white tuxedo and a much younger woman on each arm. The caption described him only as "a local businessman and two party guests." The *Tampa Bay Times* business section reported on the Kinetic Xelaron sale, but had no further details or any mention of Sandoval. The *Washington Post*'s political gossip column mentioned Sandoval only once, noting that he was a rising political fund-raiser and reporting a rumor that his name was on a short list of potential ambassadorships.

"Fund-raiser?" Sunday muttered to himself. He opened a new window on his computer and logged on to the Federal Election Commission database, which showed that Sandoval was indeed active. He had given the maximum allowable contribution of $2,700 to virtually every prominent politician in Florida and Nevada, and to the President's reelection campaign. *Nothing un-usual here,* he thought. Rich guy spreading around some cash to make friends. But $2,700 doesn't buy anyone an ambassador-ship. There must be more to Sandoval's story. More details . . . somewhere.

27.

The freshly washed pearl-white Lexus LX SUV roared up Constitution Avenue and squealed around the corner toward the dead end of 22nd Street Northwest. The driver whipped tightly around a line of waiting taxicabs and veered up onto the curb, coming to a screeching halt at the steel gate perimeter.

A Diplomatic Security officer stepped on a silent alarm and immediately raised the anti–car bomb barriers. Inside the State Department's Harry S. Truman Federal Building, all the security gates automatically locked and the reception desk computers froze. The earpieces of dozens of armed guards erupted with emergency instructions to seal all the doors and execute an immediate lockdown. Shelter-in-place orders flashed on every computer screen in the building.

The officer at the front gate unsnapped his sidearm and aimed it at the Lexus. The taxi drivers ducked into their cars as pedestrians shrieked and ran for cover.

"Driver!" the guard shouted. "Exit your vehicle with your hands up!"

He crouched and took a few steps toward the SUV. The engine cut and the door of the Lexus swung open heavily.

"Hands! Hands! Hands!" the officer shouted.

Out of the Lexus stepped a tall blond woman, middle-aged and handsome, wearing a peach-colored designer business suit.

"Driver! Hands now!"

Behind the officer, more guards in heavy Kevlar, matte black helmets, and automatic weapons emerged from the main doors. The woman threw off her sunglasses and squinted in the sun, revealing long black streaks of eyeliner running down her cheeks. She took a step toward the officer.

"Freeze! Hands! Now!"

The other guards fanned out in a perimeter around the woman.

"Down on the ground! Now! Now! Now!"

The woman showed her palms. "Don't be ridiculous," she said, wiping her cheek with her sleeve.

At that very moment, up on the seventh floor of the State Department's headquarters, a security officer burst into the office of the Secretary of State's chief of staff and slammed the door.

"What the hell's going on?" Landon Parker howled, holding a phone in each hand.

"Sir, we've got a security breach at the front gate. I'm here to lockdown your office."

"I'll call you back," Parker said, and set down both handsets. "Where's the Secretary?"

"She's not in the building, sir. She's over at the West Wing. She's secure."

"Is all this really necessary? What kind of breach?" Parker huffed.

"Unknown at this time. I'm checking now," he said, touching a finger to his earpiece.

Parker walked over to the window, pulling on the blinds.

"Sir, stand away from the window!"

Parker peered out and witnessed a dozen armed guards surrounding a pretty woman with golden hair in an orange suit. He glared as the woman reluctantly raised her hands and took several tentative steps toward the guards, igniting a round of shouting and the appearance of more officers from every direction.

"What the fuck?" Parker said to himself.

"I'm checking now, sir," the guard repeated.

Parker watched the guards swarm over the woman, force her to the ground, and handcuff her. He could see a second security team secure a pearl-white SUV parked nearby while other officers cleared the area of bystanders.

"Looks like they have it under control," Parker said. "Doesn't look like anything serious."

"Let's wait for the all clear, sir."

"I'm going back to work," Parker said, turning away from the window and eyeing one of his telephones. "Tell me, once you know what happened."

"I'm in touch with the commanding officer at the front gate right now, sir."

As Parker started to press redial, something about the woman—her shape, the color of her hair perhaps—suddenly seemed . . . familiar.

Parker set down the phone and returned to the window. The

officers were forcing the woman up to her feet. He narrowed his eyes and tried to make out her face. "Officer, I want a full report. Who is . . . that suspect?"

"Sir?"

"I just watched DS detain a woman at the front gate. I want to know who she is."

"Mr. Parker"—the officer paused and touched his earpiece—"DS is reporting that she's here to see someone on the seventh floor. She's insisting she's here to see . . . you."

Eight minutes later, Landon Parker was in a windowless room in the basement of the State Department, consoling a crying Mrs. Penelope Barrymore.

"Pippa, why didn't you just call me?"

"I did!" she wailed. Parker handed her a tissue. "They told me someone would get back to me, but of course no one did."

"I'm sorry, Pippa, I didn't know."

"You should have called me, Landon!"

"Yes, you're right. I should have, Pippa. I've been busy."

"That's why I had to just come over. Those horrible men pushed me on the ground!"

"Security is a little nervous about trucks rushing the State Department gate. You know how dangerous that was? It was stupid, Pippa. You could have been killed."

"I'm not here about me, Landon. I'm here about Brinkley. I can't believe what's happened. I need your help!"

"Yes, I know," Parker said.

"So you can help him? You can get him free from those terrible Cubans?"

"We're working on it."

"Working on it? What good are you, Landon?" she shrieked.

"Pippa, you have to be patient. We are still trying to figure out how your husband wandered into Cuban national waters."

"I don't care. I just want to know when they're going to set him free."

"I don't know, Pippa," he said.

"You *are* going to get him freed, aren't you, Landon?"

"I'm trying. The Cubans aren't saying anything yet, beyond what you've probably seen on TV."

"I saw that. Parading my Brinkley on television like a common criminal. And Alejandro, Crawford, and"—she burst into tears—"poor Dennis!"

Parker looked away as the woman blubbered.

Penelope inhaled deeply and composed herself. "Landon, how could the Cubans possibly think those fools are spies?"

"I don't know, Pippa," he said, making eye contact again. "What do you know?"

"Brinkley's not a spy." She began to whimper again.

"Of course. I know that, Pippa. But maybe you know something else that we don't? Something that could help us get Brinkley back home as quickly as possible. Anything?"

Mrs. Penelope Barrymore stopped crying and took a deep breath. "I spoke with Mariposa Cabrera—that's Alejandro's wife."

"He's the owner of the boat."

"Right. And Brinkley's friend. He coaches the girls' soccer team."

Parker leaned in close. "So what did Cabrera's wife tell you?"

"It's almost too dumb to say out loud."

"Dumber than gate-crashing the State Department?"

She shrugged.

"Tell me, Pippa, anything that might be helpful in getting Brinkley and his friends back home safe. You have to tell me."

"Mariposa . . . said something about Alejandro's family in Cuba. Before they fled years ago. They had hidden some . . . diamonds."

"Diamonds? In Cuba?"

"That's what she said. They buried them. She said Al always talked about going to get them."

"Are you telling me Brinkley got caught in Cuba hunting for . . . buried treasure?"

Pippa shrugged again. "I told you it was dumb."

"We've got a major international diplomatic incident because your husband thinks he's a pirate?"

"He's no spy," she said.

"And now I've got to rescue him?"

"Yes, you have to save Brinkley. You just have to, Landon!" Pippa Barrymore wiped the running mascara off her face and took a deep breath. "But he's no pirate either."

"He's not?" Parker asked. "Then what is he?"

28.

I could drive straight and be back in Washington, D.C. in fifteen hours, Jessica thought. Instead, she exited Interstate 95 and steered her rented convertible Mustang down Sunrise Boulevard, driving east toward the Deputy Director's house in Fort Lauderdale.

Her little errand for the Deputy Director was done. She had found Richard Green, the man connected to the missing fishing boat, but he had refused to talk. She had tracked Green back to some rich Cuban American's house, but then . . . nothing. The trail had gone cold.

It wasn't Jessica's style to give up so easy. But this assignment seemed like a waste of time. What was she supposed to do, sit in that mangrove and stake out the house? Where was this all headed? And why?

Sunday back at Langley was digging into the leads, but, really, what more could she do? *Return to vacation,* she thought. That's what she should do. *Fuck the Deputy Director.*

On cue, her phone buzzed with a text message from DANIEL DOLLAR:

> News from the Keys?

What to share with him? She could give him the name Richard Green. She could tell him that he's connected to a Ruben Sandoval. That would lead to more questions . . . and more errands.

Jessica pulled up to the driveway of the vacation house and parked. The afternoon sun was beating down and a light breeze off the ocean filled her nose with the smells of the sea. She looked down at her phone again and pressed a number.

"Hi, sweets," was the cheery answer.

"You sound happy, Judd," she said.

"Why wouldn't I? I'm sitting in my office, under fluorescent lights, reading stacks of useless government documents. I'm chasing shadows while my wife and kids are enjoying the beach. What's not to love?"

"I've been doing a little work, too."

"I thought you were going to relax," Judd scolded.

"I've got something for you."

"You do?"

"You don't sound surprised," she said.

"No comment. What've you found?"

"The missing boat . . . the fishing boat that the Cubans seized . . ."

"Yeah, I know," Judd said, looking down at a photo of *The Big Pig* and his meager files on each of the four missing Americans.

"I've got a name for you: Richard Green."

Judd looked down at the files for Dennis Dobson, Brinkley Barrymore, Crawford Jackson, and Alejandro Cabrera. "Never heard of him. Who's he?"

"He looks after the boat. Part-time."

"How'd you get his name? Are you down in the Keys?"

Jessica hesitated. *Lie Number Five?* "No," she said. *What's five lies versus four?* "No, I got it from . . . a colleague. Don't ask me more."

"Okay . . . maintenance guy in the marina." Judd scrawled down the name. "Does he know anything?"

"I don't know."

"That's all?"

"I don't have anything else on Green. I just think it might be relevant."

"Okay, thanks, sweets. I'll look into it, but you should go back to the kids. You're supposed to be on vacation."

"I have one more name for you. Does Ruben Sandoval ring a bell?"

Judd heard the name and repeated it to himself. "Ruben Sandoval . . . Sandoval . . . sounds familiar . . ." Then he remembered the name from an intelligence horse trade with his British contact the previous week. "I think Ruben Sandoval is some kind of businessman. And a political fund-raiser in Florida. He's supposed to be the next U.S. Ambassador to Egypt," Judd said.

"Egypt?"

"If I'm remembering correctly, yes," Judd said.

"How do you know that?" she asked.

Judd recalled that Serena had gotten Ruben Sandoval's name from one of her friends who worked on the State Department's seventh floor. Judd had then given that name to a British Foreign Office official in London in exchange for inside information he had needed in Zimbabwe. "Eh, I don't remember," he mumbled. "Probably just State Department chatter."

Jessica frowned. "But Egypt? That's odd."

"Sure is," Judd said. "What's our future Ambassador to Egypt got to do with the missing boat?"

"Richard Green works for Ruben Sandoval."

"Okay . . . So this Green, who we know nothing about, watches the missing boat and also works for Sandoval, who is rich and politically connected."

"Right," Jessica said. "Suspicious, don't you think, Judd?"

"Could be. But that's a pretty tenuous thread, Jess."

"It's worth digging deeper, that's all," she said. "I'm just saying that there's a connection."

"Let's assume you found something important and Sandoval is linked to the four Americans."

"Okay," she said.

"Then what are Sandoval and these poor dupes really up to? Is this a big mistake, a bunch of amateurs who got caught, or something bigger? If it's something bigger, then what? And why Cuba?"

"Good question, Judd. What the hell is going on in Cuba?"

29.

What the hell is going on in Cuba?" Melanie Eisenberg was steaming.

The Assistant Secretary for Western Hemisphere Affairs sat forward in her chair and eyed the long conference table in front of her. "Those were the very words of the Secretary of State." Several of the assembled staff shuffled papers and someone cracked their knuckles, but no one spoke. *"What the hell is going on in Cuba?"* she repeated. "We can't have it. The Secretary can't wonder what's happening. She can't have doubts about what're we doing in Cuba. It reflects badly on all of us! Does everyone get that?"

Most heads bobbed in agreement.

"I don't know what she's been hearing, but we've got to put a stop to it. I've assembled all of you now to update the team on what we know and to clarify our course of action. Sybil, put up the slides."

The screen behind Eisenberg lit up with a photo of *The Big Pig*, a long white fishing boat with a bright pink stripe along the side.

"This is the vessel that the Cubans seized. We believe it's a private U.S.-registered fishing boat. Next." The slide switched to a screengrab from CNN. "These are the four civilians who've been detained. We're still running background checks on the men, but, so far, nothing of interest. They all live in suburban Maryland, just outside D.C. As far as we can tell, the only connection between them is that their children are on the same sports team. Isn't that right, Sybil?"

"Yes, ma'am. Girls' soccer."

"Sybil, do we have anything more than what the cable news is reporting?"

"No, ma'am. But we're working on it."

"Fine." Eisenberg exhaled. "The most likely scenario is that these are just ordinary AMCITs. Regular civilians on a fishing trip and they drifted over the border. The currents in the Florida Straits are strong. I've been there many times myself. It's plausible that they just had too many beers and floated into Cuban waters. It wouldn't be the first time."

A hand went up at the table. "So, these guys are drunken yahoos and got lost—that's our story?"

"It's not *our* story, Marty." Eisenberg frowned. "Those are the facts. Human error or faulty navigation equipment . . . or something like that," Eisenberg said, scowling. "We are proceeding on this basis until we have reason to believe otherwise. I don't want the Secretary hearing rumors or paranoid fantasies. We don't want her spun up about something that's not true."

"What are the other scenarios?" asked a young woman at the end of the table.

"Excuse me?"

"If it wasn't human error or some mistake, what are the *other* explanations?"

"There aren't any other likely scenarios right now."

"What about the boat owner?" she asked. "Alejandro Cabrera could be a Cuban name. Does he have ties to Cuba? Maybe to the Miami exiles?"

Eisenberg turned to her aide, "Sybil?"

"We're looking into it."

"Good. But even if we find out this Alejandro Cabrera is the long-lost grandson of Fulgencio Batista, we're still talking about four American civilians who are now in a Cuban prison and on all the cable networks." Eisenberg pointed at the screen. The four men appeared slumped over, fear and exhaustion on their faces. "Could anyone seriously suggest *these guys* are anything other than a mistake? I mean, look at them."

"Ma'am, if the men are connected to Cuban exiles, that would change the equation," said another man at the table.

"It will certainly change how the Cubans respond," said yet another. "The conspiracy theories are going to fly."

"Even if their incursion was a mistake, if this guy is a Cuban exile, the press is going to have a field day."

"The Cubans are going to want a pound of flesh to let them go."

"Hold it!" Eisenberg snorted. "So . . . in all these scenarios, these four soccer dads were doing what? Invading Cuba? In a fishing boat? Is that what you're suggesting? I don't think even the Cubans are paranoid enough to believe that. I call that a fantasy. Anything else?"

"Ma'am . . ." The young man hesitated. "There's a rumor going around the building that one of the missing men has, um . . ."

"Yes," Eisenberg beckoned the staffer. "Spit it out."

"Um . . . friends in the building."

"What?" Eisenberg spun around toward her assistant. "Sybil?"

"There was a security incident this afternoon at the front gate, ma'am."

"And?"

"A woman crashed her car near the main entrance. I've heard she may be linked to one of the missing men."

"You've *heard*? What do we know for sure?"

"I'll check with Diplomatic Security."

"Is this the rumor?" Eisenberg asked.

The young man nodded.

"That's ridiculous. Until we have some actual facts, people, we're not changing course."

Eisenberg brushed the front of her jacket and collected herself. "Unless anyone has something else to add—*something factual*—here's how this is going to play out." She placed both hands on the table, a thick gold ring with a pale blue gemstone clacked on the wood. "We are going to issue a public call for the release of the four innocent men. No escalation, no negotiations. Let's just diffuse the situation. That's how we make this go away."

"What about Congress, ma'am? The Free Cuba Congressional Caucus has issued some pretty strong statements. Adelman-Zamora was on all the networks today."

"And the Cuba desk has been flooded with calls, ma'am."

"It's trending on Twitter."

"Twitter?" She closed her eyes.

"Yes, ma'am. Hashtag freesoccerdad4."

Eisenberg swore under her breath. "That's . . . all . . . fine," she said through gritted teeth. "Congress will make its views known. We respect that. The public, too. But we are not going to allow one lost fishing boat to become a political weapon. I won't allow this to spin out of control. It's unfortunate. But it's not in anyone's interest to escalate this incident any further. Not for Cuba. Not for the United States. Not for these men and their families. The Cubans will release them once they realize they have nothing to gain. That's it. That's our objective."

"Do we bring in the other bureaus on this, Madam Assistant Secretary?"

"Negative. We are going to put this fire out by suffocating it. By denying oxygen. We keep this within our team."

"What about S/CRU?"

"Judd Ryker?"

"Yes, ma'am. Aren't we supposed to call the Crisis Reaction Unit during a crisis?"

"Ryker, the academic?"

"Yes, ma'am."

"When someone says 'That's academic,' what do they mean?" Eisenberg asked.

"They mean 'irrelevant.'"

Melanie Eisenberg raised her eyebrows. "Meeting adjourned."

30.

The cell was built out of stone blocks and covered in a soft green moss. Brinkley Barrymore III ran his hand over the wall and felt the moistness on his fingertips. Through the sole window's iron bars, Brinkley could see palm trees and the shadows of late-afternoon light. He took a deep breath. The air smelled both fresh from the sea air outside and stale from the ammonia of the urine left behind by the cell's previous inmates.

"We're in some sort of old castle or fort," he said to the others. The K Street lawyer, usually most comfortable in a gray tailored suit, was wearing a dirty orange jumpsuit that hung on his body like an oversized sack. He shook his head. "This isn't a real prison. At least not anymore."

Alejandro Cabrera, wearing an identical jumpsuit, only tighter and even dirtier, gripped the window bars and pulled himself up to look out.

"It sure as shit smells like a real prison," Crawford Jackson said.

"No. This is for show." Brinkley shook his head.

"I don't care where we are," Crawford said. "I want to know when we're getting the hell out."

"I told you not to worry, Craw," Brinkley said. "Think about it. They have no reason to hold us. The Cubans have nothing to gain by keeping us."

"Fuck you!" Crawford barked.

"We just have to be patient. We can't panic."

"How the fuck did we let you get us into this?" Crawford clenched his fists.

"It wasn't supposed to happen this way," Brinkley said. "I'm sorry."

"You're sorry? You and Al tricked us into some bullshit fishing trip or treasure hunt or who the fuck knows what. And now we're in a Cuban prison!"

"I'll get us out. But there's no point in rehashing now what went wrong," Brinkley said. "There will be plenty of time later for an after-action. Right, Al?"

Alejandro continued to stare out the window.

"After-action?" Crawford barked. "We're in a fuck-ing prison in Cu-ba!"

"We all have to stay calm," Brinkley said. "That's how we'll get through this. That's how we'll get out. Al, back me up here."

"Look at goddamn Deuce!" The two men turned to face Dennis Dobson, sitting in the corner of the cell. He had one bandaged arm in a sling, the other arm wrapped tightly around his knees. Dennis was rocking gently back and forth, his eyes glazed over. "He's still in shock."

"Deuce will be fine," Brinkley said quietly. "Hey, Deuce!" he then shouted. "You're going to be fine! Are you hearing me?"

No reply. Just more rocking.

"Hey, Deuce! We're going to get you out of here. Do you understand?"

Still no reply.

"Why haven't they let us call the U.S. embassy?" Crawford asked. "Isn't that how it's supposed to work?"

"I don't know," Brinkley said.

"How the hell does our government even know we're here?"

"They know."

"How can you be so sure?"

"Our government isn't just going to let us rot. They aren't going to leave us in Cuba, just sitting here exposed." Brinkley shook his head.

"Are you kidding me?" Crawford's eyes were wide. "You think our government is going to save us? You don't think Washington will see us as some kind of pawn? They would sell us out without blinking if they can gain an advantage! Or just leave us here! I was in the Navy, too, you know. I know how this works!"

"They won't leave us exposed again," Brinkley said.

"Again? What the fuck're you talking about? Brink, we are in *fuck-ing Cu-ba*!"

Alejandro, who had been quiet all along, suddenly spoke up. "Craw's right."

"What?" the other two men gasped in unison.

"They're gonna do it again. No air cover. No backup. No admission. It's all happening again. Just like *mi abuelo*."

"What the fuck're you talking about, Al?" Crawford growled.

"Look, we're all under stress," Brinkley said, showing his palms. "Let's all calm down."

"It wasn't supposed to happen again," Alejandro said. "That was the whole goddamn point."

"Shut up, Al!" Brinkley hissed.

"They're going to abandon us," Alejandro said. "Just like our grandfathers."

"No they're not!" Brinkley insisted.

"What the fuck are you two talking about?" Crawford narrowed his eyes in a mix of confusion and anger.

"Nobody's leaving anyone," Brinkley said. "This isn't 1961."

31.

'm missing something, Judd thought to himself. He took a step back to examine his puzzle. He had tacked photos of the four Americans up on a whiteboard: Dennis Dobson, Brinkley Barrymore III, Crawford Jackson, Alejandro Cabrera. *Who are these guys? What are they up to?*

Landon Parker had asked Judd to help find a way to get them back without appearing to talk directly to the Cuban government. Judd was supposed to initiate a backchannel while Assistant Secretary Melanie Eisenberg was the public face of the U.S. government. So far, Eisenberg hadn't been saying much. She was playing diplomatic chess, waiting out the Cubans to see their next move. Hoping it would all go away so she could resume with her plans for diplomatic normalization. But what was Parker's angle? "I need creative thinking, Ryker!" Parker had insisted. But it didn't quite add up.

What am I missing? Judd wondered. He scrawled the name RICHARD GREEN in a box next to ALEJANDRO CABRERA and drew a solid line connecting the two men. Next, he printed a photo of Ruben Sandoval that he had found on the Internet, wrote his name underneath the picture, and attached it to the board with another solid line to Green. Above all the pictures, he wrote CUBA in a large red circle and drew dotted lines connecting the circle to Cabrera and Sandoval. He still had one more clue. In the upper corner he scribbled his best drawing of the White House and then connected dotted lines to Sandoval.

Judd stood back again and visualized the web he had just created. *Maybe this was nothing?* Maybe he was imagining some grander network that didn't really exist? A lost fisherman and his beer buddies, a Florida drifter, a yoga and juice bar tycoon, a connection to the White House. This all sounded crazy. He certainly couldn't mention any of this to Landon Parker. Judd considered wiping the whiteboard clean and starting over. He grabbed the eraser and was about to swipe when the White House gave him pause. If there was anything meaningful here, anything really treacherous, it would be the link to someone powerful. If these men were really all linked, then who was this Ruben Sandoval? Was he a power broker or a pawn? Who would know?

Judd smacked himself on the forehead. *Of course.* He dialed a number.

A few seconds later, his phone erupted. "Judd, darling!"

"Hello, Mariana. I'm sorry to call out of the blue."

"Not at all, my darling," responded Mariana Leibowitz, the Washington lobbyist who had worked closely with Judd on his missions to Mali and Zimbabwe. "I didn't expect to hear from you so soon."

"Where are you?" Judd asked.

"I'm still in Zimbabwe. I'm here with Gugu."

"You mean President Mutonga? Are you celebrating her victory?"

Mariana laughed. "Yes, President Gugu Mutonga. Of course! I don't think I've slept at all since Monday, my dear! What a ride!"

"I'm sorry I missed the party," Judd said.

"Party? Oh, Judd, you're sweet. We've been up for days because we've been *working*! The president doesn't want to waste any time. It's almost midnight here and we're still in the president's office. We're going to roll out her plan for the first one hundred days in the morning. A national television and radio address. Gugu's gonna bring it!"

"That's great. I'm doubly sorry to call, then."

"What is it?"

"I need your help, Mariana."

"Of course you do, darling. I'm impressed."

"Impressed?"

"We just finished Zimbabwe and you're already onto another crisis," she said.

"Well, not really. I have to navigate a problem in Washington and—"

"Of course, darling," she said, "after all we've been through."

"Do you know Ruben Sandoval?"

"Not personally," she said.

"But you do know *of* him?"

"Of course, Judd! What kind of lobbyist would I be without keeping a pulse on the heavy hitters?"

"Who is he? Who's he backing?"

"A better question is, who *isn't* he backing?"

"So one of them's the President?" Judd asked.

"Of course."

"Why? What does Sandoval want?"

"What do any big donors want? They want power. They want

influence. They want to stroke their own egos. They want to impress their girlfriends. Play the big shot."

"Big shot," Judd repeated.

"Why do you care about Sandoval?" Mariana asked.

"Do you need to know why?"

"Only if you want to tell me, darling," Mariana said in her most soothing voice.

"Is Sandoval connected to Cuba?"

"I'm hearing Middle East. My sources tell me Egypt or Jordan," she said. "That's about as far from Cuba as you can get."

"But I want to know if he's a player on Cuba policy," Judd said. "Do you know?"

"Then forget the White House. POTUS won't touch Cuba until it's a slam dunk. They won't make that mistake again."

"So where should I be looking?" Judd asked.

"Good Lord, Judd," Mariana said.

"Congress?"

"Do I need to spell it out for you?"

"So you're saying yes, Congress."

"Not just anyone in Congress. Start with the Free Cuba Caucus," Mariana said.

"You mean Brenda Adelman-Zamora?"

"That's her," Mariana said. "Is Sandoval connected to Adelman-Zamora?" she then asked.

"I don't know," Judd said. "That's why I called you."

"Judd, darling . . ." She paused and exhaled loudly. "Only because it's you am I doing this."

"Thank you, Mariana."

"Give me five minutes," she said, and hung up.

Judd thought about Brenda Adelman-Zamora. She was the

chair of the House Intelligence Committee. She held the press conference today about the soccer dads. She was the Cuba hawk. But was she linked to Sandoval? If so, how?

Judd wrote BAZ with a big red question mark on his whiteboard and drew a box around it. How does the congresswoman fit?

His phone buzzed with a text message from Mariana.

> Adelman-Zamora $raiser 2nite @7pm. I can get u in.

Bingo! Judd hit reply:

> Thx. Where?

> 9900 Coconut Vista, Las Olas, FL.

> I'm in DC.

> U know anyone in South FL?

32.

Jessica pulled back on the throttle of the Deputy Director's Cobalt bowrider powerboat as she approached the bright lights of her destination. The river that was the backbone of the South Florida Intracoastal Waterway was busy that evening, filled with noisy family day cruisers, long, gleaming sportfishing boats, and gargantuan party catamarans blasting hip-hop dance music.

Her target, the house at 9900 Coconut Vista Lane, was easy to find. Illuminated palm trees along the waterfront framed a brightly lit modern glass-and-steel structure that appeared to be more art museum than residence.

It had seemed absurd to Jessica to go to a party in a speedboat. She was arriving alone—wife, mother of two small children, agronomist, the furthest thing from a flashy celebrity. Her CIA training had taught her always to assume a low profile, to go unseen whenever possible. James Bond pulling up to black-tie parties in an Aston Martin was only for the movies. Real spies slipped in through the back door and then left unnoticed. Arriving at a fancy party wearing a designer wrap dress and in a luxury boat seemed precisely the wrong move.

But she had followed Judd's clear instructions from Mariana Leibowitz, who assured her that at a Florida political fund-raiser this was exactly how to fit in. With her light black skin, the party-goers would probably assume she was Puerto Rican or, even better, Cuban. No need to correct anyone's presumptions. No need to explain. Mariana had promised to tell the party host nothing more than she was sending over a rich young woman who had taken a strong interest in local politics, low taxes, and the protection of endangered manatees. That would be plenty to get Jessica in the door.

"Bienvenido a Casa Libre!" shouted a young Latino man standing on the shore, dressed in white shorts and a white golf shirt. Dozens of boats were rafted up, tied together like a marine parking lot. The valet waved for her to pull the powerboat alongside a teal-and-orange cigarette racing boat that was already secured to the dock.

Jessica idled the engine and threw him a line, which he quickly attached to a cleat, and then he stood to take her hand to help her off the vessel. A young woman, also dressed in an all-white uniform, suddenly appeared, holding a tray of champagne flutes. "Welcome to Casa Libre," she said. Energetic but soothing rhumba rhythms emanated from a band playing on the pool deck.

Jessica accepted the drink and followed the girl toward the house. Inside the parlor, voluptuous bronze women in bright pink cocktail dresses handed out drinks, while the crowd was a mix of trendy Latinos and elderly couples of all races. Along one side of the room, a long table was covered with pyramids of stone crab claws, rings of enormous shrimp, and giant wooden bowls of papaya, mango, and pineapple. Jessica stood in a strategic position by the back door, sipping her champagne, while she scanned the room. No one matched the photo of Ruben Sandoval.

She mingled among the crowd, making small talk about the hurricane season and real estate prices. She hated it. After nearly an hour, someone, mercifully, clink-clink-clinked his champagne glass, the band stopped playing, and the room hushed.

An older man stepped forward and smiled confidently at the room. His gray hair was combed over his scalp and he wore a black tailored suit over a bright red open-neck shirt, exposing a thick gold chain around his neck. The man raised his glass triumphantly.

"My friends, you are all welcome to Casa Libre! I hope you all enjoy yourselves this evening. But I must interrupt the fun for a moment to remind you why we are here tonight," he said with a slight accent that hinted at a mix of both Latin America and the outer boroughs of New York City. "Our guest of honor has just arrived and she does not have much time with us tonight. We are so very honored to have her with us this evening. I am humbled to introduce one of America's great leaders. She is the backbone of our people, a champion of freedom, and a friend of all of ours. She is just the person that we all need at this crucial time. And we are all here tonight because she also needs us. I am honored to welcome"—he paused, allowing the band a few beats for dramatic effect—"Congresswoman Brenda Adelman-Zamora!"

The crowd clapped enthusiastically as the congresswoman entered from a side hallway. Wearing a cream-colored pantsuit, she stopped and shook hands with each guest as she moved deliberately around the room, trailed by a young aide. When she arrived in front of Jessica, she warmly shook her hand as if they were old friends, "So lovely to see you again. That's a stunning Von Furstenberg dress. And thank you for your support," Adelman-Zamora said, then quickly moved to the next guest. Once she had greeted everyone, the room quieted and the congresswoman moved toward the center of the room.

"None of you are here tonight to hear a political speech, so I will be very brief, my friends. You are all here because you know of our fight. You are all here because you already know that the battle for freedom and democracy has not yet been won," she said, shaking her head. Heads around the room all shook with hers.

"You are all here because you know that the forces of tyranny and evil still exist. You all know that in the face of oppression that the United States of America must stand strong. You are all here tonight because you know that we must remain firm, even as those around us waver in the battle.

"We all are here because we seek redemption for the families who have been ripped apart by those who deny human rights and human dignity. You are all here tonight to help bring brothers and sisters together who have been torn apart by those who are threatened by freedom. You are all here tonight because we cannot allow the weak in Washington, D.C. to abandon the brave freedom fighters who live every day in fear . . ."

Jessica nodded and clapped along with the others, scanning the room for any clues she could bring back to Judd.

". . . We cannot allow the spineless bureaucrats back in Washington to forget about the courageous people who live every day with the hope that democracy will one day return to their shores. We cannot betray those brave souls who still hold freedom deep in their hearts. We cannot turn away from those who look to America for inspiration and comfort . . ."

Jessica's line of vision suddenly focused on a face hidden among the crowd that triggered something familiar. *Was it him?*

". . . You are all here today because you already know that, until I fight my very last campaign, until I breathe my very last breath, I will not rest until we have a free Cuba!"

Yes, it's him.

The crowd erupted in ovation and shouts of *"Viva Cuba Libre!"*

He cleaned up.

The party host hugged Adelman-Zamora, then turned and raised his hands. "This is why we are all here tonight. We are all here to support the reelection of Brenda Adelman-Zamora and to send a message to Washington that we will not rest until there is a free Cuba! I know everyone has come here to be generous. Checks are now being collected by the staff. Enjoy the party! *Viva Cuba Libre!*"

Jessica moved silently, eyes fixed on her target, skillfully weaving her way through the buzzing crowd, toward a skinny man in an immaculate white embroidered guayabera shirt. He was clean-shaven and his hair was pulled back into a tight ponytail. She watched the target hug the party host and hand him a thick envelope.

Once the transaction was complete, Jessica walked up and stood behind him. She could smell cigarettes and cologne.

"Hola, Ricky," she said.

He slowly turned around and narrowed his eyes. "Do I . . . know you, *chiquita?*"

"Sure you do. I'm Alexandra. We met in Marathon."

"I don't know any Alexandra," he said, turning away.

She touched his arm. "Sure you do, Ricky."

He spun back and gripped her hand on his arm.

"I remember your tattoos, Ricky," she said, squeezing his arm. "*En la Gloria de Dios.* I remember that one." Jessica traced the outlines of the mermaid on his arm with her finger. "You don't remember me?"

"I don't know you," he said, narrowing his eyes. "And you don't know me."

"And I remember this one, too," she said, touching his other arm and stroking his tattoo of a naval ship with a cross and the numbers 2506. "Ricky, are you . . . in the navy?" she asked, her eyes meeting his.

He pulled away. "You have the wrong guy. You don't know me," he said, and marched off.

Jessica waited a few seconds, then followed him through the crowd toward the back of the house. She watched Ricky talk excitedly to the valet and then climb into the teal-and-orange cigarette boat. He glanced back at the house as Jessica ducked behind one of the palm trees. From out of sight, she heard the boat fire up and roar off.

Jessica ran up to the valet, "Oh no!" she wailed. "That man who just left in the big racing boat. He forgot his cell," she said, holding up her own phone. "Do you know who he is?"

"No, señorita. I'm sorry."

"Do you know where he was going in such a rush?"

"No, ma'am. But he went that way," he said, pointing down the channel.

"South?" she asked.

"Yes, ma'am. Toward Port Everglades."

"Cast me off," she instructed, handing him a twenty-dollar

bill. She jumped in the Cobalt and started up the engine. Once the lines were free, Jessica punched the throttle, gunning the engine. This sent her wake splashing up against the waterfront and jostling the other boats. The valet stood on the shore, dumbfounded, watching the dazzling woman disappear into the darkness.

33.

Ruben Sandoval punched in the code as he had been trained to do earlier that day. The airlock to the Sensitive Compartmented Information Facility gave way with a satisfying *Tsssssss!* He pulled on the heavy steel door and flipped on the light.

The SCIF was a drab room that looked just like any standard government office. The difference was that a SCIF was a room within a room, separated by a vacuum that prevented listening devices, bugging, or any other way that communications could be intercepted.

"How do they do this?" he had asked the instructor that afternoon. "How do they suspend a room within a room?"

"I'm sorry, sir, that's classified."

"Okay. But what about the phone lines? How are those secured?"

"Also classified, sir. But I can tell you that all communications into or out of any SCIF are hardwired and we utilize the latest encryption technology. No radio or cell phone signals here.

Just a scrambled landline using exponential bit technology. It's unbreakable, sir."

Unbreakable. Ruben liked the sound of that.

He picked up the handset on the telephone and was relieved to hear a dial tone. He pulled a small piece of paper out of his pocket, unfolded it, and read the number he had scrawled in pencil. He punched in the number.

"Who the hell is this?" answered a gruff voice on the other end.

"It's me. It's Ruben."

"Why are you calling my emergency line? And what the fuck are you doing using your name on an open line? Are you fucking crazy? I'm hanging up now."

"Don't hang up! I'm on a secure phone."

"What?"

"I'm in a SCIF. I'm calling you from a secure line inside a SCIF."

"How are you in a SCIF? How's that possible?"

"I can't say." Ruben smiled smugly to himself.

"Where are you?"

"I'm sorry. It's need-to-know," Ruben said.

"Ha!" the man barked. "You hear that shit from some movie? You think you're James fucking Bond now?"

Ruben didn't answer.

"So what's the big emergency?" asked the man on the other end.

"I saw the news. How'd they get caught?" Ruben asked.

"Don't worry about it," the voice said.

"They were essential to the plan and now they're in prison. What do you mean don't worry?"

"They don't know anything. The Cubans can pull their fingernails out and they can't tell them anything."

"But what about Triggerfish?"

"Operation Triggerfish is a go."

"It's a go? They're in jail. In Havana! What do we do now?"

"Shit happens. Good operations have contingency plans. We're using their capture to our advantage."

"How?"

"You should know better than to even ask me that. All you need to know is that Operation Triggerfish is on. We're proceeding to phase two."

"Now?" Ruben asked.

"Yes. Now," the Deputy Director of the CIA insisted. "Contact your brother. Tell him to get ready. He flies tomorrow."

34.

Jessica raced down the river, the rumble of the Cobalt's engine filling her ears. Her dress clung tightly to her body and the warm wind rushed through her hair.

The sun had long set and the Intracoastal was now quieter. Most of the boat traffic was gone, just a few monstrous cabin cruisers returning from the Atlantic. Lights of extravagant homes along both banks pierced the blackness, casting spotlights on the waterway.

Jessica held the boat's wheel with one hand, her eyes darting across the water, searching ahead. Off the main river were narrower side channels, lined with more homes and moored luxury boats. *Where are you, Ricky Green?*

She pulled back on the throttle, easing off the gas just in front of a sign warning MANATEE ZONE / NO WAKE. The motor gurgled and spat in low gear. Should she stop and search the side canals or continue ahead? So many places to hide. If Ricky didn't know he was being followed, he'd probably continued downriver, toward Port Everglades, she decided. She stole one last glance down a channel and then nudged the accelerator stick with the base of her palm and the bow of the boat rose up into the air, the engine whirring back to life.

As Jessica veered around a bend in the river at full speed, the waterway widened dramatically. She could see open water ahead, the Christmas lights of gigantic cruise ships and the colossal merchant vessels of Port Everglades stacked high with steel containers.

She yanked the throttle backward, killing the engine, and the boat leveled off and sunk low into the water. Jessica cursed herself for losing him.

She found a pair of binoculars underneath the cockpit seat and searched across the open bay to the south. Plenty of boats puttering around, but nothing that resembled Ricky's flashy cigarette boat. Then she spun and checked north, back up the river. Nothing behind her either, just a large New Orleans–style paddleboat lit up like a carnival and heading straight for her position.

She turned eastward, squinting through the binoculars into the darkness, hunting for any signs of movement along the mangroves on the banks or down a slender residential canal that ran perpendicular to the river. The sounds of the crowded tourist boat, a mix of dance music and drunken hollering, got louder.

Jessica dropped the binoculars into the seat and restarted the engine. She carefully maneuvered the bowrider westward, heading toward the last of the residential channels she had yet to search. If Ricky wasn't north, south, or east, then he had to be down that last canal to the west.

As she came around behind the stern of *The Jungle Queen*, the sounds of the party were punctured by a loud crack. Jessica instinctively ducked low in the cockpit. *Fireworks? Or a gunshot?* She unconsciously reached for her inner thigh, but no holster was there tonight. Unarmed and cursing herself for the second time in the past few minutes, she peered cautiously over the side of the boat. Another three shots—*crack-crack-crack*—and she felt the rush of a bullet near her ear. *Someone is shooting at me!* Then her ears filled with a new sound, the deafening thunder of the cigarette emerging from behind the paddleboat.

Ricky Green was gripping the wheel of the racing boat with one hand and a handgun with the other. As he steadied his arm for another shot, Jessica stayed low and punched the boat's throttle forward.

The Cobalt popped up out of the water. She circled the paddleboat, using it to block Ricky's sight line and give herself a head start. Jessica then pointed her boat straight toward a marina about five hundred yards to the west, between two thick stands of mangroves. Jessica crouched down, pushing the accelerator stick as far forward as possible, blindly racing toward the marina.

Come on! Come on! she urged the engines. Behind her, she could hear screams from the tourist boat and the growls of the cigarette's motor.

She peered forward—marina dead ahead, now three hundred yards. Behind her, Ricky, in the bigger and faster cigarette boat, was gaining ground. More shots—*crack-crack-crack . . . whizz-whizz-whizz!*

She just needed to make it into the lights of the marina, now two hundred yards away. The bow of her boat slammed the water at full speed in a steady pounding rhythm.

She heard more *crack-crack-crack* then a sickening *bink-bink-bink* of the shots penetrating the Cobalt's engine. She spun the wheel to serpentine her route, but the rudder didn't respond. The boat raced straight ahead toward the concrete docks of the marina, now fifty yards away. Out of the corner of her eye, she saw a bright orange light behind her. *Her engine was on fire!*

Could she make it to the marina before the engine blew? She was still speeding ahead, unable to turn. Ricky was gaining. She took one last glance at the dock ahead, then at the cigarette, then counted . . . one, two, three . . . and dove headfirst into the water . . . four, five—*Ka-boom!*—the Deputy Director's boat exploding in a ball of flames.

35.

Where the hell is Jessica?" Judd shouted to his empty office. He slammed down the phone.

He hadn't wanted help from his wife. But he hadn't seen any option, so he'd reluctantly asked Jessica to go to the fundraiser for Brenda Adelman-Zamora and see what she could find out. He was hoping she would discover a link to Ruben Sandoval. Or at least a clue as to the political activities of the Cuban exile community in Florida. Something. Anything.

But she hadn't called him back. Jessica also hadn't replied to his text messages and now she wasn't answering her phone. It was going straight to voicemail as if her phone were turned off. Or lost. That wasn't like her.

Judd tried to concentrate on his work, on figuring out the connections between Sandoval, Richard Green, the captured Americans, the White House, and the U.S. Congress. Judd knew he was missing something, probably something big. And he was now reliant, yet again, on Jessica to find the lost piece of the puzzle.

Where they hell was she? Assist was rule one. This was why

Judd and Jessica had promised to help each other when they could. They wouldn't become entangled in each other's missions, but they were supposed to be a team. *So where was she?*

Maybe asking his wife to go to a party at a fancy house in South Florida was a mistake? *Party* . . . Judd thought. *I'm stuck here in the stale air of a State Department office while Jessica is probably sipping champagne?*

36.

The reverberation of the blast rocked Jessica's skull, but she retained consciousness.

She watched the orange fireball plume from just below the water's surface. Jessica then held her breath and waited a few more seconds, just as she had been trained, pausing to allow the smoking debris from the destroyed Cobalt to slam back to earth and fizzle. She swam underwater a few yards closer to shore, searching for a safe place to resurface. The gnarled knuckles of mangrove roots provided the perfect camouflage.

Jessica, hidden among the mangroves, grabbed a quick breath and then stealthily lowered her body again so just her eyes were above the water. Like an alligator stalking prey, she floated motionlessly, watching Ricky Green pilot the cigarette boat in circles, searching for her body, in the black water amid the smoldering flotsam. She could taste the brackish, salty water on her lips. Ricky then shut down the engine and pulled out a heavy-duty Maglite, sweeping a bright beam across the marina.

After finding nothing, he cursed loudly. An old man in a security guard uniform suddenly appeared on the marina dock. "Hey, buddy, you see that?" he shouted, cupping both hands around his mouth.

"No! I didn't see what happened," Ricky replied, shrugging. "Grab my line!" Ricky tossed the man a bowline and they tied up the cigarette. Small specks of burning embers floated where Jessica's boat had been.

"Holy moley," the old man's voice quavered. "I just saw a ball of fire. Golly, anybody on that boat?"

"I'll keep looking," Ricky said, holding up his flashlight. "You go call nine-one-one!"

Jessica watched the guard limp off as Ricky hustled across the marina to the parking lot. He checked over both shoulders, then the lights of a bright yellow Hummer flashed and she could hear the chirp-chirp as the doors unlocked. Ricky slid into the Hummer's driver's seat and drove out toward the gate.

Jessica swam over to the dock and scampered up a ladder. The old man emerged from a small shed, holding a cell phone, his eyes wide as he suddenly noticed the beautiful woman in a soaked cocktail dress. "Hey, lady, you all right?" he shouted.

"Call the police!" she shouted.

"I'm on the line right now!" he said, holding up his phone to show her.

"Give me the phone," she ordered. "You get a spotlight and start searching the shoreline."

"Where'd that other guy go?" he asked, tossing her the phone.

"I think I saw a body over there," she said, pointing toward the darkest part of the mangrove stand. "A dead body. Go now!"

As the man disappeared back into the marina office, Jessica

kicked off her shoes and sprinted down the parking lot after the Hummer.

Onlookers started to emerge from other parts of the marina. Another security guard, driving a golf cart, appeared from around a corner. Jessica hysterically pointed back toward the docks. "They need help! That way!" The golf cart sped off.

A carbon-black and cherry-red Kawasaki Ninja suddenly veered toward her. *A crotch rocket,* she thought. *Perfect.* Jessica waved both her arms and the motorcycle came to a violent stop right in front of her.

"There's been an accident! They need help!" she cried, pointing behind her. The rider yanked off his helmet. His blond buzz cut, muscular build, and thick neck told Jessica immediately that he was an athlete or ex-military. "What, lady?" he squinted at her. "What are you saying? Are you okay?"

"There!" she shrieked. "Give me your helmet. They need you there!" She kept pointing behind her.

The man thrust his helmet into her grasp and ran in the direction of the dock. Jessica took a deep breath, composed herself, then slid the helmet on her own head. She carefully tightened the chin strap, mounted the Ninja, and slipped the old man's cell phone into her bra. Jessica twisted the throttle grip twice, feeling the vibrations of the racing engine surge through her body. Then she kicked down on the gearshift and zoomed off.

Once she cleared the marina gate, Jessica leaned into a tight turn toward the main road. She righted the bike and assessed her options. *Where'd you go in such a hurry, Ricky?* Then she saw a sign for the highway, I-595 West. *That's it.*

Jessica rocketed up the highway on-ramp. She weaved carefully through traffic, keeping her eyes far ahead. After a few minutes, she spotted the school-bus-yellow Hummer cruising in the far left lane. Jessica eased the Ninja behind a black SUV in the same lane a few vehicles back.

She tailed Ricky at a safe distance for fifteen miles until he followed the highway onto the Everglades Parkway. He was taking Alligator Alley, the flat road that cuts across the vast swamps of southern Florida. *Where the hell are you going, Ricky Green?*

Jessica dropped farther back as the traffic lightened, just enough to keep Ricky's taillights in view. Soon, they were deep into the Everglades, an endless horizon of pitch-black nothingness on both sides.

The hypnosis-inducing road left her alone with her thoughts . . . On the orders of the Deputy Director of Operations, Jessica had gone to Marathon in the Florida Keys to figure out what happened to *The Big Pig* and the four American fishermen. She had traced Ricky Green and the seized fishing boat back to Ruben Sandoval, but then . . . nothing. She hit a dead end. She had Sunday back at Langley still digging. Then, out of the blue, her husband called to ask her to go to the fund-raiser for Brenda Adelman-Zamora to look for any clues linking the congresswoman to Sandoval. And, of all people, Ricky Green turns up at the party! Did that make sense? Was Ricky the connection between Adelman-Zamora and Sandoval?

She should call Judd and tell him what she knew. But Jessica also knew she couldn't tell her husband what had just happened—that she had almost gotten killed while doing his favor, that she had wrecked a powerboat, that she was now on a racing motorcycle, chasing a man who'd shot at her, into the deepest swamps of South Florida while a total stranger was watching their children. No, she couldn't tell Judd anything until she knew more. Until she knew where this was all headed. What was she really dealing with? *Who was Ricky Green? And what the hell was 2506?*

37.

Sunday set down his phone and checked the clock on his classified computer screen. His assessment of potential links between Iran and underground Somali banking networks was
due by midnight if a summary was going to make it to the Director of National Intelligence's morning briefing. He had promised
his boss that he'd have something for the DNI on time. He had
never missed a deadline.

Sunday had been nearly finished and starting to dream about
finally climbing into bed when his phone had rung. It was a number he didn't recognize, but the 305 South Florida area code was
enough of a coincidence that he answered. It was Jessica Ryker
with an urgent request.

Sunday had listened carefully to the Purple Cell leader. When
she was done speaking, he set aside his DNI project, forgot about
sleep, and opened a new window on his computer. Figuring out
if "2506" meant anything relevant should have been easy. A

search of the CIA databases should have turned up the answer in a few minutes. But today . . . nothing. He rubbed his eyes. It was almost as if he were being deliberately blocked from the Agency's archives. *Or were the records stripped?*

Sunday logged off of the CIA network and on to a Department of Defense database of covert operations. Again, nothing of use.

"Hey, you still chasing the Ayatollah's Somali pirates?" boomed a voice from above Sunday's head.

"Go away, Glen," Sunday said, shaking his head at his colleague, who was leaning over the cubicle wall.

"Aw, don't be like that, S-man. If you're still here digging, that means you haven't finished your assessment." Glen waddled around the wall and peered over Sunday's shoulders at the computer screen. "You need some help?"

"No." Sunday turned off his screen. "If you want to help me, you can start by going away."

"You're no fun anymore, Sunday. I thought Nigerians were supposed to be party animals."

"I'm American."

"Whatever."

"I grew up in California."

"Yeah, I know, I know. So that's why you're no fun?"

"No time for fun. I've got to finish this by COB."

"The CIA doesn't have a 'close of business,' Sunday. Didn't they tell you that, like, on the first day?"

"Go away."

"No, sir," Glen said with a mock salute. "We are twenty-four/seven! We never close! Not the Central fucking Intelligence Agency. Not even on Christmas."

Sunday turned his back on Glen.

"Hey, if you're Muslim, they probably have you working on Christmas, right? Used to call that shift the Jew Crew around here."

"I'm ignoring you," Sunday said.

"I guess it's more Muslims than Jews now, dontcha think?"

"Glen, I'm going to turn my computer back on and finish my work. If I turn around again, I expect to see that you've gone away."

"Okay, okay," Glen huffed. "Don't get so damn testy, Sunday. I thought you Nigerians were supposed to be laid-back."

Sunday waved Glen away over his shoulder. "Shoo."

"I know you're supposed to be compartmentalized on this Iran thing, but I'm not going home yet. If I can help, let me know. Maybe run some Google searches or something." Glen laughed to himself and wandered away.

Google?

Sunday closed the Pentagon database on his classified computer and opened a web browser on his unclassified machine. Into Google he typed *2506*. The search results were long lists of addresses. Nothing notable. He was about to close the window when he glanced at the search results at the bottom of the screen. There was something he didn't expect: an orange-and-blue flag of a silhouetted soldier with a bayonet-tipped gun and a banner reading BRIGADA ASALTO 2506.

A Spanish Assault Brigade 2506? He typed this into a new search field and the result:

Brigada Asalto 2506 was a CIA-sponsored group of Cuban exiles formed in 1960 to attempt the

military overthrow of the communist Cuban
government.

Ay! He carried on reading.

It carried out the abortive Bay of Pigs invasion
landings in Cuba on 17 April 1961.

The Bay of Pigs?

38.

Jessica blocked out the bone-deep cold she felt from wearing a damp cocktail dress on a high-speed motorcycle for the past ninety minutes. She had tailed Ricky Green all the way from Port Everglades, onto Highway I-595, down Alligator Alley, and again when he turned south toward Everglades City. The road was so flat and straight, Jessica turned off the Kawasaki's lights and just followed the red rear lights of the Hummer.

As she passed the WELCOME TO EVERGLADES CITY sign, she thought "City" might be an exaggeration. The town was more like a small island with modest sixties-style clapboard houses, amply spaced on large plots of land. Sure, it was late, but the streets were wholly abandoned.

They passed the turnoff for the Everglades Airport, and just as the town appeared to end in darkness, Ricky veered off the main road and down a dirt driveway.

Jessica waited until the lights of the Hummer had disappeared from view, then she hid the motorcycle in the bushes and followed the dirt path on foot. After about a hundred yards, she came upon the parked Hummer and could see moving lights through the brush in a clearing ahead. She could hear Ricky banging on metal and grunting but couldn't see what he was doing. Jessica pushed deeper into the brush to try to get a better look.

Suddenly, she heard a motor start up, followed by an incredibly loud hum, like a giant hair dryer. A second later, she was blasted by a gust of warm tropical air. Jessica shielded her eyes and backed away from the bushes. Was he taking off on a seaplane? Or a boat? It sounded like both.

As the noise and wind receded, she returned to the Hummer and ran down the path that Ricky must have taken toward the machine. She arrived at the shoreline just in time to see Ricky strapped high in a chair at the front of a low, flat boat with a massive spinning fan at the back. *A fanboat.*

Fuck! Where the hell is he going now? Jessica wondered as Ricky evaporated into the infinite darkness of the Florida swamps.

39.

Judd still hadn't heard anything from Jessica. He had hit a dead end trying to uncover more on the Americans from *The Big Pig.*

Judd turned away from his whiteboard, with its photos of the men and the lines of the web that still didn't make sense. *Maybe I'll never know the truth,* he thought. Even if he didn't know who these guys were or what they were up to, he knew he had to focus on his task: a hostage negotiation strategy for Landon Parker. He still needed a backchannel to Havana. And he needed a plan before the end of the day.

Judd had discovered in the archives that every White House since John F. Kennedy had tried to establish a secret dialogue with the Cuban government. LBJ, Nixon, Carter, Bush, Clinton— they all tried. And they all failed. Even the coldest of the Cold Warriors, Ronald Reagan, had attempted to find common ground with Havana by negotiating to end the presence of Cuban troops in Africa. Reagan had to strike a deal with El Jefe. The result of eight grueling years of talks was the departure of Cuban troops from Angola, a withdrawal of South African forces, and the creation of a newly independent Namibia. It was a complex triple agreement of historic proportions. But that diplomatic success in Africa never led to a broader détente between Washington and Havana. Instead, the Angola negotiations followed the same pattern as other attempts at dialogue: Small steps in confidence building eventually gave way to animus.

Judd had read through the history of failed diplomatic overtures to Cuba. It was a long record of missteps and misunderstandings. Minor advances toward compromise were simply swept away by political expediency. Hard-liners on one side or the other had found it too easy to scuttle any progress. *Why should Landon Parker believe I can do better? Why should I think I can?*

Judd had scrawled down the basic outlines of a plan on a single sheet of paper.

1. *Good faith*
2. *Discreet negotiations*
3. *Plausible deniability*
4. *Incentives to deliver*

Judd was stuck on number one. What kind of new gesture could the United States make that might entice the Cubans but not enrage Capitol Hill? How to thread the needle between the old men in Havana and the old men in Miami? How to find common ground between El Comrade Presidente and Brenda Adelman-Zamora? Judd jotted down a list of the least-controversial options that he could present to Landon Parker:

music, baseball, biotech sugar.

It was a pitiful list. Sugar might even be too contentious. Judd changed it:

~~biotech sugar~~ *tropical agriculture.*

Still pathetic. But at least it was something to propose. The topic was beside the point, he reminded himself. It could be anything. He just needed to manufacture a new reason to talk to the Cubans. Any cover for making a deal to recover the Americans.

Were they hostages? Or ploys? Or pawns? The uncertainty burned at him. Judd turned back to his whiteboard, staring at the photos of the four men. What were they really doing in the Florida Straits? Why was Landon Parker so anxious to help them? What was their connection to Ruben Sandoval? And who was Richard Green?

Who the hell were these people?

40.

Sunday dug deeper into the CIA archives on the Bay of Pigs. Most of the records on Brigada Asalto 2506 had been redacted or were so old that they had been boxed up and taken to off-site storage, probably some warehouse in a nondescript office park off a northern Virginia parkway. There was no way he'd get to the original records tonight.

The CIA had increasingly been relying on "open source intelligence," what government officials called any material that was also available publicly. Crucial nuggets of information could often be found in newspapers or on websites that were just as reliable as clandestine sources. Sometimes open source was even better.

So far, Sunday had confirmed from open sources that Brigada Asalto 2506 had, in fact, been a group of Cuban exiles that formed the core team of a covert paramilitary CIA operation to invade Cuba in 1961. The plan, hatched by the Agency's Deputy Director of Operations at the time, Randolph Nye, was to have 2506 land at Bahía de Cochinos and establish a beachhead. They would then make contact with a local underground force, inciting a popular counterrevolution and eventually retaking power in Havana. Assassinating the Cuban leader was not a formal objective of the plot, but all members of 2506 knew that wealthy Cuban exiles in Miami had placed a large bounty on the head of El Jefe.

Sunday read in the historical records that President John F. Kennedy had approved the Bay of Pigs operation, but so much had gone wrong that day. The element of surprise was lost after invasion plans leaked. The Bay of Pigs was supposed to be one of America's most covert operations, but it was spoken about openly in the cafés and bodegas of Little Havana in Miami.

On the fateful day of the operation, Brigada Asalto 2506 attacked a well-armed Cuban force and quickly ran out of ammunition and supplies. The first-wave teams on the beach were trapped and outnumbered. The underground counterrevolutionary cells were also neutralized before they could activate. The promised cash never arrived.

In the end, more than a hundred men from Brigada Asalto 2506 were killed and more than a thousand were captured. The detainees were then publicly paraded back in Havana, a humiliation that was only worsened by a show trial the following year. The leaders of 2506 were executed, while the rest were given lengthy prison sentences. Most of the men were eventually released in a prisoner exchange in late 1962. They returned to Miami, longing for home, seething with hatred for the communists, and burned by the betrayal of the U.S. government.

Sunday found several historians who concluded that Nye's plan was doomed from the start not by operational mistakes but rather by a flawed premise of popular support. Few academics believed that the Cuban public was ready at that time to support an American-backed invasion.

But among the exiles in Miami, Sunday learned, that one factor rose above all else as the reason for the debacle: Kennedy's denial of Nye's request for U.S. air support. *The planes never came.*

Fascinating, Sunday thought to himself. But what do Randolph Nye and Brigada Asalto 2506 have to do with today? How is this ancient history possibly connected to the Americans captured on *The Big Pig*?

Sunday kept digging. He learned that after the Bay of Pigs failure, Nye resigned, moved to a ranch in Texas, and quietly disappeared from political life. Sunday unearthed his brief 1991 obituary in the *Waco Tribune-Herald*, which noted his lifelong service to the United States government but made no mention of the CIA or of Cuba. Sunday also found a photo of Randolph Nye in the 1932 archives of the *Yale Daily News*, but he was wearing a football helmet so his face was hidden. The only other picture of Nye that Sunday could find was in a long-defunct Spanish-language newspaper of South Florida, *La Gloria*. The grainy photo from February 1961 showed several men around a table at a restaurant. The caption read *Líder local Héctor Cabrera se reúne con Randolph Nye del gobierno federal.*

The name Cabrera lit up on the page like a neon sign. Sunday double-checked his notes and, yes, one of the hostages, the owner of the boat, was Alejandro Cabrera. Sunday quickly searched the open source database for Héctor Cabrera and found an obituary in the *Miami Herald* from 1979:

Héctor Cabrera, a beloved figure in Little Havana . . . Born in Santa Cruz del Norte, Cuba . . . A successful diamond dealer . . . Moved to Miami in 1959 . . . Cuban patriot active in local politics and charitable organizations . . . a champion for democracy and human rights in his homeland . . . Survived by his grandsons, Alejandro Cabrera and Ricardo Cabrera . . . Donations can be made to the Kiwanis Club of Little Havana . . .

Sunday sat back in his chair to absorb what he had just read. The captured American, Alejandro Cabrera, was the grandson of a Cuban exile linked to the architect of the Bay of Pigs. A coincidence? Or did a young Alejandro listen to the war stories of his grandfather and was somehow seeking to redeem his family's past? Could the seizure of the fishing boat be yet another mistake in a long line of ill-advised covert operations by exiles against the Cuban government? Or by the Central Intelligence Agency? Or, most likely, was Sunday inferring conspiratorial connections that didn't really exist?

Sunday decided he needed more information on Alejandro before taking any of this back to Jessica. He logged on to the FBI database and found that Alejandro Cabrera had a long list of minor criminal infractions but nothing serious. From what Sunday could tell, Cabrera seemed to be a genuine real estate agent from Maryland, the father of three girls, a second-generation immigrant who was living the suburban American dream. Maybe the historical Bay of Pigs link was a fluke?

Sunday carefully reread Héctor Cabrera's obituary. What was he missing?

Héctor Cabrera . . . Born in Santa Cruz del Norte . . . A successful diamond dealer . . . Cuban patriot active in local politics . . . Survived by his grandsons, Alejandro Cabrera and Ricardo Cabrera . . .

Ricardo? The FBI files showed that Ricardo Cabrera of Miami had been arrested at age eighteen during a drug bust in Everglades City, Florida, in 1983. After that, the records stopped. No tax filings, no police rap sheet, nothing. Sunday checked for a death certificate but came up blank. Ricardo Cabrera ceased to exist in 1983. It was probably nothing, just a criminal who disappeared underground. Or maybe incomplete records, Sunday told himself.

It was now after eleven o'clock and Sunday knew the Purple Cell team leader was waiting to hear from him. Plus he still had to finish his Iran-Somalia assessment for the Director of National Intelligence. Sunday made a mental notation to follow up on Ricardo Cabrera once he got time rather than chase another ghost tonight.

Sunday started to call the number Jessica had given him as her temporary phone in Florida. But before pressing the final digit, he suddenly knew exactly what she would say. Sunday set the phone back down. He couldn't miss anything obvious.

Sunday pulled up research on Dennis Dobson. Software engineer, family all clean, nothing of note. He found the same for Crawford Jackson, a former Navy SEAL, now a contractor at Carderock Naval Surface Warfare Center, with the highest level security clearances. His background was scrubbed every year, no blemishes, nothing suspicious.

The last man, Brinkley Barrymore III, was probably the least likely to have something big to hide. Barrymore was ex–Naval Academy, Georgetown Law, a JAG naval lawyer, now a partner at a prestigious D.C. law firm. Open sources reported that his grandfather was the scion of a well-known Annapolis family that claimed lineage back to one of the original settler families at Jamestown, Virginia. The style pages of the Washington press were filled with stories of the Barrymores at Annapolis Yacht Club regattas, at black-tie charity galas, symphonies at the Kennedy Center, and other socialite events of the Washington-Annapolis blue-blooded glitterati.

Brinkley Barrymore III's wedding to Penelope Anderson of Memphis was covered in a gaudy half-page spread in the *Washington Post*. In the story, buried among the achievements of the Barrymore family, was a small notation that Brinkley's maternal grandmother, Henrietta Nye, had also attended the wedding.

Ay! Sunday's eyes nearly popped out of his head. *Nye?*

41.

The ringing phone startled Judd, shaking him from his intense concentration. Without checking caller ID, he snatched the handset, "Sweets! Is everything all right?"

"Dr. Ryker, it's me, Sunday."

"Oh, sorry," Judd said, deflated. "I was . . . waiting for a call."

"Is everything okay, sir?"

"Yes, it's fine. My wife's away with the kids and . . . It doesn't matter . . . It's good to hear from you, Sunday. I . . . I appreciate your work on Zimbabwe last week. You were a huge help."

"I can't believe you pulled it off, Dr. Ryker. It's really something."

"*We* pulled it off, Sunday. No way Gugu Mutonga would be president without you," Judd said. "You sent me just the right information at just the right time. Right when I needed it."

"I'm just happy to help out," Sunday said, suddenly wondering if calling Judd Ryker had been the right move.

"You seem to have an eerie intuition, Sunday." Judd knew he was pressing too far, but couldn't help it. "A magic touch."

"I'm, um . . . just an analyst doing my job, sir."

"Well, we made a pretty good team, didn't we?"

"Yes, sir, we did."

Judd weighed his options on whether to ask the question he really wanted to ask, but Sunday quickly changed the subject.

"Sir, I'm actually calling you for a favor."

"You're asking me for a favor? I think I owe you quite a few."

"I'm working on a special project right now—"

"Don't tell me you're working on Cuba!"

"Um . . . no, sir," Sunday said. "I'm not supposed to discuss details of any of my special projects, but . . . it's not Cuba . . . Is that what you're working on, Dr. Ryker?"

"I'm not supposed to say either, Sunday."

"I understand. I'm sorry to have to ask you a favor. *A big favor.*"

"Okay, shoot."

"In Zimbabwe, you had a Department of Justice official on your delegation, didn't you?"

"Isabella Espinosa?"

"She's the one. Is she . . . any good?"

"Isabella is five feet four inches of twisted steel who hunts war criminals. If you're a bad guy, she's one hundred and five pounds of pure devastation. Are you chasing monsters?"

"Not exactly. But I'm tracking a suspect and I've hit a brick wall. I need someone inside Justice to help me break through.

Someone at DOJ who might be willing to take a risk and help a friendly CIA analyst on the side."

"An unofficial inquiry?"

"Yes. Someone discreet. Someone I can trust."

"That's Isabella. I'll set it up."

42.

The chill was turning to pain. Jessica pulled off the highway at an empty rest stop, parked off in the shadows near a picnic table, and killed the engine on the Kawasaki Ninja. Jessica lifted off her helmet and shook out her hair. *Some fucking vacation,* she thought.

The swamp in front of her was pitch-dark. The loud croaking of frogs and clicking of cicadas filled the night. *Damn, it is late.* She still had over an hour of riding left to get back to Fort Lauderdale and her children. She knew she still had to call Judd. Now was as good a time as any.

"Hello?" he answered.

"Hi, sweetheart, it's me," Jessica said.

"Oh, thank God . . . What number is this?"

"Oh, sorry. Yeah, my phone died. I'm using a new one."

"Died? What happened? I've been leaving you messages."

"It got wet," she said, imagining her phone sitting at the bottom of the Florida Intracoastal. "I picked up a burner to use while I'm still down here on vacation. I'll get a new phone when

I'm back in Washington. I'm sorry, I didn't get any of your messages."

"A burner?" Judd scoffed. "You sound like a drug dealer."

"You're cute." She forced a laugh. "Everything's fine, Judd. I'm sorry I didn't call earlier. You know how crazy it can get putting Noah to bed."

"I've been waiting to hear what happened at the fund-raiser," Judd said impatiently.

Jessica paused. "Yes, I went to your party in Las Olas. It was quite a house. A palace, really."

"Did you find anything? Did Adelman-Zamora show her face?"

"Yes, she was there. Gave a rousing stump speech. Lots of cash changing hands. I'm sure she raised lots of money tonight."

"So, what did you find? Any connections to Ruben Sandoval?"

"I'm sorry, sweetie, I . . . didn't see any. There were so many people there . . . so many rich people . . . I could have missed him. I don't think I found you any new leads." *Lie Number Six.*

"What about Richard Green? The maintenance guy on *The Big Pig* that you told me about. Any links to him?"

She paused again. "I'm . . . not sure. I mean, I gave you his name, but I don't know what he looks like." *Lie Number Seven.* "I thought you'd be looking into him, Judd. What have you found out?"

"Me? Nothing yet. I've been focusing on the hostages for Landon Parker. I'm working on a plan for some kind of quiet diplomatic negotiations."

"I'm sorry, Judd, I wish I had more for you."

"I'm sorry, too, Jess. I'm sorry I had to ask you to go to some stupid party while you're on vacation with the boys. I shouldn't have asked you to do it. I broke our rules of engagement by dragging you into my work problem. It was wrong. It won't happen again."

"You didn't break our rules," Jessica said. "We're allowed to help each other. *Assist*, remember?"

"I'm just glad you called and you're okay. I was starting to get worried."

"I can handle myself," she said, glancing down at the motorcycle.

"How did your phone get wet?"

"I was on a boat," she said with a wry smile, thinking of the bowrider, now bits of scattered flotsam on the waters of Port Everglades.

"A boat? Whose boat?"

"Judd, sweetheart, I'm *exhausted*," she said. "Maybe we can talk tomorrow?"

"Uh, yeah, that's fine."

"Love you," she said.

"Love you, too."

After ending the call, Jessica twisted her fingers in her hair, deciding if she should make the next call or not. There was only so long you could avoid the inevitable. She knew that was true at home—and at work.

She punched in a number that she had long ago memorized.

"Coney Island Pizza," a bored woman answered.

"Coney Island Pizza? I have a special order for urgent delivery," Jessica said.

"Would you like our special—pineapple and Italian sausage?" the woman asked flatly.

"Yes, extra-spicy," Jessica replied.

The phone beeped twice, she heard a click-click, and then a gruff voice said, "Where the fuck've you been?"

"In Marathon," she said, "running your little errand."

"And?"

"I can't work this issue."

"What? Why the hell not?" the CIA's Deputy Director of Operations snarled.

"I told you I won't play my own husband. I told you I won't run him. That was part of our deal."

"Who's asking you to run your husband? He's not even in the game. Jack's a goddamn civilian."

"It's Judd. And he's *working on* Cuba," she said.

"Not my goddamn fault. You were on this Cuba business first. Tell your Jack or Judd to go complain to Landon Parker."

"I can't do that."

"Why the hell not?"

"He doesn't know. He still thinks I'm on vacation."

"Again, not my problem," he said. "What'd you find in Marathon?"

Jessica paused. "Looks like four fishermen got lost."

"That's all? You've been missing for the past eight hours and that's all you got?"

"As far as I can tell, it looks like a straight-out mistake. Just like they said on the news."

The Deputy Director grunted into the phone.

"What aren't you telling me, sir?"

"Compartmentalized information, Jessica. You know that."

"Is this an operation? Are these lost fishermen *your guys*?"

"You should know better than to even ask that question."

"I can't help you if you don't tell me what you're trying to do here, sir," she said.

He paused, then coughed, before speaking again. "You ever heard of O?"

"The letter *O*?"

"The man O!" the Deputy Director snapped.

"No, sir."

"O is Oswaldo Guerrero. The one who cracked Operation Rainmaker."

"I wasn't part of that operation, sir."

"So you've never heard of him?"

"Not really. I've heard there's a ghost called O. A creation of the Cuban intelligence services. Just something to keep us guessing. But I never thought he was a real person."

"O's no ghost."

"Is that who you're chasing?" Jessica whispered, "Is that why I'm down here in Florida?"

"Not anymore."

"I can stand down, sir?"

"You want off, you're off. Enjoy the rest of your vacation. We'll talk about what's next once you're back online."

"Yes, sir."

He sighed and his voice softened. "Have you had a chance to try out my bowrider yet? Isn't she a beauty?"

43.

The frantic beat outside his window was loud enough to wake him. Ernesto rolled over gently, brushing against the mosquito netting hung above and around his bed. He checked the clock: 5:38. It was a bit earlier than he normally arose, but he didn't mind. The sudden music wasn't an annoyance; it was a soothing comfort. The sounds that filled his ears, an eclectic meld of Cuban rhumba and African techno pop, was a calming reminder of where he was living. And where he was from.

Lying in his bed, the doctor listened to the *musseque*, the shantytown that had been his home for so many years, coming alive for the day. The banging pots, the chatter of old women, the crowing roosters—they all reminded him of his childhood. The smells of burning charcoal and rotting garbage also invaded his bedroom through the bars on his window and evoked memories of his previous life.

Dr. Ernesto Sandoval had been working in Angola so long that he had begun to wonder if he would ever return to his true home. The sprawling capital of Luanda had been a disaster when he had first arrived all those years ago. The war, the corruption, the dysfunction, had all conspired to create one of the world's most desperate and unhealthy places. That's why his government sent armies of doctors to Angola. To help the sick. To show solidarity against the imperialists. To broadcast the benefits of Cuba's socialist revolution. Ernesto was one of the foot soldiers in the battle against tropical disease and, coincidentally, Cuba's ideological war against the Americans.

Not long after Ernesto arrived in Angola, so, too, did a tidal wave of oil money. And everything began to change. Extravagant high-rise hotels sprang up along the luscious cove of Luanda Bay. Luxury SUVs crowded the palm-lined Avenida 4 de Fevereiro, the beachside parkway honoring the start of the war of independence from colonial Portugal and the beginning of thirty years of nearly endless conflict. The grand avenue celebrating Marxist popular revolution was now synonymous with flashy opulence. Grilled lobster and imported French champagne could be consumed in a *pescaderia* in the shadow of Fortaleza de São Miguel, the fort built by European explorers nearly five centuries earlier. The hub of the transatlantic slave trade, a symbol of all that was supposed to be wrong with global capitalism, had become a scenic backdrop for lavish excess. This was the affluent new Luanda, the modern capital of oil executives, sovereign wealth fund managers, and mind-bogglingly rich politicians. *Too much money.*

The glitzy waterfront of the capital wasn't the real Angola,

Ernesto knew. A closer look at the skyline revealed many sky-scrapers were only half built, teeming not with beautiful people but packed tight with poverty-stricken squatters. These crowded vertical slums housed thousands of the poor, the very ones his government had sent him to help. These people, living in the real Angola, were his patients.

Ernesto stared at a water stain on the ceiling and wiggled his toes, thinking about the many flights of stairs he would climb yet again today. He groaned as he sat up in bed. It was meaningful work, he knew. His life's passion. At least for now.

Ernesto slipped out of bed and began his usual morning routine by turning on a small gas stove to heat water for coffee. As he brushed his teeth, he noticed the lines on his face had grown sharper and patches of his short hair had become grayer. He spat in the sink and stared at himself in the cracked mirror. He wondered how much longer he could wait. Was he getting too old? *Would the call ever come?*

No time for such doubts. He had too much work today. His patients needed him. Checkups, vaccinations, perhaps he might even deliver another baby. Yesterday he helped deliver a healthy baby boy in the stairwell on the fourteenth floor of a half-finished building that will one day be a bank headquarters. The mother, out of gratitude for the doctor's care, named the boy Che. *His* nickname. The thought made him blush.

Despite the poverty and desperation of the slums, Ernesto loved the work and loved his patients. And the views. From the upper stories of the squatters' towers, he could see across the city, behind the soaring buildings, to what felt like the entire world.

He could see the open spaces that had once been the dense shacks of those fleeing the countryside for the relative wealth and safety of Luanda. *The problem was too little money.*

From the top of the towers, Ernesto could also recognize the place that had once been his first assignment, his first home in Africa. Boavista had been one of Luanda's poorest slums, but it was erased. The official orders from the Minister of Public Health claimed the bulldozers were deployed to protect the people from cholera and rainy season mudslides. But Ernesto, like everyone else in the capital, knew that the true reason was to clear land for a new commercial real estate project by a member of the ruling party's politburo. Again, *money.*

Ernesto could also spy, up high on a ridge overlooking the waterfront, what had once been Roque Santeiro, Africa's largest open-air market, where not long ago one could buy everything from used shoes to the latest satellite dish. No more. Now it was fenced off and crowded with construction cranes covered with Chinese lettering.

Although these changes made him angry and sad, he knew the future of Angola was not his fight. He would have to wait for his chance for that. For now, he consoled himself with small victories, keeping his patients alive, bringing babies into the world, and waiting patiently for his chance to do something great. To be consequential.

Ernesto finished getting dressed, grabbed his medical bag and stethoscope, and stepped out into the noisy street. His neighborhood was a series of narrow, densely populated alleys. The homes were made of sand-colored concrete, interspersed with specks of yellow and pink, the peeling paint of a more hopeful time. In between the formal structures were inventive shacks of plastic and liberated bricks, topped with rusty metallic sheeting. Down the center of the dirt road ran a steady stream of milky water and cellophane wrappers. At this early hour, the roads were not yet jammed with people and the battered blue-and-white minibuses, but Ernesto knew they were coming.

As Dr. Ernesto Sandoval began his hike to his clinic, tiptoeing through garbage, the cell phone in his pocket buzzed. The number was a series of zeros, something he had never seen before. He decided to answer anyway.

"Alo?"

"*Hermanito?*"

"Ruben?" Ernesto's pulse quickened.

"*Mi hermanito Che?* Is that you, my brother?"

"Ruben? Is that you?"

"Yes, Che. It is me."

"How are you, Ruben? Is there news?"

"It's time."

"Now? Are you saying this is it?" Ernesto's heart pounded in his chest.

"Yes, *mi hermanito*. This is it."

Ernesto's eyes began to water. "I can't believe it, Ruben. After all these years and so much dreaming. Are you certain it is now?"

"Yes, Che. This is the call. It's finally time for us to all come home."

44.

Judd Ryker had finally decided that the best approach to the Cubans would be through baseball. The Cubans were obsessed with baseball. And what was more American? And how could Congress possibly object to a State Department diplomatic effort built around sports? Yes, that would be his pitch to Landon Parker—a low-key initiative to diffuse tensions, build confidence, and allow secret negotiations for the hostages from *The Big Pig*. It sounded stupid, but maybe stupid just might work. The U.S. helped break the ice with China with Ping-Pong, so why not baseball in Cuba?

More to the point, he didn't have anything else. And it was nearly midnight. Judd began drafting talking points for Parker about the potential for baseball diplomacy:

Abner Doubleday, inventor of baseball
Baseball and apple pie

American troops bring baseball & democracy to Japan
Ping pong détente with China
Chance of success: ~~25%~~ 50%

What would Landon Parker think about this? Judd wondered.

"What do you have for me, Ryker?" Parker said. Judd spun around to find the Secretary's chief of staff standing in the doorway.

"Mr. Parker. I wasn't expecting you. I am just finishing talking points to present to you."

"So what do you have?"

"I've been digging into the archives to see what's gone wrong with so many previous attempts to talk quietly to the Cubans."

"I don't need a history lesson, Ryker. I need a plan."

"I'm developing a four-phase strategy. It starts with a low-profile good faith gesture, something noncontroversial. And then we use that as a cover for negotiations. If it all goes wrong—"

"What's your good faith gesture?" Parker interrupted.

"Baseball."

"Sports, Ryker? I asked you for creative and you're giving me—"

"Yes, I know. Baseball doesn't sound like much. But sports worked in the past," Judd tried to explain. "When the Nixon administration needed a way to talk to the Chinese—"

"No time for that, Ryker." Parker shook his head. "It's a hell of an idea. I love baseball as much as the next man. I've got box seats at the Nats, for God's sake. But your plan will take weeks. We don't have weeks. We need something right away."

"Okay, sir."

"I thought S/CRU was built for speed?"

"It is. That's the whole point of the Crisis Reaction Unit. But you asked me to strategize a way—"

"What's the final phase?"

"Sir?"

"Your strategy, Ryker. Maybe we can jump straight to your final phase. What is it?"

"Incentives to deliver."

"You're back to Adam Smith? I thought we agreed there's no time for academic theories inside government."

"Incentives are just ways to make sure everyone is motivated to follow through on their promises. We don't want to give away everything up front. It's better to hold back. If we got to the final phase of incentives—"

"Look, Ryker," Parker interrupted, "I know what I said before. That I asked you for new ideas. But things are moving fast. Melanie Eisenberg is holding a press conference tomorrow morning. She's going to declare that the capture of innocent Americans in international waters is an illegal act and that the United States won't negotiate. She's shutting down any possible overture we can make publicly until this thing cools off. Your baseball idea is dead. Forget it."

"So you want me to work on another plan? Something covert?"

"No time for that either, Ryker."

"So . . . what do you want me to do, sir?"

"I need someone I can trust to go talk to the Cubans directly. Like, right now."

"You're sending me to Cuba?"

"In a way, yes."

Judd stood up from his chair. "Should I go pack?"

"No," Parker said, shaking his head with impatience. "The way you're getting there, you can't bring a suitcase."

"How am I going?" Judd didn't like the sound of this.

"You'll see, Ryker," Parker said, revealing nothing with his facial expression. "You're leaving in five hours."

"When?"

"I've arranged a special undercover departure out of Andrews at oh five hundred. When you get there, you need to negotiate the release of the four men from *The Big Pig*. I want them home as soon as possible. That's your new assignment."

"What, exactly, am I offering the Cubans in exchange for the hostages?"

"You'll figure that out with O."

"What's O?"

"Not what, Ryker, *who*. Oswaldo Guerrero, Cuba's head of military intelligence."

"I'm going to meet Cuba's chief spy?"

"That's right, Ryker. Face-to-face. You're going to be the first American to ever meet O."

45.

Oswaldo Guerrero sipped his tiny cup of thick coffee. The breeze off the Bay of Havana kept him cool, but he didn't feel at all relaxed tonight. The café overlooking the beach was still jammed with locals enjoying a warm evening and loud conversation. Despite the crowd, Oswaldo sat alone and undisturbed. The staff—the few that mattered—knew to give this regular customer his privacy. Even those who weren't directly on his payroll knew to give the short man with powerful arms plenty of space.

After the waiter silently delivered another cup, Oswaldo dropped a white sugar cube into it and slowly stirred with a dainty spoon for nearly a full minute. The ripples of the muscles on his tan forearm highlighted the scars of past battles. His flat, crooked nose, dead black eyes, and a shiny gold front tooth suggested this was a man with an eventful past. He gently set the spoon aside and took a sip.

Off in the distance, the lights of Morro Castle taunted Oswaldo. *The Americans. Los yumas. Los yanquis.* These gringos rotting in his cell didn't know anything. Just more fools. He should slit their throats and toss them back in the sea where he had found them. They should die like the dogs that they are. Just like all the others that came before them trying to poison his homeland with their money and their selfish ways.

If the Americans were going to call him El Diablo, then why not show them what a real Devil can do?

"Ach!" he scolded himself for being emotional. Those four dupes in Morro Castle were nothing. But what about their reckless bosses back in Washington? He knew the Americans were up to something. They always were. Their bravado, their crude schemes, the arrogance and ignorance of *los yanquis*. How did such a country become so rich and powerful when they couldn't even see through the lies of the traitors in Miami? How could they not see the dance of the exiles? How could such a country be so mighty yet unable to keep a simple secret? The United States was a lumbering beast, a giant shadow hanging over his beautiful island, his *Cubita bella*. The fools in his prison cell were just another insult!

Every four years, a new team of American politicians arrived with new ideas, some new gesture that was supposed to impress him, some new threat that was supposed to scare him. Now they were trying to lure Cuba into capitalism by pretending to be friends. The gringos called it *normalization*. None of it will work. He sipped his coffee.

Oswaldo Guerrero could see through it all because he had seen it all before. The gringos didn't know their history. That had been his comfort in the past. But history was precisely what unsettled him about tonight.

Something was different. Was today a genuine opportunity? Or was this just another gringo trick? Was this latest incident real? Or just more scheming by scoundrels in Washington, D.C.?

Oswaldo sipped his coffee again. Deep down, he knew what had really changed was not the Americans. They were very much the same. *Los yumas.* Overconfident, inept, stupid.

What had changed, what he could never admit except within his own private thoughts, was Cuba. *His Cuba.* As certain as *los yanquis* were about themselves, Oswaldo was certain that the Cuban Revolution was coming to an end. Their allies in Moscow had abandoned them. Beijing had become a den of capitalists. And their last remaining friends in Caracas had lost their minds. Even at home, his great leaders were on the verge of death. One thing the Cuban Revolution could never defeat was mortality.

And the youth, the engine of the revolt, the fuel that burned the fire of revolution, was different today. They just weren't like him and his peers. They were distracted. They were selfish. They were weak.

Oswaldo Guerrero, from the time he first joined the secret intelligence service at the age of sixteen, had been a loyal believer in the cause. His mother had thrown flowers on the rebel jeeps when they first arrived in Havana. Oswaldo attended special state schools to learn Cuban revolutionary values. By the time he was five years old, he had memorized El Jefe's "Declaration of the Socialist Character of the Revolution." At the age of seven, he joined the Union of Rebel Pioneers, then graduated to the Rebel Youth Association when he turned thirteen. He was working for the state before he even learned to shave.

Oswaldo Guerrero was raised on *patria o muerte*—nation or death! That was his motivation for continuing to fight the

Americans. To always be on watch, to uncover their plots, to be ruthless with the enemies of the revolution. Above all, to protect Cuba's independence. The Americans had occupied Cuba in 1898, 1906, and 1917. They tried to invade again in 1961. And *los yanquis* kept trying. But men like him had always fought back. Patriots like him had always defended Cuba's total independence.

While Oswaldo was an idealist, a son of the revolution, he wasn't blind. He saw what was happening to his own country. One of the benefits of being at the top of the national intelligence services was a unique window into what was really going on inside Cuba. He could see, underneath the peeling paint, the shiny new tourist hotels, the smiling faces, there was growing unhappiness. Under their breath, in the corners of the plazas and cafés, people complained about the revolution.

Dissent was in the air. It was getting louder. The hardships of life, the sacrifices, were all becoming too much for the masses. And, worst of all, the lure of the bright lights of American consumerism was too much for ordinary people to resist.

He knew that Cuba, despite men like him, was slowly losing its independence. It wasn't *los yumas* who were taking it. No. Cuba was giving away its total independence by rotting from the inside out.

Several years ago, when Oswaldo first concluded that the revolution was doomed, he knew the best option was to repair relations with their big neighbor. To find some way to reach an accommodation to avoid a cataclysmic rupture. He would do this on Cuba's terms. On *his* terms. But how to trust them? How to know which gestures were tricks and which were real? *They were all tricks.*

So what was different about this latest offer? Who was this Judd Ryker? Oswaldo had nothing on him in his files except some useless academic publications. If the Americans were serious this time, then why were they sending some professor? Was this his final opportunity to make history? Oswaldo drained his coffee and motioned to the waiter for another.

Or, maybe he should slit this Judd Ryker's throat? Sending their envoy back in a body bag would get their attention in Washington! That would let them know that they still have something to fear from El Diablo! That Cuba hasn't yet given up. That the Americans can keep trying but they haven't beaten Oswaldo Guerrero.

He leaned forward on the table and laughed to himself, his gold tooth flashing like one of the city's lights. When the gringo professor arrives, he decided, he knew what do to with him.

PART THREE

FRIDAY

46.

Judd Ryker felt like Jonah being swallowed by the whale as he stepped onto the steel ramp yawning open at the back of the massive C-140 Hercules. The cold gray plane was mostly empty, his footsteps echoing through the vast cavern of the cargo bay.

"Good morning, sir!" snapped a young Air Force officer who had suddenly appeared.

"Good morning," Judd replied wearily. "I'm Judd—"

"Yes, sir. Dr. Ryker from State. We're expecting you, sir."

"You're taking me to Cuba in this?" Judd waved his arms around the empty cavern.

"My orders are to brief you on our exact destination only when we are wheels up."

"But you are taking me to Cuba?" Judd narrowed his eyes and rubbed his neck, which was starting to ache.

"I couldn't say, sir. I'm just following orders."

"I don't understand." Judd winced at the confusion.

"It's nearly oh five hundred," the officer said, showing Judd his watch. "Preflight checks are complete. As soon as you get strapped in, we can go. I have to ask you to remove any cell phone."

Judd handed over his phone reluctantly, but he ran through in his mind the most important numbers that he had memorized: the State Department's Operations Center hotline and Jessica's temporary cell.

"I'm ready." Judd steeled himself. "Anything else I need to know?"

"No, sir."

"I don't have any baggage," Judd said.

"Of course not, sir. I'll be back once we're in the air."

The officer exited the plane and Judd buckled himself into a jump seat along a side wall of the C-140. He watched the giant ramp close, leaving him alone in the dark in the belly of the whale. A pang shot through his spine. *What have I gotten myself into?*

A few seconds later, a fluorescent light flickered on, illuminating the cargo hold, but not relieving Judd's sudden anxiety. He then heard the engines fire up and the loud whirring of the four huge propellers.

After a long taxi, the giant plane rumbled down the runway, the walls shuddering violently during takeoff. Within moments, the C-140 reached altitude and leveled off, allowing both the plane's fuselage and its sole passenger to relax.

Judd slumped back in the jump seat. Exhausted, alone, and ensconced in the white noise of the engines, he fought off the urge to sleep. He hated tight spaces. It wasn't quite claustrophobia, but, growing up in rural Vermont, he was always more comfortable out in the open, plenty of air, plenty of sky. Tightly packed trains were bad; small, crowded airplanes were worse. At least he wouldn't have to worry about that in the back of the cavernous C-140. At least—

"Sir!"

Judd opened his eyes.

"Sir! We are beginning our descent."

Judd blinked a few times. He realized that he must have dozed off.

"Where are we?" Judd asked.

"Sir, you need to put this on," the officer said, handing him an orange jumpsuit.

"I'm not wearing this. It looks like a prison uniform."

"I don't know, sir. My orders are to have you wear it before we allow you to deplane."

"What? I don't even know where we're landing."

"Yes, sir. We will be arriving at GTMO in"—he checked his watch—"fourteen minutes."

"GTMO?"

"Gitmo, sir."

"You're taking me to Guantánamo Bay?" Judd's eyes widened and his heart raced.

"Yes, sir. That's our destination."

"Why would a State Department official wear a prisoner uniform at a military detention camp?"

"I couldn't say, sir. I'm sure you'll be briefed on arrival," he said. "I only know that I have strict orders that you wear it before getting off the plane at Gitmo. The jumpsuit and this." The officer held up a small black cloth hood.

A hood! Judd's abdomen convulsed. *What the hell have I got myself into?*

47.

ssistant Secretary for Western Hemisphere Affairs Melanie Eisenberg tapped the microphone on the podium and checked her hair in the monitor. The Press Room was littered with television cameras and journalists. Behind Eisenberg, the back wall was covered with a navy blue curtain and an oval sign showing the world map and DEPARTMENT OF STATE / WASHINGTON. An American flag rested on its pole, perfectly positioned to appear over Eisenberg's right shoulder in the television frame. The front of the lectern displayed a circular State Department logo, an eagle gripping an olive branch in one talon and arrows in the other.

"Are we ready?" Eisenberg barked at an aide off to the side of the stage, who nodded.

"Ladies and gentlemen," she began, holding her chin high, "we have a simple statement this morning. As many of you know, Cuban authorities seized a private American fishing vessel operating in international waters on Wednesday evening. In the interest of prudence, we have refrained from making any public statements until we had ascertained all the facts."

Eisenberg made eye contact with a boyish reporter sitting in the front row. "We now can confirm that four American citizens have been detained by the Cuban government." She stared directly into the camera. "This illegal act undermines the progress we have made establishing dialogue with the government in Havana. It has put at risk all of the efforts to date to resolve our diplomatic impasse that goes back more than half a century. We hoped this incident would be quickly resolved in a peaceful manner, but that has not happened. The United States cannot stand idly by as our citizens are treated in this manner."

Eisenberg held up a scolding finger. "I would like to remind this audience and the American people that while we have removed Cuba from the list of official state sponsors of terrorism, this administration will continue to uphold our policy of not negotiating with hostage takers. Let me be very clear: There will be no negotiations."

She grabbed both sides of the lectern. "We call upon the Cuban authorities to release these Americans immediately and unconditionally. The United States of America stands with these innocent men, their families, and the Cuban people, who only yearn to be free." She paused. "I will take a few questions."

The room erupted.

"Yes," she said, pointing to the young man in the front.

"Domingo Campesino, *Miami Herald*. Can you confirm the identity of the four men?"

Eisenberg shook her head. "Out of respect for the privacy of their families, we are not releasing their names."

"But several television networks are reporting these men as: Dennis Dobson, of Rockville, Maryland; Crawford Jackson—"

"The Department of State cannot at this time confirm any unsubstantiated news reports," Eisenberg interrupted. "As soon as we have more information, we will let you know, Domingo . . . Next?"

"Amanda Haddad, Fox News. Are you declaring this an act of terrorism?"

"I didn't say 'terrorism.' I said 'illegal.' We stand by our policy of never negotiating for hostages."

"So Cuba is no longer a state sponsor of terrorism, but you're not denying that their seizure of the fishing boat might be an act of terrorism?"

"Don't parse my words. I stand on what I've previously indicated . . . Yes?"

"Jasmine Chepenik, *Orlando Sentinel*. What are the Cubans saying about this incident? What do they want in return for their release?"

"You'll have to ask them."

"They haven't told the U.S. government anything?"

"I just told you, Jaz," Eisenberg huffed, "we aren't negotiating. We will not pay ransom of any kind. That's not the American way . . . Who's next?"

"Van Wagner, *Politico*. The reaction from Capitol Hill has been swift and aggressive. The Free Cuba Congressional Caucus issued a statement yesterday morning that was essentially the same position that you just articulated. What's taking the administration so long?"

"We respect Congress and their rights to come to whatever

views they choose. That's why we have separation of powers, Van. That was the vision of the Founding Fathers."

"But your position is essentially the same as Chairwoman Adelman-Zamora. Is the administration now in lockstep with her on Cuba policy?"

Eisenberg bit her lip. "We agree with all those who believe the Cuban people have a right to determine their own government, to enjoy the basic freedoms that all Americans enjoy, and to decide their own future."

"So this is a shift in administration policy? Are you taking a more hard-line stance?"

"Van, I'm not going to debate Cuba policy with the press. I believe I've made our position clear . . . Last question . . . Mikaela?"

"Mikaela Rinehart, *Washington Post*. Even if the administration says no direct talks with the Cubans, there is a long history of sending third parties to negotiate hostage releases. Chairman Bryce McCall of the Senate Foreign Relations Committee has played this role in the past, for instance last year in West Africa. I understand that Senator McCall has made a private offer to the White House to go to Havana in order to broker an agreement. Is that under consideration?"

"That's a red herring."

"Is that a no?" she asked.

"Let me make this perfectly clear, Mikaela." Eisenberg failed to hide a grimace. "We will not negotiate. There will be no secret deals. There is no American envoy being sent to talk with Cuba."

48.

Detainee 761!" the officer shouted.

Judd couldn't see any light through the hood. No shadows. Nothing. His breathing quickened. *Calm down,* he told himself.

"Opening the cargo bay door!"

Judd winced as he was pulled to his feet, the plastic handcuffs pinching the skin on the wrists. He heard the loud whirring of the door opening and a hollow thunk. Judd tried to slow his breathing.

"Let's go," the officer said roughly. He guided Judd down the ramp and out onto the tarmac. Once outside, Judd immediately felt the heat of the sun.

The officer led blind Judd for another two hundred yards, then stopped. Judd heard new voices.

"What's your cargo today, Captain?"

"Detainee 761," the officer said. "Transfer from Camp Romeo."

"Welcome to Gitmo, 761," someone sneered, tapping Judd on the shoulder.

"What's the security level for this detainee?" asked another voice.

Judd tried to speak but the tight hood made it difficult. "Hey," he tried to say.

"Should I check SIPRNet?"

"Negative. TS/SCI. Special protocol for this one."

"Hey!" Judd tried to yell again, but the men ignored him.

"Roger that. I'll take him into holding cell Zebra, before a transfer to Camp Delta."

"Hey! Hey!" Judd tried again. "Hey!"

"I don't think he's going to Delta."

"Echo or Iguana?"

"Neither."

"Where do I take him, then?"

"Put him in the black hole."

"Hey!" Judd shouted as loud as he could. "I'm—"

A firm hand pressed to his throat. "You got a screamer. Better get him there quick."

Judd felt the hand slide to the back of his neck. "Quiet, 761! You'll have plenty of time to talk once we get you to the hole."

What the hell is going on?

Judd was bundled into a vehicle and driven for several minutes. Then he was yanked out and forced to stand. He could hear *beep-beep-beep* and then the click-clack and woosh of a door release. Judd was shoved forward and felt the sudden coolness of air-conditioning. He was shuffled down a corridor, then through another door lock, and finally into another room.

"Seven sixty-one is here. Your special protocol from Romeo."

"Leave him."

Judd could hear the other men depart and the door shut and

lock. Once they were gone, the hood flew off his head. Judd shut his eyes against the sudden bright lights.

"I'm sorry, Dr. Ryker." He felt the handcuffs release. "You're safe here."

Judd rubbed his wrist and squinted, trying to see who was in front of him.

"Who are you?" Judd asked.

"It doesn't matter," said the man.

"You know who I am," Judd said. As his eyes adjusted, he could make out the silhouette of an older man, with short hair, a neatly trimmed beard, dressed in civilian clothes—black T-shirt, blue jeans.

"I could tell you my name—any name—and it won't matter. You will never see me again. And I'll never see you again."

"What the hell is going on here?"

"My orders are to make you invisible. That's what I'm doing, Dr. Ryker."

"Whose orders?"

"I can't say."

"What are you, State? DOD or CIA?"

The man shrugged. "I can't say."

"Are you another agency?"

"Please, Dr. Ryker."

"So where am I?" Judd asked. "What's the 'black hole'?"

"Here. You're in a SCIF at Guantánamo Bay Naval Base. You don't need to know any more. You are totally safe and secure, sir."

"Safe and secure? You just hooded and frog-marched me off an airplane?"

"Yes, sorry about that, sir. Couldn't be avoided."

"I don't understand."

"The Cubans monitor all our incoming flights. They've even got moles inside the base. I had to make it look like you were Taliban or ISIS. Even to our own guys."

"That's insane."

"It's an insane world, Dr. Ryker. This is the only way to get you onto the island and be one hundred percent certain you've arrived undetected. We used to bring people in via Canada under tourist cover, but we couldn't take that risk with you. You'll need to change identities before you leave this room."

"What identity?"

"This is your new cover, sir," he said, pointing to a baby blue linen suit and a straw sun hat.

"I have to wear *that*?" Judd asked.

"And *this*," he said, holding up a fake beard. "You're going native."

"I don't understand," Judd said. "Where am I going?"

"We can't send you over the wall, as the Cubans mined everything beyond our fence line with locally made POMZ. The commies were good at laying mines, but they didn't bother to map them. We hear them burn off every once in a while. Flying cooked goat. We find it charred to the fence. Sometimes a dog."

"You're saying Cuba is a minefield?"

"Yes, sir. That's why you need this suit and beard. You'll go in during the regular shift change with the local staff. Only a few old guys left, so you'll need to look elderly to avoid being noticed."

"I'm not sure I understand," Judd said.

"Sir, we can't send you over the fence. It's too dangerous. So you are going into Cuba the safest way we know. You're going to walk out right through the front gate."

"And then what?"

"And then *this*." The man handed Judd a sealed envelope. "Don't open it until I leave and you are alone. Read it. Then burn it," the man said, and tossed Judd a book of matches.

"What is this?" Judd asked, holding up the envelope.

"Your mission, sir."

49.

Sunday blew gently on his cup of coffee, the freshly roasted Ethiopian variety that he always bought from Swing's whenever he was near the White House. The coffeehouse had been packed with National Security Council staff, badges around their necks, discussing work in subdued tones and nonspecific code.

Sunday crossed 17th Street, walked between the thick car bomb barriers, and onto the pedestrianized Pennsylvania Avenue. To the south was the Eisenhower Executive Office Building, where the President's foreign policy staff worked in a grand edifice that reminded Sunday of a giant haunted house. To the north was Blair House, the President's official state guest residence, a tasteful, early-nineteenth-century townhome used by only the most prominent VIPs.

Sunday entered Lafayette Square, the park directly across from the White House. The square was not yet filled with tourists or protestors. At this early hour, it was mostly government workers on their way to EEOB or the U.S. Treasury or the West

Wing. *This was a stupid place to meet,* he thought. Too many eyes and ears. Too high a chance of running into someone who might recognize him. Or her.

He circumnavigated the park twice, then, satisfied no one was watching him, settled on an empty park bench overlooking a statue of President Andrew Jackson, riding a horse and surrounded by cannons. He slipped on sunglasses, pulled a Boston Red Sox cap from his jacket and placed it on the bench.

After a few minutes, a petite, dark-haired woman sat down next to him and opened the *Washington Post.* She flipped through the paper, then stopped on the sports page.

"What's the score of last night's Red Sox–Yankees game?" Sunday asked the woman while looking straight off into the distance.

"The Nationals beat the Mets, five to four," she said, and turned the page again.

"Thank you for coming on short notice," he whispered.

"I'm not supposed to be here," Isabella Espinosa said. "In fact, I'm *not* here."

"Yes, ma'am, understood," Sunday replied without making eye contact.

"The only reason I even took your call was because I owe Judd a big one."

"I'm indebted to Dr. Ryker, too."

"Let's make this quick," she said.

"Did you find anything on Ricky Green?"

She shook her head.

"Nothing at all?"

"Doesn't mean there isn't something there," Isabella said, "just that I couldn't find it."

"Maybe witness protection?"

She shook her head again. "I can't get access to that. And if I could, telling you would be a felony."

"What about Ricardo Cabrera?"

"He was in the system. Low-level drug trafficker. Grabbed in Operation Everglades."

"What's that?"

"Massive interagency drug sweep. The Feds flooded Everglades City. It was the biggest cocaine bust in South Florida history. I'm talking FBI, DEA, IRS, the U.S. Marshals, Customs. Even the Coast Guard and DOD got involved. I've never seen anything like it."

"So you were there?" Sunday asked.

"I sure hope not," she said.

"I don't understand."

"I was a kid. Operation Everglades was in 1983."

"They caught Cabrera way back in eighty-three?"

Isabella nodded.

"And then what?" Sunday asked.

"Then nothing. He just disappeared."

"Cabrera's been gone since 1983?"

"Him and the cash."

"What cash?" Sunday raised his eyebrows.

"During the bust, the Feds seized almost a million in cash. But some of those arrested later claimed that there was more. A lot more."

"How much?"

"One of the ringleaders who went to prison was later caught on a wiretap claiming that *los federales* had stolen *two hundred million cash* that he had hidden in the Everglades."

"Why would anyone hide that much cash in a swamp?" Sunday asked.

"The Everglades have always been a magnet for criminals. It's close to the Caribbean and far from authorities. In the 1920s, rumrunners used to bring the stuff into the swamps from Cuba and Jamaica. In the 1980s, it was cocaine and marijuana. Whatever the mob runs into the United States. Makes sense they would try to keep their operations in a place that's remote and impenetrable, but also not far from the source. And close to Miami. That's the Everglades."

"Anyone ever find the two hundred million?"

"Probably never existed," Isabella said. "Just another Florida swamp legend. They still catch guys trying to find it. Modern-day treasure hunters."

"More pirates," Sunday said.

"What pirates?"

"Never mind," Sunday said. "It's quite a coincidence that Ricardo Cabrera goes missing at the same time as a huge amount of money, don't you think?"

"I don't know." Isabella shrugged. "What's your interest?"

"I'm trying to find Ricky Green. Could he be . . . Ricardo Cabrera?"

"Can't help you," Isabella said.

"You already did."

50.

Judd stared down at the page in front of him.

TOP SECRET/EYES ONLY: JUDD RYKER

Via Station Jtf-Gtmo

Take the blue and white Chevy Bel Air taxi from the Northeast Gate at 10.00. You will meet your contact at a neutral location. Seek release of innocent Americans. Maximum approved offer: $1 million and baseball exchange. No prisoner exchange. No change in US policy. Find a good faith gesture and explore breakthrough on other issues. Good luck. –LP

Landon Parker? What the hell is this? What kind of instructions are these? And what happened to Oswaldo Guerrero? Judd tried to open the door, but it was locked.

"Hey!" he shouted. "Let me out!"

The door lock clacked and a soldier in uniform blocked the

doorway. "I can't allow you to take that out of the SCIF, sir," he said, pointing at the paper in Judd's hand. "I'm under orders to assist you, but only after you have destroyed that document."

Judd took a deep breath, read it one more time, memorized the key details, then struck a match, lit the paper, and watched it burn.

"Where's the other guy?" Judd asked.

"What other guy, sir?"

"The one with the beard. The one who—" Judd stopped himself. "I need a secure phone right now."

"Right there, sir," he said, pointing to a black phone on a desk in the corner. "That's an encrypted line to Washington."

"I need five minutes. And then a ride to the Northeast Gate."

The soldier nodded and closed the door.

Judd started to punch in the number for the State Department Operations Center, which could connect him to Parker. *What kind of horseshit assignment was this?* He stopped just before he hit the last number. He set the phone down. *Wrong move.* Judd snatched the handset again and tapped in another number.

"Who's this?" Jessica answered.

"Me, sweets."

"What number is this? Where are you?"

"I'm on a government phone. It's a secure line."

"Is everything okay?" Jessica sounded worried.

"Yeah. You said we should speak tomorrow. That's why I'm calling you."

"I'm at the pool," she said breezily. Judd glanced at the concrete-block walls of the room at Guantánamo and imagined his wife, sunbathing in a bikini, beside a crystal-blue pool, sipping a fruity tropical drink. "I'm rereading *Treasure Island*. It's just as wonderful as I remembered, Judd. I'm up to the part where they've hired Long John Silver as the cook for the voyage to the Caribbean."

"I remember that part. Little do they know, right?"

"When are you coming to join us?" Jessica asked.

"Soon. I'm . . . stuck at work."

"Is that why you're calling? Do you need me to go to another party or something? I'm good at that," she joked.

"No . . ." Judd said, "Not that. You ever heard of someone named . . . Oswaldo Guerrero?"

Jessica was silent on the other end of the line.

"Jess?"

"I'm still here," she said.

"Well, have you? Does the name Oswaldo Guerrero mean anything to you?"

"What have you gotten yourself into, Judd?" Her breeziness was gone.

"So you *have* heard of him?"

She paused. "No." She winced at *Lie Number Eight*. "Judd, I thought you were trying to get those fishermen free?"

"Yes, that's right. The Soccer Dad Four in Cuba."

"I . . . wouldn't assume they're soccer dads," Jessica said.

"Why do you say that? How would you know, Jess?"

"The one who owns the fishing boat—"

"*The Big Pig?* Alejandro Cabrera."

"Yes, him," Jessica said. "He's Cuban American."

"So? What does that mean?"

"He's not just anybody. The Cabreras are well connected in Little Havana and in the exile community in Miami. Alejandro's grandfather was a leader of Brigada Asalto 2506."

"Twenty-five oh six? What does that mean?"

"The Bay of Pigs invasion."

"So . . . what are you saying?" Judd asked.

"And one of the other men—"

"Dobson? Jackson?"

"No, the other one," she said.

"Brinkley Barrymore? The lawyer?"

"He's the grandson of Randolph Nye," she said.

"Who's Randolph Nye?"

"Back in the early years of the Cold War, he was the Deputy Director of . . . a three-letter agency. The Bay of Pigs was *his* operation."

"How do you know all this?"

"Don't you get it, Judd?" she asked, ignoring his question.

"So Cabrera and Barrymore have family history tied back to the Bay of Pigs. So what? What are you suggesting, Jess?"

"Think about it, Judd."

"Are you saying that a bunch of soccer dads, or whatever they are, who were out fishing in Florida were actually trying to invade Cuba . . . to redeem their grandfathers?"

She didn't reply.

"Are you telling me," Judd continued, "that the four middle-aged guys from suburban Washington were trying to launch *another* Bay of Pigs?"

"I don't know, Judd. But I think you need to find out."

"I'll add this to the list of things that don't make sense," he said. "But, Jess, how . . . do you know all this?"

"Once you told me you were working on the hostages, I did a little research."

"What else do you know?"

"Judd, dear," she said, trying to calm him down. "You need to be careful. Very careful. I know Landon Parker asked you to take this on and you're working hard to show S/CRU can be a success. But I'm worried you don't know what you are getting yourself into."

"You're worried?"

"I'm worried about *you*, Judd."

"Well, don't be. I can handle this."

"Cuba policy is a minefield in Washington."

He looked around at the room again, the old suit, the fake beard he was supposed to wear, and thought, *I'm definitely not in Washington.*

51.

We aren't going to let them take away Social Security!" Brenda Adelman-Zamora was speaking too loudly into her Bluetooth headset as she walked through the arrivals lounge. "I'm just getting off the plane now . . . I don't give two shits what committee he sits on . . . No deal. You tell him I said that!"

Behind her trailed a young woman pulling two suitcases, a travel dog bag slung over one shoulder with the head of a black-and-tan Yorkshire terrier poking through the top flap. The girl struggled to keep up with the congresswoman, who was barreling through the crowded terminal.

"No . . . No . . . Hell no!" Adelman-Zamora shouted into the phone. "I won't allow it! You tell Arnie that I said it's not happening until hell freezes over."

Travelers, aware of the approaching storm but avoiding eye contact, gave the woman wide berth.

"He's offering how much more for Everglades restoration?" She stopped dead in her tracks. "What about federal funds for widening I-95? Do we dare? Oh my goodness! Hold!"

Adelman-Zamora spun around, lowering her brow as she searched the throng for her aide with her luggage and her dog. The young woman finally appeared.

"Where have you been? Never mind. Leave the bags and little Desi Arnaz here. I'll watch them. Bring me one nonfat peach yogurt for the car. Not the disgusting one with the granola, the one with the fresh fruit. I need a copy of the *Washington Post*. And I see the newsstand has the CIA T-shirts back in stock. They love those at the constituent office in Fort Lauderdale. Bring me four in the red and two in the blue." She paused. "And two in the pink. All size small. Hurry. Go."

The congresswoman shooed away the aide and turned back to her phone call. "If we can get that deal, let's take it! I'll be in soon. I'm just leaving the airport, if I can get through these dreadful crowds. It's just too busy. I can't stand the airport this time of year. Don't worry, I'm on my way into the office!"

52.

Ma'am, I'm just on my way back into the office," Sunday said into his headset.

Sunday had left downtown Washington, D.C. after his clandestine meeting with Isabella Espinosa from the Department of Justice. He had driven along Constitution Avenue, between the Lincoln Memorial and the U.S. Department of State headquarters. The Eisenhower Bridge then took him over the Potomac River. He was driving northwest on the parkway when Jessica Ryker called.

"Do you know anything about an Oswaldo Guerrero?"

"Never heard of him, ma'am."

"Also known as O. Anything?"

"I'm sorry, ma'am."

"I need you to find out ASAP. It's urgent. Anything you can find on Oswaldo Guerrero or O. The minute you're back."

"Yes, ma'am. I'm on it."

"What else have you got for me?"

"I met with your husband's Justice Department contact. That's where I'm coming from."

"She give you anything new on Ricky Green?"

"Not exactly, ma'am. I think I have something better."

"Spill, Sunday," she said.

"One of the missing men from the fishing boat, Alejandro Cabrera, had a brother Ricardo who dropped off the radar in 1983."

"Keep talking."

"I found him in the records, but they stop in 1983."

"So what happened in eighty-three, Sunday?"

"That's where it gets interesting. Ricardo last appears to have been arrested in a drug bust in South Florida in 1983 and then he just vanishes."

"So he was killed? Drug dealers disappear all the time. Especially in Florida."

"This wasn't local police, ma'am. It was a major federal interagency operation. I'm talking about FBI, DEA, and at least half a dozen other agencies."

"So you're thinking Ricardo was flipped by the FBI? That he disappeared into witness protection?"

"Maybe. DOJ won't say. But now his brother suddenly appears on our radar? Alejandro's fishing boat is captured in Cuban waters, he's the grandson of a leader from the Bay of Pigs, and this mysterious Ricky seems to be in the middle of it all. Seems awfully coincidental, ma'am."

"This drug bust. Don't tell me it was in—"

"Everglades City, ma'am."

Jessica was silent on the line for moment, then spoke up. "You're thinking . . . Ricky Green *is* Ricardo Cabrera."

"Yes, ma'am. I'm pretty sure of it."

Jessica was quiet again.

"Ma'am, that's not even the best part," Sunday said, just as his car passed the exit sign for the GEORGE BUSH CENTER FOR INTELLIGENCE.

"What else?" Jessica asked.

"A large amount of cash went missing," he said. "Drug money that should have been seized during the bust . . . it just disappeared."

"Happens all the time."

"But this haul was huge. Could be as much as two hundred million dollars in cash."

"Who keeps that much cash?"

"Operation Everglades took down a major cocaine cartel. It's plausible."

"Okay . . . So, how do two hundred million ghost dollars fit with Ricardo Cabrera going into witness protection and becoming Ricky Green? Why would the FBI even allow that?"

Sunday pulled onto the exit ramp past a sign warning AU-THORIZED CIA EMPLOYEES ONLY.

"Ma'am . . . I don't think it was the FBI."

53.

Are you in the goddamn CIA?" Crawford Jackson poked his fingers hard into the chest of Alejandro Cabrera.

"Let's not get crazy here," Brinkley Barrymore III said, stepping between his two friends. "We can't turn on each other."

Crawford's eyes locked with Brinkley's. "I asked Al a question."

"Just look at him," Brinkley said. Alejandro was slumped in a chair, his belly stretching the filthy orange jumpsuit. "Al's not CIA."

"Are you?" Crawford narrowed his eyes.

"This is just what *they* want," Brinkley said. "To make us turn on each other."

"You didn't answer my question, Brink," Crawford said.

"I'm not even going to dignify it," Brinkley shot back.

"The gear, the boat, the last-minute trip—"

"Bonefish," Dennis Dobson spoke up, his first words since they had been detained some forty hours ago.

"What?" The others all turned to face Dennis.

"Bonefish," Dobson said again. "You told us we were marlin-fishing, but then you changed your mind and had us go after bonefish in the Seminole Flats. That's how we wound up in Cuba. That's how you got us into this. *Bonefish*."

"See!" Crawford shouted. "Deuce's with me. What the fuck're you two really up to?"

"And the bonefish turned into diamonds. But, why did you need all those guns, Al?" Dennis was waking up.

"Is this another Agency clusterfuck? I'm the SEAL. Dennis is, what, the techie? What's Al supposed to be? Is this your half-assed operation, Brink?"

"This was all a huge mistake," Brinkley insisted. "A big misunderstanding."

"Either you are a fool or someone set you up, Brink," Craw said. "Someone set us all up. No other way to explain it."

"All that matters is that we're getting out of here soon," Brinkley insisted.

"I don't care what you and Al are up to. Go ahead, get yourself killed on some weekend warrior yahoo bullshit," Crawford said. "But why would you drag us into it?"

"I want to know what we were really doing?" Dennis shrieked. "If we weren't fishing, and we weren't treasure hunting, then what the heck were we really doing out there?"

No one said anything.

"Al? Brink?" Dennis squealed. "I almost died. You have to tell us!"

No reply.

Dennis calmed his voice to a whisper. "What is 1961?"

Brinkley shook his head and turned away. "We're all getting out of here alive."

54.

The yellow school bus carrying Judd passed by a large concrete pillar wrapped in barbed wire, ENTER IF YOU DARE painted on the side. The bus climbed a hill and then stopped. The hydraulic doors released with a pucker and swung open.

"Northeast Gate! Last stop for Cuba!" shouted the driver, a uniformed Marine, who eyed Judd warily in the rearview mirror. Judd, wearing the old suit he had been given, pulled down his hat and stroked his false beard. It was a convincing disguise, but he was beginning to sweat and the beard tickled.

"Just you today, Grandpa?" the driver asked.

Judd shrugged and rose to leave.

"Can't believe you old guys are still working after all these years. Helluva commute, *señor*."

Judd coughed, his hand covering his face, as he descended the steps. Outside the bus, a modest gatehouse was surrounded with yellow-and-red concrete barriers, the closest ones painted with the letters USMC. A six-foot-high fence topped with razor wire ran in both directions as far as the eye could see.

"Make sure you stay on the road, Grandpa!" the Marine shouted. "It's a minefield out there!" He laughed as he closed the door and pulled away.

Judd turned back to the security gate in front of him. On the other side of a narrow no-man's-land was a second gate about eighty feet away. A friendly, soft-pink-and-white building with a prominent, not-so-friendly sign: REPUBLICA DE CUBA / TERRI-TORIO LIBRE DE AMERICA.

Judd walked slowly, with a slight hobble, and, as promised, was waved through both gates without incident. On the other side, tall cacti grew on the hills overlooking the border post.

Where's my taxi? He was sweating more. His beard was itching fiercely. He had no phone, no ID, no money—nothing. He was standing in Cuba, alone, waiting for a car that might never come. *Then what?*

Judd looked up to the sky. Vultures flew high above in wide, lumbering circles. At least his back spasms had settled down.

Just then, he heard the soft rumble of a car's engine. Through the vapors of the hot morning sun on the road suddenly appeared what looked like a smiling face. The mouth of a shiny chrome grille, the bright eyes of the headlights, a V-shaped nose in the center. Just above the nose was the giveaway: CHEVROLET. Judd rubbed his eyes as a 1957 Chevy Bel Air rolled to a gentle stop in front of him. The car was an immaculate turquoise blue like the Caribbean Sea, with a white roof, the insets of the rear wings also a perfectly polished white.

The door swung open with a slight creak. Judd bent over to peer into the car at the driver. A short Hispanic-looking man with muscular arms and black eyes looked back at him.

"Taxi, *señor?*"

55.

The bottle was calling him, but he knew it was too early for scotch. The Deputy Director of Operations needed something else to calm himself. This often happened just as an operation was moving into the critical phase. It was mostly an adrenaline rush, he knew, but he didn't want the excitement of the moment to cloud his judgment. He would need to make important decisions in the coming hours. He needed to have a clear mind.

His ex-wife used to make him protein shakes with a raw egg on the mornings when she knew he was hyped-up. But now she was making breakfast for an investment banker in Chicago. His second wife, he barely even saw her anymore.

The Deputy Director swore to himself then flipped on a headset. He touched his earpiece. "Connect me to Romeo Papa Eight."

A few moments later, his earpiece clicked and he heard a familiar "Sir?"

"What's your status, Romeo Papa Eight?"

"We've got an inbound bird, ETA Luanda, Angola, in just under an hour. They can run an accelerated turnaround and

be wheels up by 1800 local time departure. That's 1200 Eastern, sir."

"What's the bird?"

"Dassault Falcon 7X."

"Meets all our specs?"

"Yes, sir. It's right at the limit of the range, but Luanda to
Cuba can be done nonstop if the load is light."

"One passenger."

"No problem, sir."

"Fingerprints?"

"The Falcon is registered to a Brazilian agroprocessing firm,
via São Paulo, Dubai, and the Caymans. Pilots are from Odessa,
hired through a third party in Cape Town. It's so clean, you can
eat off the fuselage."

"Better be," he said, and tapped his ear to hang up. He opened
his drawer, pulled out a short glass tumbler, and set it on the desk.
He ran his finger around the rim as he tried to slow his breathing.

The Deputy Director tapped his ear again. "Connect me to
Oscar Sierra Two."

Seconds later, he was on the line with another of his operations teams.

"What's your status, Oscar Sierra Two?"

"The package is being extracted. Bravo Zero is on his way to
the site. It'll be ready to fly in two hours."

"What's the weight?"

"Two hundred and four pounds total."

"Bundled how?"

"Just as you requested, sir. Five cases, forty pounds each."

"That's two million per case?"

"Yes, sir. Ten million total. Do you need more? We can pack whatever you need, sir."

"Ten will do for now. But be ready in case we need a second shipment."

"Yes, sir."

"I want it at the gator drop near Homestead by twenty-one thirty. That's as far as I need Bravo Zero to take it."

"Yes, sir."

He hung up. The pieces were falling into place. He had compartmentalized the entire operation. He was the one person on the planet who knew how it all fit together. That was the only way to make it work, he knew. That was the downfall of Rainmaker, Pandora, Pit Boss, and all the other operations that had failed before. Too many cooks, too much groupthink, too many leaks. The only way to beat Oswaldo Guerrero in his own backyard was to do it all *himself*.

One more tap of the ear. "I want Yankee Tango Four."

While he waited to connect, he walked over to an antique credenza on the far side of his office. He opened one of the doors and extracted a bottle of eighteen-year-old Oban Single Malt Scotch Whisky. He had bought that bottle on a long-ago trip to Scotland, an excursion after visiting GCHQ in Cheltenham. He'd been waiting for a reason to celebrate.

Click-click! "What's your status, Yankee Tango Four?" he asked, returning to his desk and setting the bottle next to the tumbler.

"No bread tomorrow."

"Are you sure?"

"Wheat stocks are down. The imports won't be arriving.

We've made sure of that. When Mama Bear goes to the cup-board, the cupboard will be bare."

He poured two fingers of scotch into the glass.

"And the streets?" he asked.

"Yankee Tango Four is ready in Santiago. Just waiting for the payouts to arrive."

The Deputy Director nodded to himself and took a healthy sip of the Oban.

"Operation Triggerfish is a go."

56.

Jessica tried to concentrate on *Treasure Island*. Her sons, Noah and Toby, were splashing in the pool, the sun was hot, the day was perfect. Except that Judd wasn't there.

Late the previous night, she had told the Deputy Director of the CIA that she was opting out of his Cuba operation, whatever he was up to. She had fed Judd a few clues and had Sunday digging for more back at Langley. She had helped her husband because he asked. That was their deal. *Assist*. But don't get too close. Jessica was pulling back from Cuba. She was putting an end to the unavoidable lies. *Eight lies already was enough.* This was the only way.

Jessica tried to relax. That was why she was here in Florida, she told herself. She stared at the words on the page. But she couldn't concentrate. She couldn't read. She couldn't clear her mind.

The Deputy Director had agreed to let her off . . . too easily. That wasn't his way. He must have sent her down to South Florida for . . . something else. It couldn't have been to just check out one missing fishing boat. He could have sent a rookie operative to do that. Hell, he could have sent Aunt Lulu. No, Jessica was certain there was something else going on here and that the Agency—*her Agency*—was deeply involved.

She had pieced together a lot and had told Judd what she knew. She had gone to the fund-raising party for him, too. That was the deal. *Did that make up for the lies?* Then Ricky Green had tried to kill her at the party. She had decided not to tell Judd about that. And now Judd—*her Judd*—was in the middle of some murky diplomatic backchannel. It didn't add up. It made her nervous. But she had decided to let it go. *To avoid.*

Then Judd had called that morning and asked about one Oswaldo Guerrero. That was why she couldn't relax. The web of lies—to her boss, to her husband, to herself—wasn't clearing. *It was thickening.* That wasn't the plan.

The deal with Judd was supposed to unburden herself. *Assist, avoid, admit.* Rather than rise above all the lies, she was somehow getting in *deeper.* And the more she tried to pull back, the farther in she waded. There was nothing left to do but . . . to push through and come out the other side.

She stared again at the pages of *Treasure Island* without seeing the words. She was plotting. She decided the logical next step was figuring out exactly who Judd was meeting. How to help him succeed one more time so they could start all over again? So many unanswered questions, but right now what she needed to know most of all was . . . *who is this Oswaldo Guerrero?*

On cue, her phone rang.

"It's me, ma'am," Sunday said.

"Why are you out of breath?"

"I ran into the parking lot to make this call. It's not good."

"What's not good?"

"You asked me to look into O. To find out what I could about Oswaldo Guerrero."

"I'm worried that he isn't real. Don't tell me you found *nothing*."

"Just the opposite. The file on O is as thick and ugly as I've seen."

"What does that mean?"

"Guerrero is the Cuban military intelligence chief. The one who's foiled virtually every U.S. covert action to destabilize the regime over the past twenty years."

"So O's smart," she said.

"More than that. O's ruthless. You ever hear what went wrong in Santiago?" Sunday asked.

"Tell me," she said as her heart rate quickened.

"An op that went bad a few years ago. The last real attempt to incite a counterrevolution in eastern Cuba. In the city of Santiago. We sent in some of our people and it was"—Sunday coughed and cleared his throat—"a bloodbath."

She exhaled loudly. "Rainmaker," she whispered.

"Yes, ma'am. Our operatives walked right into O's trap," Sunday said.

"And?" Jessica's heart raced.

"That's why they call Oswaldo Guerrero . . . El Diablo de Santiago."

57.

The taxi had driven in silence, away from the gate at Guantánamo Bay. For the past fifteen minutes, the '57 Chevy Bel Air had wound down a dirt road that cut through the hills of rural Cuba. Judd tried to keep track of their direction—first northeast, then east, then north again—but he lost his bearings in the twists and turns of the road. He tried to memorize markers just in case he needed to make his own way back to the base. He made a mental note of a small tobacco farm, a pink-and-blue dilapidated shack, an abandoned church.

Judd eyed the driver. "Where . . . are we going?"

The driver shrugged without turning around. Then he reached forward to the dashboard. Judd could see scars along the driver's muscular forearms and a nose that must have been badly broken at least once. An ex-boxer, perhaps? The man grabbed the radio's knob, twisted, and suddenly the cab was filled with the rhythmic drums and a wailing trumpet of Cuban rhumba.

"Are you taking me to Oswaldo?" Judd asked over the music.

The car screeched to a halt.

Judd looked through the windshield. *Nothing in the road.* He looked out the windows both ways. *No homes. No buildings.* They were in the middle of nowhere.

"Why are we stopping?"

The driver silently opened his door and stepped out of the still-running car. He slowly turned and opened the back door. Judd saw a pistol in the driver's hand. *No witnesses.*

Judd showed his palms. "Easy."

"Out!" the driver demanded.

Judd exited the car, his hands above his head. *Am I being robbed?* "I have no money," Judd said, trying to remain calm. The driver shoved the barrel of the gun against Judd's cheek.

"Turn!"

Or kidnapped? Judd spun around. "I'm American," he said.

The man pushed the gun into Judd's kidneys. He slapped handcuffs on one wrist and pulled down one arm, then the other.

"I'm here to see Oswaldo Guerrero," Judd insisted, his hands now bound together. He twisted his neck to try to see the man's face and that's when, for the second time that day, a dark hood was slipped over Judd's head.

58.

oney Island Pizza? I have a special order for urgent delivery . . . Yes, extra-spicy . . . What the fuck have you gotten Judd into?" Jessica spat into the phone. "Tell me right now!"

"I don't know what you're talking about," the Deputy Director said so calmly that it only enraged Jessica further.

"With respect, sir, I don't give two fucks about your compartmentalization. Tell me what you're doing that's put Judd in danger!"

"Remember who you're talking to, little lady," he shot back.

"Sir." Jessica took a deep breath. "I told you I wouldn't run an operation on my own husband. I told you when we eventually reactivated Purple Cell that I wouldn't do it. These were our new ground rules and you're breaking them already."

"I didn't break any rules. Purple Cell isn't reactivated."

"You're forcing me to lie to Judd again."

"I didn't force you to do anything."

"I already told you I'm out. And now you're dragging me back in."

"I don't know what you're talking about," he said flatly.

"You know *exactly* what I'm talking about. My whole family is now in the middle of your operation."

"What kind of business do you think we're in, Jessica?"

"I told you I wouldn't lie to him anymore. I wouldn't do it. We agreed that I'm out."

"That's right."

"Now Judd's life is in danger. He's been sent into the clutches of . . . the Devil."

"What do you mean 'the Devil'?" he snapped.

"O. Oswaldo fucking Guerrero. El Diablo! You've sent Judd right into the hands of the Devil of Santiago!"

"Shit!" he hissed. "Are you saying Judd's gone into Cuba?"

"I don't know yet. I think so. He's cooking up some convoluted backchannel. This is all your fault."

"I didn't send him to Cuba. You should be chewing out Landon Parker, not me."

"Landon Parker didn't pull me into this, you did," she shot back.

"What's Parker up to?"

"I have no idea," she said.

"He's going to fuck everything up," he said.

"Fuck *what* up?"

"Jessica," he calmed himself again. "Why is the goddamn State Department running operations in Cuba? What's Parker's game?"

"I told you, I don't know."

"I need you to find out."

"No, sir, I'm out. I want nothing to do with this."

59.

ound and hooded in the trunk of the antique Chevy, Judd
tried to calm his breathing for the second time that day. His
stomach rumbled. His neck throbbed. He pushed away the
fake beard with his tongue and tried to moisten his lips. *If the
driver was going to kill me, I'd be dead already.*

The engine of the old car whined as it climbed a hill. Judd
used his feet to brace himself as he rolled toward the back of the
trunk with a painful thud.

*If he's not going to kill me, then what? Ransom? Does the
driver even know who I am? Did I get in the wrong taxi? Who
is the driver?* These questions raced through Judd's mind in the
darkness and stale air of the trunk.

The car drove for another fifteen minutes, methodically twist-
ing and turning along a road that had become increasingly bumpy.
*I'm not heading into a city. He's taking me farther into the
wilderness.*

Just as Judd decided his only course of action, the car rolled
to a halt. *Silence.* The driver was in no rush. Then Judd heard the

door open and slam shut. The man's steady deliberate footsteps came closer. The trunk popped open.

"Take me to Oswaldo Guerrero!" Judd demanded through his hood.

The driver didn't hesitate. He yanked Judd out of the trunk by his arms and dragged him away.

"You don't know who you are dealing with!" Judd shouted. "I'm here to see Oswaldo Guerrero!"

The man pushed Judd forward. He could feel gravel under his feet give way to soft sand. As they walked farther, Judd could hear the gentle splashing of waves, could smell the sea air. *Where am I being taken?*

Judd trudged along the sand in silence until the man grabbed his wrists to hold him still. The sun was hot on Judd's skin. Then Judd felt a violent shove and, unable to balance with his hands, he felt himself going down.

In the instant that he fell, he didn't scream or yell or cry. He didn't think about the cliff or the hole or the rocks that could be below. He didn't think about Cuba or Landon Parker or his mission. In that flash of an instant, handcuffed and hooded, in the hands of an unknown assailant, in some unknown corner of a forgotten island, as he fell helplessly to his fate, the only image in his mind: *Jessica.*

That's when Judd hit the soft rubber and bounced gently. *An inner tube?* Then the unmistakable sound of an outboard motor being started. *Now what?*

60.

Mommy!" Noah whined from the pool.

Jessica didn't hear it. She had just hung up the phone on the Deputy Director of the Central Intelligence Agency. She had just told her boss—the man who held the future of her career in his hands, one of the most powerful men in Washington, one of the most powerful people in the world—to fuck off. She had refused to help him find out what Landon Parker was doing in Cuba. What Judd was doing. She had refused to spy on her own husband.

Was she being righteous? Or just stupid?

"Mommy! Mommy!" her son cried again, now standing next to her, soaking wet and dripping.

She had put herself at risk. Hell, Ricky Green had shot at her. He'd tried to run her down in his cigarette boat just the night before. But Jessica wasn't worried about the risks to herself. She could handle that. What tore at her was the idea that she had put Judd in danger. That somehow her actions, even if she thought she was helping, had helped to deliver Judd into the arms of the Devil.

"Mommy!" Noah poked her.

"Yes, Noah," she said, snapping out of her thoughts, "what is it? Are you hungry?"

"Cold," he said as he danced in place, the water pooling in a puddle beneath him. His older brother Toby was still splashing obliviously in the pool.

"Well, let's get you all nice and warm," she said soothingly as she wrapped him in a large blue towel and pulled him onto her lap into a bear hug.

"Is that better?" she asked. "You're all warm and safe now. Mommy's got you."

Noah nodded. "When's Daddy coming?"

"Soon, baby."

"When?"

"I don't know, Noah." She kissed him on his head. His hair smelled of coconut sunscreen and chlorine. "I hope Daddy's coming soon, baby."

61.

The Zodiac bounced up and down rhythmically as it raced out to sea. Judd sat low and braced his feet against the soft sides of the watercraft to keep his balance. He hadn't heard any other people, so Judd assumed he was still in the custody of the taxi driver, but the man hadn't spoken another word. All he could hear through his hood was the high-pitched whine of the motor and the sound of the wind.

After what seemed like an eternity, the engine roar eased and the bouncing slowed. Distant shouting in Spanish, the thunk of banging metal, the splash of waves, and then Judd was hauled to his feet.

"*Arriba! Arriba!*" someone demanded, and Judd was lifted up by the armpits until his feet settled on a hard metallic surface. *A ship?*

"My name is Judd Ryker," he said firmly. "I am here—"

"*Silencio!*" demanded a brusque voice.

Judd was pushed along the steel deck. He could feel the gentle rocking of the swell. *Yes, a ship. But where?* He was led down a flight of stairs and through a door, then forced into a chair by firm hands. He heard a heavy metal door slam shut and the clang of a lock. *Am I alone?*

Then Judd heard the gentle breathing of someone nearby.

"My name is Judd Ryker," he said. "I am here—"

The hood was snatched off and Judd shut his eyes to the sudden bright lights. As he squinted hard, he felt the handcuffs releasing. Adrenaline rushed through his body. Without looking, Judd turned and swung hard with a primal roar, his fist colliding with the side of someone's skull. He ignored the pain in his hand and pivoted for another blind roundhouse punch just as arms wrapped him tightly. Judd twisted to break free from the vise, but the other man was stronger.

"*Relajé!*" the voice whispered. "Relax, amigo."

Judd thrashed for a few seconds more, but the adrenaline surge receded and the futility of struggling sank in. Judd dropped his head and exhaled.

"And remove that ridiculous beard," said a voice with a heavy Spanish accent.

Judd took off his disguise and forced his eyes open. He focused on the face now in front of him. Black eyes, chiseled jaw, broken nose, a short man with thick arms. *The taxi driver.*

"Who—?" Judd started.

"I apologize," the man interrupted, rubbing his jaw. "This is not how we treat guests in Cuba. It could not be helped."

"Where . . ." Judd started to ask, noticing with relief that he wasn't in a cell. There was a table set for a meal, a desk, a bar with an array of bottles. This looked like a captain's quarters.

"Dr. Ryker, you are on the *Granma Nueva*. Welcome."

"What's this?"

"*Granma Nueva* is a special ship of the Cuban navy. *My ship.*"

"I don't understand," Judd said. "I thought—"

"Are you hungry, Dr. Ryker?" he said, pointing to a plate of rice and black beans on the table, neatly set with polished cutlery. "I have cold beer, too. I understand that you like beer, Dr. Ryker."

"How would you—" Judd stopped himself. He rubbed his wrists. "Yes, I'll have a beer. If you'll have one with me."

"Of course, Dr. Ryker!" the man replied with a forced smile, revealing a shiny gold front tooth. "We are going to have many drinks together today."

"You know who I am," Judd said. "So, who are you?"

The man returned Judd's glare, but his silence was answer enough.

"Oh . . ." Judd whispered to himself.

The man blinked.

"You're Oswaldo Guerrero," Judd said aloud.

"Your Caribbean Special Projects Unit calls me El Diablo de Santiago," he said. "I hate that name."

"The Caribbean Special *what*?" Judd was confused.

"It wasn't my fault, Dr. Ryker. What happened in Santiago was your mistake. The CIA's mistake. Not mine."

Judd shook his head. "I'm not CIA. I don't know anything about—"

"Never mind, Dr. Ryker. You are my guest. You are welcome."

"You can call me Judd. You know why I've come to Cuba. I'm here on behalf of the Secretary of State—the United States government—to negotiate the release of our citizens. I've been authorized—"

"No, Dr. Ryker," Oswaldo shook his head.

"What do you mean no?" Judd cocked his head to one side. "I'm not leaving without the Americans. That's why I came here. That's why I agreed to meet with you."

"Those four fools I'm holding in Morro Castle? The spies we caught throwing guns into my sea?" He waved his hand as if swatting a fly. "You can have them."

"I don't understand."

"You aren't here for those fools, Dr. Ryker."

"I'm not?"

"You're here for something much more important."

Judd tried to hide his surprise. "And what is that?"

"Are these men relevant? No. Is hostage negotiation your expertise, Dr. Ryker? I don't think so."

"How do you know me?"

"Why would Parker have sent you all the way here?"

"Landon Parker?" Judd's poker face broke. "How do you know Mr. Parker?"

"Come, have a beer, Dr. Ryker," Oswaldo said, popping the caps off two bottles of Bucanero Fuerte and handing one to Judd. Judd examined the label: a smirking unshaven pirate in a bright red shirt and hat.

"*Salud!*" Oswaldo said, holding up his bottle.

"*Salud!*" Judd said before knocking back a swig.

"My country may be small and poor," Oswaldo began, "but *mi Cubita bella* hasn't survived for this long without understanding you *yanquis*. You may be big and rich, but you don't understand Cuba. You never have."

"Why are you telling me this?"

"After so many battles. So many failures—the Bay of Pigs, the blockade, the strangling of our people, your pathetic attempts to create a revolt, to bribe our patriots—you thought you could incite the masses in Havana, in Matanzas, in Santa Clara. They all failed, no?"

"And Santiago?"

Oswaldo lowered his eyes and shook his head. "You didn't come all this way to talk about history."

"Why did I come, then?"

"It's time for a better way," he said, sitting up straight in his chair. "That's why Parker has sent you here. That's why Parker sent you . . . to me."

"How do you know the Secretary's chief of staff?"

"That's not the question you want to ask me," Oswaldo said as he took a long swig and then slammed down his empty bottle. "You want to ask me about the future of my country."

"Are you saying that the Cuban government . . . is ready to change?"

Oswaldo opened two more bottles of Bucanero Fuerte. "The Cuban people are ready for something new. *I am ready for something new.*"

"Democracy?" Judd ventured.

Oswaldo snorted and handed Judd a beer.

"A new leader of Cuba? Is that what you're proposing?"

"I'm not proposing anything. We are just two new friends talking, no?"

Judd took another drink. "You? Are you next in line after ECP?"

Oswaldo looked puzzled.

"ECP," Judd said. "That's government-speak for your president. So are you next after El Comrade Presidente?"

"No, no, no!" Oswaldo laughed. "I am a man of the shadows. I am like you."

"If not you, then who?"

"Answering that question can get a man killed."

"Killed?"

"Asking that question can get you killed, too," he said, his smile suddenly disappearing.

"What do you mean by that, Oswaldo?"

"Have another beer, Dr. Ryker. We are going to be here for a long time. If today ends well, you will leave here drunk and victorious. If not, then . . ." He trailed off.

"Then what?"

"After beer, we will have Cuban rum, Dr. Ryker! I have a bottle of the best in the world. Handmade especially for El Jefe."

"What are you talking about, Oswaldo? What, exactly, do you think we are negotiating?"

"Cuba's next leader must carry on the revolution." He raised a bottle of rum triumphantly. "This comes from Santiago. Aged for thirty years."

"But our next leader must also be acceptable to the *yanquis*, too," he declared, untwisting the cap.

"Yes . . . I agree," Judd said. "A political transition is most likely to succeed with a compromise. Someone who can bridge both sides."

"Of course!" Oswaldo said, pouring the golden rum into two shot glasses.

"So . . . who?"

"We need a president who would be seen as a brother in Havana." He handed a shot glass to Judd. "And as a brother in Miami."

"So who could that be?" Judd asked.

The two men downed the rum, the sugary liquor burning the back of Judd's throat. Oswaldo stared into Judd's eyes and then shook his head. He grinned and held up his empty glass.

"No one knows."

62.

Dr. Ernesto Sandoval stood on the runway, staring over his reading glasses at the private jet in disbelief. The shiny-white Dassault Falcon 7X vibrated like a chained tiger ready to pounce.

"Is that for me?" Ernesto asked the pilot, a stocky Ukrainian with a flattop buzz cut and thick neck.

"Yes, Dr. Che," the pilot said in stilted English. "Where are your bags?"

Ernesto shook his head.

"Yah," the pilot grunted. "We go."

Ernesto climbed up the small staircase and into the jet's cabin. Instead of the usual rows of seats, this plane had been outfitted with just six leather captain's chairs. The walls were paneled with polished cherrywood, with multiple television screens. Along one side was a fully stocked bar and a tray of seafood canapés.

"What's this?" Ernesto asked.

"Yours, Dr. Che," the pilot responded. "Sit. We complete pre-flight checks and then we go."

"Who paid for all this?"

The pilot shrugged and winked, then marched away.

Ernesto settled into the first seat, the soft leather caressing his skin. He buckled the strap and looked out the window. Beyond the lights of the airstrip was pure darkness. Nothing. He was excited and nauseated at the same time. This was the moment he had been waiting for all those years but also, at his core, the moment he dreaded most.

Ernesto didn't remember much about his father or his brother from his life back in Cuba. He had heard all about his big brother, Ruben, from his *mami*, about his heroic flight to America, his big success in the big country. Then his mother passed away and he was, not for the last time, all alone.

But the stories of his family were more legends than anything real. Like the fictional adventures from his boyhood love of *King Solomon's Mines*, *Robinson Crusoe*, *Treasure Island*, and, of course, his favorite: *Peter Pan*.

The rest of his life had been a virtual flash: grade school, the army, a failed marriage, medical school, deployment to Angola. He was ecstatic to be sent to Africa, hoping that his life would become meaningful. That his own voyage would rival that of Allan Quatermain into the darkest bush. That he would earn his nickname Che, just like Ernesto Guevara, another doctor who traveled to the deepest jungles to fight poverty and injustice.

Yet Angola hadn't turned out to be anything like he expected. It wasn't exotic or daring. In fact, it was a lot like back home in Cuba, only a bit poorer. Ernesto made the best of his duty and embraced a simple life that was worth living. But the African chapter of his life had passed quickly. And now it, too, was nearly over.

Suddenly, before Ernesto knew what had happened, what his life had become, nearly six decades had elapsed and he had grown from orphan to old man. It was all honorable, a life of small victories in the slums of Luanda, but was it meaningful? Was it genuine? He didn't know yet.

The call, so many years ago, had been a jolt.

Hermanito, it's me. Ernesto, it's your big brother, Ruben."

The tears had flowed. That contact had come, out of the blue, just as Ernesto's marriage was crumbling, he was embracing the rigors of medical school, and he was trying desperately to put his life together again for the second time.

"I have a business in America. I have *money*," Ruben had told him.

"I don't need money," Ernesto had replied.

"Soon, I will have power." Ruben told him to be patient. "I have a plan."

Ernesto's role in the plan was to finish medical school, to become a doctor. To build a reputation. To complete his duty. And, most of all, to lay low until Ruben called again. Until it was time.

That time was now. The second call had finally come.

As the Falcon rumbled down the airstrip and zoomed westward over the Atlantic Ocean, Ernesto sensed this was the beginning of his third life. A life that would bring him back to Cuba, back together with his brother Ruben, back to a life of true meaning, of a true patriot. Of greatness.

"Flight time to Santiago will be eleven hours and forty-six minutes," the intercom announced.

Ernesto anticipated a glorious return. Heaving throngs at the airstrip as he descended the steps, waving and shouting his name—*Che! Che! Che!* Housewives, working men, pretty girls, the real Cubans. *His people.* Ernesto wasn't used to the limelight, but the idea was beginning to electrify him.

Just one question nagged at Ernesto as he watched the lights of Luanda disappear forever, despite assurances from Ruben that everything had been taken care of, that all the pieces were in place, that he would be welcomed home as a hero. Dr. Ernesto "Che" Sandoval, sitting comfortably in a luxury seat on a private airplane, was flying home to Cuba still wondering, deep down, whether his big brother's plan would actually work.

63.

The sun was beating down fiercely on Ricky, but the wind kept him cool. He pulled on the brim of his Marlins baseball cap with his left hand since his right hand was firmly on the fanboat's steering stick. Lashed to the seats of the boat were five identical black hard-shell suitcases. All empty.

Ricky expertly piloted the fanboat through the infinite swamp, past reeds and sawgrass that looked identical in all directions, to a place that didn't appear on any map outside of Ricky's own memory.

Out here, in the middle of the Florida Everglades, static maps were mostly useless. The swamp ebbed and flowed, changing with every storm, the landmarks always shifting, always evolving. This is what made the Everglades the perfect place to hide. Or to get lost.

Ricky turned sharply at a stand of cypress trees and then killed the motor. The bow of the boat grounded softly in the grass. Ricky grabbed one of the suitcases and hopped onto a small wooden platform that led to a tiny enclosed structure.

When he first came here, Ricky had been told the site was an abandoned blind for hunting wild boar. Then he was later told no, it was originally a secret outpost of the Seminole Indians for one of their three wars against the U.S. Army. Ricky didn't bother to ask more questions. He didn't care about the location's history. All that mattered was that it was hidden among the trees deep in the swamp and no one could ever find it. It was undetectable to the naked eye at water level from every direction. And, most important, invisible from the air.

Ricky scanned the horizon through binoculars for any signs that someone had followed him. He listened for any sounds of an engine. All clear. But he couldn't relax.

Ricky knew from experience that all clear could change. Without warning.

That day, way back in 1983, was like a zombie movie. One moment, all was quiet; the next, they were coming at him from everywhere. The beasts, black head to toe, snarling faces hidden behind black shields and black helmets, swarmed like it was the Apocalypse. They came by land, they rose out of the water, they dropped from the sky. There were so many, he couldn't count.

Ricky's mind was dizzy and time slowed to a crawl. A cocktail of narcotics and adrenaline churned through his bloodstream. The flashbang, the shouting, the swarm, the pain—it was all a blurry haze.

The next thing Ricky knew, he was in a room, collapsed in a metal chair at a metal table. He was cold but could taste warm salty blood from his busted lip. A beefy man in some kind of police uniform was glaring at him.

"Who are you working for, Ricardo? Who's the big boss, Ricardo? We already know everything. We just want to hear it from you."

Ricky had looked around the room, confused and scared. It was bare except for the table and chairs, a single lightbulb in the ceiling. And a long mirror along one wall.

"Where am I?" Ricky slurred. "Who . . . is 'we'?"

"Fuck you, Ricardo. We ask the questions."

"Who's behind the mirror? Who am I really talking to?"

"Your worst fucking nightmare, Ricardo. Who are you working for?"

"I . . . don't know anything."

"You don't know? You don't fucking know? You're carrying all those drugs and you don't know?"

"I don't know anything. I . . . I . . . I'm just a kid."

"You're eighteen, Ricardo. You're in deep shit. You're gonna be charged as an adult. Narcotics trafficking, racketeering, conspiracy, assault on a federal officer. This is some heavy shit."

"No . . ." Ricky muttered.

"You're gonna do some serious time in a serious place. They're gonna love you in the hole at Pensacola. You know what a skinny eighteen-year-old Cuban boy looks like to a monster serving life in federal prison?" The interrogator licked his lips and chortled.

"No . . ." Ricky whimpered.

"Then you better answer my goddamn questions. Have you ever met Escobar?"

"I don't know him. I mean . . . I've never seen him."

"We know you were carrying for him. You know what Escobar's going to do to you in prison when he figures out how much money you've cost him?"

"No . . ."

"You know what happened to the last kid?"

"No . . ."

"You want me to help you, Ricardo?"

"Huh?"

"You stupid fucking shit-eating punk. If you want me to help you, then you have to help me."

"Like what?"

"Give me something. What do you know?"

"Are you DEA? FBI?" Ricardo wheezed. "I want witness protection!"

"You think you're gonna get witness protection? For what? What can you give me, dipshit?"

"I know where the money is."

"What money?" asked the man, stealing a glance at the mirror.

"The big money. More than you can imagine. I know where it is. I know where—"

Before Ricky could finish his sentence, the lights went out.

"Hey, what's going on?" he squealed.

"That's enough," said a new, deep voice. "We'll take it from here. He's the one."

Ricky was blindfolded and taken away.

"Hey! Hey!" he shouted into the dark, but no one replied.

He was then thrown into the back of a car and driven for what could have been five minutes or five hours. The next thing he remembered was his feet being bound and the sudden rush of blood to his head as he was hung upside down. A few seconds later, the blindfold was removed and Ricky found himself staring straight down into the yawning jaws of an alligator.

"Ahhh!" he screamed and wriggled, his pants suddenly

soaked with the warmth of his own urine. "I'll tell you whatever you want!"

The gator hissed and snapped.

"I know you will," said the deep voice, attached to a man he'd never seen before.

"I'll take the deal! I want witness protection!"

"You've got the wrong guys, Ricardo," said the man. "We don't do witness protection. You're going to take us to the money."

Ricky winced at the memory of the gator and that day that everything changed.

He pushed open the door and darted inside the empty wooden hut. The air was humid and thick. Mosquitos buzzed his ears. He waved them away and then began tapping on the floorboards until he heard a comforting change in pitch. *Bingo!* Ricky lifted up a panel to reveal a black metal hatch with a small plexiglass screen. The old combination lock had long ago been replaced by a modern electronic keypad. Ricky tapped in the code and pulled opened the heavy metal door with a hollow thud.

The sight of all that money still gave Ricky a rush. He took a deep breath, wiped the sweat off his face, and checked over his shoulder through the door one more time. Then he carefully counted out two million dollars and stacked the bills in the suitcase. Satisfied, he shut the case and spun the lock. *One down, four to go,* he thought.

Ricky checked his watch. Right on time.

64.

Judd Ryker and Oswaldo Guerrero had each finished their plates. The table was covered with empty beer bottles and spilled rum. The two men had talked around in circles, probing each other, trying to find common ground, never quite trusting the other. The alcohol was helping, a convenient diplomatic lubricant.

"What happened to your tooth, amigo?" Judd asked his host.

Oswaldo tapped his golden front incisor. "The same way I broke my nose." He rubbed the end of his nose. "Boxing." He held up two meaty fists. "I was a champion of the Rebel Youth Association."

"We don't box much back in Vermont," Judd said.

"You don't fight, *asere*? More of a lover, no?" He smiled and winked.

"I wouldn't say that."

"You were wise to give up trying to beat me," Oswaldo bellowed, slapping Judd forcefully on the back. "You *yanquis* are just playing cowboy games. We Cubans are fighting for survival."

He held up his fists again and shadowboxed. "If you lose to me, you just go back to your shopping malls and your hamburgers. We have no choice. We cannot afford to lose."

"We should finish," Judd suggested, directing Oswaldo's attention to a scrap of paper in front of him. Judd had scrawled the outlines of their agreement so far.

hostage release → wheat
private enterprise → travel & trade
free elections → recovery package

"Okay, Oswaldo, this is what we've agreed. Three phases, three steps."

Judd was feeling confident that he was close to a breakthrough. He'd bonded with Oswaldo Guerrero over beer and baseball while they negotiated their countries' futures for hours on a ship floating off the coast of Cuba. The events of today were also deniable. If it all went wrong, Judd wasn't even officially here. No one would even know . . . And now Judd was sealing the deal with a simple package of incentives. Cuba does this, America does that. Everyone was out for themselves, all in the service of the common good. Whatever Landon Parker and Melanie Eisenberg would have thought, Adam Smith would have been proud.

"Once you release the prisoners, we'll deliver enough wheat to refill your stocks," Judd stated. "Once you allow—"

"Yes, yes, Dr. Ryker. We'll let businesses open and you'll end what remains of the blockade. We've agreed to all of that." Oswaldo poked Judd's paper with his finger. "We haven't dealt with the toughest problem at all. The big thing that will stop us all from success."

"The return of seized private property." Judd nodded to himself. "I was hoping that we could leave that tricky issue for the very end. The exiles in Miami are going to insist on something. My thinking is that Cuba would commit to full restitution in exchange for new credit—"

"No, no, no. Not the exiles. Not the traitors. They're not the issue."

"Then what?"

Oswaldo threw back another shot of rum. "The boss."

"El Comrade Jefe?"

Oswaldo shook his head. "El Comrade Presidente. ECP."

"Are you saying ECP isn't on board?"

"If the *Comrades* knew I was here talking you, I would be . . ." Oswaldo dragged a finger across his neck.

Judd sat back in his chair to digest this new piece of information. "You're rogue?"

Oswaldo poured the two of them another drink. "I'm rogue, Dr. Ryker? What about you? You came to me in disguise, hidden from your own people. Why didn't you just fly into the airport at Havana? Why are you dressed like a peasant and not a diplomat?"

"Discretion, Oswaldo. Your people are watching the borders."

"Of course!" Oswaldo laughed. "I must control any knowledge of your arrival. Or we'd both already be"—the Cuban grabbed Judd by the throat and pretended to choke him—"dead."

"So"—Judd pushed Oswaldo's hands away—"on whose authority are you negotiating with me?"

"I should be asking you that very same question."

"I don't think so, Oswaldo." Judd scowled. "I'm representing the U.S. Department of State. The American government."

"Are you certain of this, *asere*?" He waved a scolding finger at the American. "That's not what the television says."

"I have authority. I was sent here by Landon Parker. You know that. I have instructions from him to negotiate and bring a deal back to Washington," Judd said.

"How are you certain Parker will agree? Or that Parker can get your Secretary and your President to agree to this?" Oswaldo shook Judd's paper with the three points. "Or your Congress?"

"I know my limits. It's my problem to get everyone on board," Judd said. "I know how to get my side to agree."

"So do I," Oswaldo shot back.

"So . . . how will you get ECP to go along?"

"You leave that to me," Oswaldo said with a wave of the hand.

Judd stood up from the table. "Before we go any further, I need to know how."

Oswaldo shook his head.

"That's it? The whole plan depends on me just . . . trusting you? Your secret?"

"Precisely. The whole plan depends on me," Oswaldo said, his eyes widening. "The future of Cuba depends on me. I am glad that you finally understand, Dr. Ryker. And that's why I need something very important from you."

65.

Don't hang up."

Jessica already regretted answering the phone when it flashed DANIEL DOLLAR. She had told herself she wouldn't answer the phone, wouldn't talk to her boss, until she was back in Washington. She wasn't going to allow herself to be used anymore. She wasn't getting dragged back into his operation, blind and manipulated.

Jessica had spent the morning at the pool with the boys. Now they were walking on the boardwalk, enjoying the sun, Toby and Noah losing a battle with melting soft-serve ice cream. Doing what normal vacationers did. That was the whole idea, right? But something in the back of her brain, something deep down, compelled her to push the button and answer his call.

"I told you, I'm out," she said.

"You're never out, Jessica," the Deputy Director said. "You should know that by now."

"You sent me on vacation," she said, stepping off the board-walk onto the soft white sand. "That's the order I'm following."

"Well, the situation's changed. I need you now. It's an easy job. A-B-C. In and out."

"Easy?"

"I need you to go to Homestead and collect a package and then drop it off. That's it. You'll be done before midnight."

"Homestead? The air base? What am I flying?" Jessica asked.

"Need-to-know," he said.

"Where's the drop?"

"Need-to-know."

"What's the package?"

"Jessica, you should know better. You'll know all of this soon enough. All you need to do is go to Homestead tonight."

"I'm not flying another one of your missions into Havana, sir. I'm not dropping another good operative to his death. I won't do it."

"The drop isn't Havana."

"Don't tell me it's Santiago!"

"Not exactly. The package isn't an operative."

"Sir?" Jessica took a deep breath and started to speak again when he cut her off.

"Cash," he said. "Hard cash."

"I'm delivering money?"

"I need you to deliver ten million dollars in unmarked bills to a contact in Baconao Park. It's a mountainous reserve about half-way between Gitmo and Santiago. It's how we channel cash to sleeper cells on the streets of Santiago. That's the mission. A cash drop in a park. I told you—easy."

"Why physical cash? What happened to the electronic money operation? Isn't that what BesoPeso was for?"

"I don't want to talk about it," he snarled. "Cash is the only way."

"The Cubans blocked BesoPeso?" she asked.

"That's why I need you," he said, fighting to cool his temper.

"Mommy, I need you!" Noah cried. She looked up from her call, a swirl of chocolate and vanilla ice cream coating his face and dripping down his arm.

"I'm sorry, sir," she said. "Like I told you, I'm out."

66.

C ash."

"Money?" Judd was taken aback. "I thought you were a socialist?"

"Twenty-five million dollars. Nothing less. Untraceable. It must be in unmarked, nonsequential bills," Oswaldo Guerrero said, looking satisfied with himself.

"Twenty-five million dollars in unmarked, nonsequential bills?" Judd winced. "Where did you get that, O?"

"Hollywood," Oswaldo said with a smirk. "I've seen your movies."

"What movies?"

"All of them."

"Well, movies are made up," Judd said. "I don't know where you expect me to get that much cash. That's not how it works in Washington."

"You are rich." Oswaldo snapped his fingers. "Twenty-five million is nothing for the American government. Twenty-five million is nothing even for those Cubans living in Miami. I should ask you for more. I should ask for *a hundred million*." Oswaldo rubbed his chin. "But, no. *I am a socialist.* I am not greedy. I only need twenty-five million."

"What for?"

"For me. For my independence. For my total independence. What else do free men truly desire, Dr. Ryker?"

"Free men?"

"I can see where my country is going. I don't want to be the last one. I want to live, *asere*."

"I need another Bucanero," Judd said. He accepted a beer bottle from Oswaldo and popped the top. "Even if I could get you the money—and I'm not saying I can—but if I could, it would have to be in an account somewhere."

Oswaldo shook his head.

"We could set it up wherever you want," Judd continued. "In Miami or New York or maybe . . . Mexico City—"

"No!" Oswaldo slammed his beer down. "You think I would fall for another *yanqui* trick?"

"Why would I trick you, Oswaldo? What would I have to gain?"

"With respect, Dr. Ryker"—Guerrero calmed himself—"you are nothing. You can say whatever you want here. But you cannot guarantee that the money will appear. You cannot promise to deliver. No. I've seen it all before."

Judd started to reply. "What if I—"

"Untraceable cash." Oswaldo rubbed his thumb and forefingers together. "Right here. I need to feel it. Or we are finished negotiating. You are finished."

"That's unreasonable, Oswaldo."

"If you are finished, there is nothing left to discuss. I go back to Havana. I cut the throats of your four American fools at Morro Castle. I feed their flesh to the sharks. And you?" Guerrero forced a grin that sent a chill through Judd's spine.

"Oswaldo, you can see *I have nothing.*" Judd showed his palms and patted his pants. "How can I just make twenty-five million dollars appear?"

Oswaldo stood up and stumbled over toward a desk. He carefully pulled open the top drawer and reached inside, feeling around clumsily for something.

Panic rose within Judd. *A gun?* Judd thrust his hands into the air. "What are you doing!?"

"You will make the money appear." The Cuban turned back and tossed something black and rectangular. Judd caught the object. A satellite phone.

"Call Parker," Oswaldo demanded.

"I thought satphones were illegal in Cuba?"

"They are. Tell Landon Parker twenty-five million. Unmarked, nonsequential bills."

67.

Jessica was still steaming when her phone rang. No matter what the Deputy Director says, she decided, *I'm still out*. But the number displayed on her phone started +882 and then a string of random numbers she didn't recognize. An anonymous satellite phone.

"Hell-o?"

"State Operations Center? This is Judd Ryker with S/CRU," her husband's voice said. "This is an urgent call. Please connect me to Landon Parker."

"Judd, it's me," she said. "You called your wife."

"This is a priority one call," Judd replied. "Yes, yes, thank you. I'll hold for Mr. Parker."

"Judd, can you hear me? It's *Jessica*."

"Yes, I can hear you, Mr. Parker," he said. "I'm still in Cuba, but we've got a situation and I need your help."

"I'm listening," Jessica said.

"I've met with our contact. I'm with him right now . . . Yes . . .

Yes . . . We're making progress . . . I'm feeling good . . . Historic, yes, sir. There's just one problem."

"I'm listening," she repeated.

"I need twenty-five million dollars."

Jessica then heard some muffled noises. "Judd? Judd?"

"Twenty-five million in unmarked, nonsequential bills. It has to be untraceable, sir. That's what I need right now or it's all over."

"Judd, is this for real? Is your life in danger?"

"Yes, yes. That's correct," Judd said. "I know it's impossible, Mr. Parker. That's what I told our contact, but he's insisting that you can make it happen. If I don't come up with twenty-five million, we are dead in the water. That's why I'm calling you."

"Judd, I have an idea."

"That's what I thought, Mr. Parker . . . Very well . . . I will pass that message . . . Yes, I can give you my location."

More muffled noise. "Here are the GPS coordinates . . ."

Jessica wrote the digits that her husband recited on her arm with a pen and then quickly hung up. She dialed another number.

A young female voice answered. "Coney Island Pizza."

68.

The woman strode briskly down the alley toward her next target. Two men, middle-aged, with identical black mustaches, sat on wooden crates, playing chess. They each held chipped enamel cups of black coffee and they were sharing a plate of roasted pork covered in onions.

"*Jaque-mate!*" one shouted with glee.

"*Puta!*" the other man cursed. He slapped his hand down on the board and swept away the pieces. He drained his coffee and scowled.

The winner held his belly and laughed. "*No más*, comrade?" he joked.

When the men spotted the woman coming their way, they stopped their conversation and their faces turned serious.

She stopped in front of them and looked them up and down warily. "Are you ready?"

The winner of the chess game nodded. "We are waiting for your signal."

"Here," she said, passing him a few local pesos.

"What is this?" he scowled. He showed the money to his friend. "What can we do with this?"

The other man shook his head.

"More is coming. American dollars tomorrow," she said. "That will be your signal. You need to be ready. You need them all to be ready."

"Manuel, Domingo, Arianna," the man counted out on his fingers. "Louisa, Marisela, Ramón Grande, Ramón Pequeño. All of our barrios in Santiago are ready."

"Very good," the woman nodded.

"When?" the man asked.

"Eight o'clock tomorrow morning."

The man smiled with approval. "Where?"

"The Plaza de la Revolución," she answered. "Are you certain you're ready?"

"Of course," the winner said. "We have been ready for a very long time. We are now only waiting . . . for you."

"*Viva Cuba Libre!*" she whispered.

"*Viva Cuba Libre!*" the two men repeated in unison.

And she turned on her heels and fled the alley to find her next target.

69.

Jessica pulled the white convertible Ford Mustang off U.S. 1 and turned sharply to the west down another wide, flat Florida avenue. After several more turns, she pulled into the parking lot for the Gator Grill, a fast-food stand advertising fried frogs legs and alligator tacos. At this hour, the place was already closed, and the seating area, a cluster of picnic tables beneath a thatched roof, was abandoned. She backed the car into a space facing the main road and turned off the engine. The land around her, horizontal emptiness in every direction, was punctured only by a sliver of moonlight and the chirping of cicadas.

The Deputy Director had been less surprised than she hoped when she called him back to accept the drop mission. Jessica realized the moment she heard his voice on the other end of the line that he had expected her to call back. He knew she would cool off and eventually relent. They both knew it.

"I'll do it out of my loyalty to you," she had said, "for everything you've done for me." He pretended to accept her lie graciously and countered with a fabrication of his own. "Apology accepted. You know I wouldn't knowingly entangle you in a mission that involves family." Then, gratuitously, "You have my word on that, Jessica."

She bit her lip. "Yes, sir."

The lies were out in the open and mutually ignored. She had to focus. She used to wall off her emotions effortlessly, but it was getting harder. Now Jessica had to forget how she felt about her husband, her family, her boss, her future. Just focus on the mission.

The Deputy Director of Operations explained that Jessica's task was to deliver ten million in cash to a Cuban opposition cell leader. Using the code name Alpha Nine Nine, she was to meet a contact code-named Bravo Zero at the Gator Grill in Homestead, accept the package, and take it to the nearby Air Reserve Base, where she would fly to Guantánamo Bay Naval Base, following regular flight patterns. Just after the approach at Gitmo's Leeward Point Field, Jessica was to pull up and veer to the south into Cuban airspace to meet a second contact, code-named Charlie Three, in a remote part of Baconao Park. Her instructions were to deliver the money to Charlie and then return immediately to Florida. "In and out," the Deputy Director had said. "Alpha, Bravo, Charlie—easy."

His reassurances had the opposite effect. She couldn't help but wonder what he wasn't telling her. But what made Jessica really anxious was what she wasn't telling him.

Jessica watched two headlights appear in the distance and then bound toward her location. She stepped out of her car and leaned casually on the hood.

The approaching lights turned into the Gator Grill parking lot and then went dark. An oversized cherry-red Ford F-150 pulled up next to her and a skinny man with long dark hair stepped out of the pickup truck.

The moment he was out, Jessica leapt at him, unleashing a lightning front snap kick to his groin. He groaned and doubled over just as she thrust a palm heel blow to his nose. The man screamed and held his face, blood gushing between his fingers. She snatched one of his wrists and twisted violently, forcing him to spin. Jessica grabbed a fist of hair at the back of his head and jammed his face against the pickup truck. His blood smeared the side of the red cab.

"What are you doing here?" she snarled.

The man coughed and wheezed.

Jessica punched him hard in the kidneys. "I said what are you doing here, *Ricky*?"

"I'm—" he began.

She unleashed another blow to the back of his head and then forced him to the ground.

"How did you find me, Ricky? Or should I say Ricardo Cabrera!"

"Alpha . . . Bravo," he moaned.

"You're . . . Bravo Zero?" she gasped, releasing her knee from his back.

"In the cab . . . your packages," he groaned.

Jessica checked over both shoulders. They were still alone. "Don't move!" she hissed, pushing her foot against his neck, his face rubbed into the gravel. Ricky nodded and winced.

Jessica slowly backed away from Ricky toward his truck. Satisfied that he wasn't getting up, she clicked open the cab door. Inside she saw five black hard-shell suitcases piled on the passenger seat. She turned back to Ricky, now in a fetal position.

"Don't you move, Ricardo." He shook his head.

Jessica transferred four of the cases into the trunk of her Mustang, the fifth she strapped like a child into the passenger seat. She returned to Ricky and bent down close to his ear.

"I should kill you right now," she hissed.

"No," he moaned. "I didn't know we were on the same side."

"Never say that!" she barked, and kicked him again in the kidneys. "I don't care who you think you work for. We are *never* on the same side." She got into her car, slammed the door, and revved up the engine.

As she pulled out, Ricky sat up, coughing and spitting blood into his palms. The Mustang suddenly jolted to a halt and the door swung open.

Jessica stepped out, marched over to Ricky, and stood over him. He looked up at her and raised his bloody palms. She snap-kicked him just under the jawbone, sending him sprawling flat on his back in the gravel parking lot.

"I'm Alpha."

70.

When the black Audi A6 veered off the parkway and into the scenic overlook, the white Cadillac Escalade was already there.

"She's early," the Deputy Director of the CIA said aloud. He pulled into the space next to Adelman-Zamora's SUV and cut the engine. He removed the batteries from each of his three cell phones and shoved them in the glove compartment of his wife's car. Then he exited the Audi, checked that no one was watching, and opened the Escalade's passenger door.

"What the hell's going on?" she chirped before he had climbed in.

"Madam Chairwoman—"

"If you don't stop calling me madam, I'm going to throw you into the fucking Potomac," Brenda hissed. "Where are we with our goddamn operation?"

"*My* operation," he said slowly, "is proceeding. It's all going according to plan. We are moving into the final phase now."

"What kind of tradecraft bullshit is that? Why don't you tell me again in English."

"OPSEC."

"What?" She scowled.

"Operations security. We agreed that I shield you from the details and just give you the big picture. That's what I'm doing. It's for the safety of the operation. And just in case something goes wrong."

"What's going wrong?"

"Nothing's wrong," he said.

"I don't believe you," she said. "Those four soccer dads? They have to be yours, right?"

He looked at her, giving nothing away.

"Don't give me that blank-stare spook crap," she scoffed. "I've been around long enough to know their capture can't be a coincidence. They have to be yours. And if one of your teams is sitting in a Cuban jail, then something went god-awful wrong."

The Deputy Director blinked. "Yes they're mine, some of them. But, no, nothing went wrong. I told you, it's all going according to plan."

"You sent a team into Cuba to be captured *on purpose?*"

He didn't reply.

"Who would possibly agree to such a high-risk kamikaze operation?"

He continued to stare coldly.

The look of confusion on her face slowly melted away. "You evil fucking genius," she whispered. "You played on their emotions. You knew that they'd want redemption for their grandfathers. You duped them into a failed invasion to create an international incident."

He blinked.

"Don't tell me you promised them"—she swallowed hard—"air cover."

He shook his head. "They knew the risks. They just didn't know the bigger picture."

"So, now what?" she asked, bouncing in her seat. "You have to tell me what's next. I have to know!"

"We're moving into the final phase."

"That's all you're going to say?"

"I've got multiple people in the air as we speak. It's all converging. Everything is a go. That's all I'm going to tell you. Anything more might compromise the operation."

She exhaled loudly.

"You do your part and I'll do mine," he said. "That's how we achieve mission success. That's how we finally make history."

Brenda Adelman-Zamora knew that the Deputy Director was right, but she pouted anyway. "At least tell me how long I have to wait. *When* can I expect good news?"

"Tomorrow."

"Tomorrow?" Her eyes brightened and she licked her lips. "We're that close?"

He nodded, suppressing a smug grin that was like a baby bird trying to break out of its egg.

"Is our candidate on his way already? I mean, he's in the air and coming home?"

"I shouldn't say," he whispered as he flashed her a wink.

"Do you promise . . . tomorrow?"

"There are no promises in covert operations. You know that already. But confidence is high."

"Good." She spun her wedding ring on her finger. "I want you to update me as soon as you have some news."

He nodded.

"You're going to make a brilliant CIA Director. Think of everything we will do together."

He nodded again.

"Who knows? Maybe you'll go higher. Like the next Director of National Intelligence. How would you like that?"

"One step at a time."

"I can't believe it's finally happening," she said, reaching down and squeezing his inner thigh. "After all these years, it's *finally* happening." She leaned in to kiss him.

The Deputy Director turned his head and removed her hand from his thigh.

"I'm sorry," she said, looking away. "I don't know what I was thinking."

"Don't apologize, Brenda. It happens when an operation reaches its climax. People get excited."

"I'm not regular people," she insisted.

"Everyone responds differently under stress," he said.

"I still shouldn't have done that."

"No, you shouldn't have," he said. "Not here."

71.

She'd never seen anything like it before.

"Here she is," said the young man proudly. "The latest Sikorsky S-97 Raider."

Jessica eyed the helicopter, a shiny black beast with a narrow nose like a shark. She, too, in a skintight black flight suit with black combat boots, looked like an animal ready to attack.

"Actually," he whispered, "this baby is the S-97 Raider X2. Experimental prototype."

"I've flown Black Hawks, Apaches, and Little Birds. Even an old Huey." Jessica tried to hide her childish excitement. "But I've never seen her. What's with the double rotors?" she asked, pointing to the two sets of rotor blades stacked on top of the fuselage.

"Yes, ma'am," said the Air Force lieutenant, who Jessica thought had barely started shaving. "The main rotors spin in opposite directions, which negates the need for a tail rotor. Instead, you have the propulsion propeller at the back. It gives the Raider a shitload of velocity." The lieutenant suddenly looked embarrassed. "Pardon my French."

"What's her speed?" she asked.

"Cruising speed is 235 knots."

Jessica's heart raced with anticipation.

"That's almost twice as fast as a conventional helicopter, ma'am."

"So where's my pilot, soldier?" Jessica asked, looking around an empty airfield.

"Tampa, ma'am."

"Excuse me?" she scowled.

"We don't have pilots here at Homestead who are cleared to fly the Raider. We're just an Air Reserve Base. This helicopter isn't even officially here."

"I need to be airborne right now!" Jessica demanded. She knew that a missing pilot would derail the whole plan.

"Yes, ma'am. I was told you were a chopper pilot."

"That's right. But never a bird like this one."

"The Raider controls are similar to the Black Hawk. This X2 version is configured for a single pilot or can be piloted remotely."

"Remotely?" She narrowed her eyes.

"You'll be flying it with a copilot at MacDill Air Force Base up in Tampa."

"My copilot is with SOCOM?"

"I don't know, ma'am. Could be Special Operations Command. Could be regular Air Force. Could be . . . another part of our government. That information is way above my security clearance. I only know that your copilot is briefed at MacDill and ready to go. You'll communicate through the headset. I'll show you."

Jessica opened the door of the Raider and climbed into the pilot's seat. It smelled like a new car.

The lieutenant began pointing out the various cockpit controls. "The navigation and flight controls are all based on the Black Hawk layout. The pilot at MacDill will handle most of this, but here's how you control the rotors. The pitch is here. And your secure comms are over there. And here," he said, pointing to a bright red switch above her head, "is how she goes into stealth mode."

"Stealth in a helicopter?"

"This's the experimental part. It's now set to normal operations mode. Push this down one click and she'll be invisible to radar. It also scrambles the electronic communications with MacDill, so your signal can't be picked up by the enemy."

"What's the third mode?" she asked, pointing to the switch.

"In an emergency, if you need to go totally radio silent, push it down again to here." He snapped the switch down two clicks. "That kills all onboard external communications. The electronic footprints completely disappear to anyone on the ground, including base."

"She goes full black?"

"Full black," he said with a smile.

"How does that work on a helicopter?"

"Above my grade, ma'am." He shook his head.

Jessica put the headset on and oriented herself around the cockpit. *Yes, I can do this,* she thought, nodding to herself.

The airman started to leave when she grabbed his arm. "Lieutenant, where are the controls for enabling the remote pilot?"

"Right here, ma'am." He tapped a box underneath the pilot's seat, with its purple wire that ran into the floor. "When this is on," he said, touching a flashing purple light next to the analog altimeter, "MacDill is your copilot. Just as if they were sitting right here next to you. Make sure this light stays on or you're fly-ing on your own."

Jessica nodded. "Lieutenant, I've got five cases in my vehicle, four in the trunk, one up front. Can you load them into the Raider while I run prestart?"

"Yes, ma'am," he saluted and marched off.

Once the airman was out of earshot, Jessica tapped a button on the ear of her headset. "This is Alpha Nine Nine. Can you hear me?"

"Roger, Alpha Nine Nine. Good evening. This is Whiskey Base Seven. Are you ready for prestart checks?"

"Affirmative, Whiskey Base Seven. Have you locked in our destination coordinates?"

"Doing that now."

"What's our flight time?"

"One hour forty-two minutes to Gitmo, Alpha Nine Nine."

Perfect. "Let's go, Whiskey."

72.

The Dassault Falcon 7X landed, its wheels squeaking sharply on the airstrip as it touched down. Ernesto Sandoval's heart raced as he felt the jolt of the land, his arrival back in Cuba. He could almost hear the crowds already: *Che! Che! Che!*

The masses, unable to contain their love and admiration. Just like Pope Francis in Revolution Square.

The plane taxied for a few minutes, Ernesto's nose pressed against the window for his first glance of home, his first sight of *his people.*

The pilot rolled the Falcon away from the main terminal and parked at the far end of the tarmac near an empty cargo hangar. The engines shut down and the door opened with a satisfying pop.

Ernesto poked his head out of the door.

"Welcome home, Dr. Che!" said an elderly woman surrounded by half a dozen shabbily dressed middle-aged men.

"Where is everybody?" Ernesto asked, frowning.

"I'm sorry, Dr. Che," the woman said, forcing a smile, "you

arrived too late for a welcoming party. The cells will be activated in the morning."

"Cells?"

"The crowds will come tomorrow, Dr. Che."

"Tomorrow?" Ernesto knew he should hide his disappointment, but he couldn't help himself.

"For the bread rally," she said.

"Bread?"

"Our *Cubita bella* is running out of wheat. There is no bread. The government has failed us again." She tisked. "Mass protests are planned for tomorrow. In the Plaza de la Revolución. That's when the crowds will come. That's when the people will hear you, Dr. Che. That's when we will begin a new chapter for Cuba!"

"I was expecting a crowd here. Tonight."

"Tomorrow, Dr. Che. Tomorrow is your day!"

73.

lpha Nine Nine, prepare for final approach to Leeward Point,"
said the voice in Jessica's headset.

"Preparing for approach, Whiskey Base Seven," Jessica
replied, seizing the cyclic control stick with one hand and the
collective with the other. She spied the red lights of the airstrip
dead ahead and, at its very end, the green circle of the helicopter-
landing pad. Beyond the airfield, she could see the brightly illuminated fence line that separated Guantánamo Bay Naval Base
from the mainland. The official border between Cuba and
America.

"I have a visual of the helipad, Whiskey," she said. "I have the
controls."

As the Raider crossed into official American military airspace,
the copilot announced, "Negative, Alpha Nine Nine. We've got
you. We're putting you in a ten-foot hover."

"Roger that, Whiskey," she conceded.

The Raider slowed until it was just floating in midair over the landing pad, the engine vibrating but the helicopter motionless. Jessica reached up and pushed the red switch to activate stealth mode, scrambling communications with Tampa and, she hoped, vanishing from Cuban radar screens. The plan assumed that the Cuban military tracking incoming American flights would conclude that the helicopter had landed at the base. *Nothing to see here.*

Jessica followed the next step in the plan, turning the Raider to the south and accelerating forward at low altitude. Within seconds, she was over the fence line and in Cuban airspace. Jessica was flying straight for the drop point with Charlie Three, an isolated location nestled within the hills of Baconao Park adjacent to the naval base.

"ETA four minutes, Alpha Nine Nine," said the voice in her headset.

"Roger that. Four minutes, Whiskey Base Seven."

Unlike the bright lights of the naval base, the park was pitch-black. Jessica could barely see the ground with the naked eye, relying instead on the Raider's night vision capabilities to fly low and fast.

After three and a half minutes, Jessica tapped her ear again. "Approaching Charlie Three."

"Roger that, Alpha Nine Nine. We see you. We're putting you back in a ten-foot hover."

The target was blinking on her navigation screen and the helicopter slowed to a midair halt.

"Roger, Whiskey Base Seven," she said. Jessica then reached up to the red stealth switch above her head and rubbed it between her fingers. She looked out the window into a total void of light. Jessica couldn't see anything, but she knew Charlie was down there somewhere.

"I see movement on the ground. Whiskey Base Seven, can you confirm that's Charlie Three?"

"Checking now, Alpha Nine Nine. Stand by."

"Negative," she said. "Whiskey, I'm going full black."

"Negative, Alpha Nine Nine. Repeat, negative. We advise—"

Jessica clicked the switch down, cutting off her copilot in Tampa in midsentence. She then reached down underneath her seat, feeling for the box and the connecting wire. She gripped it tight.

"Good-bye, Whiskey," she said, and released a guttural roar as she ripped the cable out of the floor. She examined the purple wire, limp in her hand, and then tossed it behind her, satisfied she now had full control of the Raider.

Jessica pushed back her sleeve to read the new coordinates written on her arm. She typed them into the navigation system and then spun the nose of the Raider to the east.

"Sorry, Charlie," she said aloud as she pitched the helicopter forward and shot off.

74.

The Deputy Director flipped up the collars on his jacket and pulled the Nationals baseball cap lower on his head. It had been stupid to risk exposure at a high-profile hotel like the Willard InterContinental, just a stone's throw from the White House. He cursed himself for his weakness. *And at a time like this.*

The lobby of the Willard was full of foreign agents and, boy, would they love to have spotted him here. How many times had his operatives found valuable information in the walls and wires of that very building. The same hotel where Abraham Lincoln had stayed, where Martin Luther King, Jr., had written his famous "I have a dream" speech, where countless business deals, foreign plots, even revolutions, had been hatched.

But he couldn't allow his own activities at the Willard that evening to become part of history. The secret cables back to Moscow, Caracas, Beijing, London—they all had to be clean.

She had insisted on a suite at the Willard, one she promised had been arranged for inconspicuously. With a few basic precautions, no one would ever know. It was safer than risking a U.S.

park policeman knocking on the fogged-up window of a Cadillac Escalade. So they had arrived separately, through different doors, and taken distinct paths to the suite. Now that it was time to leave, he had changed his clothes and departed first, taking the elevator down two floors, then a flight of the stairs, then crossed the hallway and took another elevator. Once on ground level, the doors opened with a cheery ding. He brushed his shoulders and double-checked his fly.

The Deputy Director walked briskly, making no eye contact with the clusters of businessmen, diplomats, and tourists milling around the lobby. He reached the main revolving door facing Pennsylvania Avenue, pushed hard, and, without slowing down, jumped into a taxi and sped off.

He knew that someone in that lobby would have killed to spy a juicy nugget like the Deputy Director of Operations of the Central Intelligence Agency slinking out of a downtown hotel late on a Friday night. He would have to be more careful once he was CIA Director. And even more so if he became DNI. He was warming to that idea.

For now, the Deputy Director was just grateful that no one had recognized him in the lobby. And he hoped, in five minutes or so, that no one would recognize the nine-term congresswoman from Florida either.

75.

Jessica was back over the Caribbean Sea en route to her new target. Flying at low altitude in the dark was easier over open ocean without the perils of dodging the rolling mountains of eastern Cuba. She kept the Raider's nose tucked forward like the head of a charging bull.

A visual of her target soon appeared on the horizon. The single white star in the distance quickly multiplied into two, three, four lights, then, eventually, the clear outline of a naval ship bobbing in the sea.

She slowed her speed and circled the vessel from fifty feet away. GRANMA NUEVA / HAVANA, was painted on the stern, just below a raised deck and a dark gray helicopter pad. "Honey, I'm home!" she announced to no one.

Soldiers on the ship began to emerge, crowding the top deck and pointing weapons menacingly at the helicopter. *Not everyone is expecting me.* She briefly considered turning the communications system back on and radioing to the captain but decided against it. She hovered just off the stern, sliding side to side like a hummingbird approaching a flower.

This seemed to agitate the Cubans further, until a short muscular man in civilian clothes appeared. At his command, the soldiers lowered their weapons and scampered into a tight circular formation. The man jogged out to the middle of the landing deck and waved his arms, then crossed them forming an X in front of his body—the universal signal to land.

Jessica eased the Raider gently down onto the helipad, cut the engine, and showed her palms to the men gathering around her.

As she opened the door, half a dozen soldiers again raised their rifles. Jessica stepped out cautiously, her hands high over her head. The Cubans stared in disbelief at the woman in the tight black jumpsuit who had emerged from this spaceship.

"Oswaldo Guerrero," she demanded. "Where is he?"

"You are welcome aboard the *Granma Nueva*," the man said, bowing his head. His eyes locked on hers. "This is an honor—"

"Save it." Jessica dropped her arms. "Where's Oswaldo Guerrero?"

The man touched his chest with his palm, his forearm muscles tensing. "I am O." He bowed his head. "And who are you?"

"Where's Dr. Ryker?" she demanded.

"Very well, you don't have a name. But when the American government sends me such a beautiful agent—"

"Where's Ryker?" she barked, and tightened her fists. She could smell rum on his breath.

"He is safe, my angel. Where is my package?"

"Not until I see Judd Ryker."

Oswaldo dismissed the soldiers with a wave and led Jessica

through the ship, her boots pounding hard on the steel deck. They passed through a hallway, down a flight of stairs, to a heavy door. Jessica ducked her head to enter the cabin.

She was expecting the worst but was surprised to find Judd sitting happily at a table covered with dirty plates and empty bottles.

"Dr. Ryker?" she asked.

Judd flashed a momentary look of relief but maintained a steady poker face. "Ma'am," he said as stiffly as he could.

"Dr. Ryker, your cavalry is here," Oswaldo announced with a wide smile. "You *yanquis* and your cowboys!" He turned to Jessica. "You can see your Dr. Ryker is very safe. Now, where's my money?"

"In the chopper."

"Unmarked, nonsequential bills?"

Jessica nodded. "Everything all right here, Dr. Ryker?" She raised her eyebrows and pursed her lips, the same face she made when her children were naughty.

"Yes, ma'am. Now that you're here, now that the money is here, everything is *perfect*." Judd turned to Guerrero. "Isn't that right, O? We're done. Now that you have your money, we have a deal."

"I knew you *yanquis* were rich. That you could make money appear from the sky. Delivered by an angel. I knew it, Dr. Ryker. Just like your movies. Twenty-five million dollars." He snapped his fingers.

"We have a deal," Judd said, standing up to leave. "You have your money. You'll release the hostages and take care of . . . the other business you promised."

Jessica cleared her throat and both men turned to face her. "About the money . . ." she said. "I brought *ten* million, not twenty-five."

Judd's eyes widened and his heart sank.

"You think . . . you can play games with me, *yanqui*?" Oswaldo hissed, his eyes darkening.

"Just ten?" Judd rubbed his neck.

"Don't play that cowboy game with me, Dr. Ryker. Our deal is dead. You are all dead."

"Oswaldo"—Judd placed both his hands on the table— "we've been talking for the past"—Judd pretended to check his watch—"twelve hours. We've made a breakthrough. Ten million is a lot of money. Don't get greedy now. Are you going to throw that all away?"

"Our deal was *twenty-five* million." Oswaldo turned his back and reached deep into his pocket.

"O! Don't do it!" Judd said, trying to stay calm. "We have a deal. Cuba's future. Your future. What more do you want?"

"I want this!" he said, spinning around. Judd blinked just as Jessica grabbed Oswaldo's arm, twisted him around, and forced him to the floor in a flashbang of violent grace. A metallic clang rang out as a heavy object hit the floor.

"What are you doing, *mi bella*?" Oswaldo laughed to himself as Jessica dug her knee into his back.

The Rykers both glared at the object—not a gun but a satellite phone.

"A phone?" Jessica said.

"Call Parker," Oswaldo groaned. "That's what I want."

"You want me to . . . call Landon Parker?" Judd's heart was still pounding as Jessica released Guerrero from her clutches.

"Of course. When you needed money a few hours ago"—
Guerrero stood up and brushed off his pants—"you called him."
He snatched the phone off the floor. "You called him with *this*
phone. And then"—Oswaldo winked at Jessica and flashed his
gold-toothed smile—"this angel flew from the clouds onto my
ship with ten million dollars in cash. Do it again."

"I don't think it's that easy to just . . . reach him," Judd said,
shaking his head.

"Yes. It is. This is a *magic* phone," Oswaldo said with a shrug.
He pushed redial. "I'm calling Landon Parker. As you did." Oswaldo pressed his ear to the speaker. "It's ringing."

Judd and Jessica exchanged glances of surprise as the phone
in Jessica's pocket erupted in song.

Oswaldo Guerrero glared at Jessica, then down at her ringing pocket, then at his phone. His expression turned to a snarl.
"What kind of *yanqui* trick is this?"

76.

The abrupt light broke the darkness. The clang of the cell door jolted the men awake.

"*Mueve se!*" a guard shouted, poking the end of his gun into Dennis Dobson's ribs. "Move it!"

Deuce groaned and held his shoulder, still pulsing with pain from where the Cuban navy doctor had removed the bullet.

Crawford Jackson scampered to his feet and stepped between them. "Hey, man! What are you doing?"

"*Silencio!*" The guard shoved Crawford away and waved his weapon menacingly at the others.

"Easy . . . Easy . . ." Brinkley Barrymore III held up his hands. "*No problema . . . No problema, señor.*"

"What do you *hijos de puta* want now?" Alejandro Cabrera growled.

"Al, please," Brinkley pleaded. "Not helpful."

"I don't give a fuck," Al said, standing up to full height and leering at the guard.

"*Mueve se!*" the guard scowled, pointing his gun at Alejandro. "Let's go, *yanqui* spies! Move it! *Mueve se!*"

"They think we're spies, Brink!" Dennis cried as Crawford helped his friend to his feet.

"*Dónde vamos, señor?*" Brinkley asked.

"*Silencio!*" the guard snapped, and rammed the butt of his gun into Brinkley's gut. The lawyer doubled over, the wind knocked out of him, coughing and spitting.

"*Puta!*" Alejandro snarled, and rushed the guard.

Within seconds, more guards flooded the cell and wrestled all four men to the floor. The Americans' hands were all tied behind their backs and they were wrenched back to their feet. Each was blindfolded and then they were led roughly out of the cell in single file.

"Where're they taking us, Brink?" Dennis begged blindly. "Where?"

"Shut up, Deuce," Alejandro quipped. "They took our brave brothers to the firing squad. Go with honor."

"What?" Dennis shrieked. "What firing squad?"

"*Silencio!*" a guard ordered as he punched Alejandro in the kidneys.

"Be strong. It's gonna be all right," Crawford whispered.

"We aren't spies!" Dennis wailed. "Tell them, Brink! Tell them!"

"Shut the fuck up!" Alejandro barked.

"They're just messing with us, Brink?" Dennis wept. "Are they gonna kill us, Brink? Or is this a trick? We're gonna be okay, right?"

"I don't know, Dennis," Brinkley said as they were shoved out the door, forced to walk deeper into the darkness. "I just don't know."

77.

I s this another dirty *yanqui* trick?" Oswaldo's body shuddered with anger.

"No tricks, Oswaldo." Judd held up his hands.

Guerrero bent over and pulled a Makarov pistol from an ankle holster.

"What are you doing?" Judd gasped.

"Don't give me more of your American bullshit," Oswaldo spat, flashing the Soviet-era handgun. "You never called Landon Parker, you called . . . her!" Oswaldo pointed the Makarov straight at Jessica's head.

"Oswaldo!" Judd stepped in front of Jessica. "Listen to me. You're drunk. We have a deal. A good deal. For you and for Cuba. You don't want to do this."

"You lied," he hissed. "Just like all the others before you. Stinking *yanqui* liar."

"You're right. I never called Parker. *But your money is here.* Your money was delivered as we agreed. We still have a deal, Oswaldo."

"Twenty-five million was our deal, not ten! You think I'm a fool? You think Cuba will fall again for your tricks? You think false promises with a few beers can outsmart me? There's a reason your CIA calls me El Diablo. Our deal is dead."

Oswaldo aimed the pistol directly at Judd's chest.

"You are both . . . *dead*."

78.

The Deputy Director never felt so alive. He had tipped the taxi driver generously and was now sitting in the driver's seat of his wife's Audi, feeling smug satisfaction over the events of that evening. Operation Triggerfish had gone as smoothly as he could have hoped. All his moving parts—the money, the planes, the teams of operatives, his candidate—had come together under his personal direction. He was a chess master. He was on the verge of triumph.

His deployment of Jessica Ryker had been an especially brilliant move, he thought to himself. She was the perfect operative to send into Cuba for the money drop. Yes, he was going to definitively exorcise the ghost of Randolph Nye and the Bay of Pigs. He was going to be the one to redeem the CIA after half a century of failure in Cuba. He was finally going to beat Oswaldo Guerrero.

The only unplanned incident so far that day had been his rendezvous with Brenda Adelman-Zamora at the Willard Hotel. A delicious, warm-blooded bonus, he decided. "Maybe you'll go higher," she had suggested. "Like the next Director of National Intelligence." For the first time, he allowed himself to consider the possibility.

The Deputy Director turned over the ignition and popped open the glove compartment. He reinserted the batteries in his cell phones, humming to himself and feeling on top of the world.

As the phones sprung back to life, they flashed a long list of urgent messages. All the warmth in his heart turned to ice.

Charlie 3 reporting no show from Alpha 99

Alpha 99 not responding

Bravo 0 hospitalized

Alpha 99 still not responding

Charlie 3 aborting

Oscar Sierra 2 aborting

Yankee Tango 4 aborting

Alpha 99 gone black

Triggerfish dead

79.

Nothing is dead, Oswaldo." Judd stepped slowly toward the Cuban intelligence chief. "Our deal is still very much alive. You have ten million dollars now."

"No," Oswaldo insisted, pushing the pistol into Judd's chest. "Our deal was twenty-five."

"That's right. And you'll get the other fifteen. After you deliver."

"After?" Oswaldo took a step back.

"We never pay it all up front," Jessica said, sliding out from behind Judd. "Dr. Ryker should have explained. In the United States, we always insist on"—she looked straight at her husband—"aligned incentives."

"Incentives?" Oswaldo narrowed his eyes and looked Jessica up and down. "Who *are you*?"

"She's my partner," Judd said, shielding his wife again. "And she's right. In America, deals work best when both sides are— how do I put this?—*motivated*. Ten million now. You'll get the rest once everything else is done."

Oswaldo Guerrero didn't respond.

"We still have a deal," Judd said, unsure what was going through Oswaldo's mind. "This is all in your interest. And in ours."

The silence was broken by a soft chuckle. Oswaldo's laugh built louder and then he stopped abruptly. "Self-interest promotes the common good," he said.

"That's . . . right." Judd nodded as he and Jessica exchanged glances.

"Man is an animal that makes bargains," Oswaldo announced.

Jessica shot Judd a look of confusion.

"No complaint is more common than that of a scarcity of money!" Oswaldo bellowed, waving the gun wildly.

Judd shrugged back at Jessica.

"Little else is requisite to carry a state to the highest degree of opulence from the lowest barbarism but peace, easy taxes, and a tolerable administration of justice," Oswaldo declared. "All the rest comes about by the natural course of things!"

Judd's face suddenly relaxed. "Adam Smith . . . ?"

"A good soldier always studies his enemy, Dr. Ryker," Oswaldo said with a hint of a grin. "He seems appropriate at this moment, no?"

"So, are you saying . . ." Judd said as the fear and bewilderment in his chest was being replaced by a warming satisfaction ". . . we have a deal?"

Oswaldo shoved the pistol into his waistband and stuck out his hand. "Even communists respond to incentives."

PART FOUR

~~~~~~~~~

SATURDAY

80.

Oswaldo, you look terrible, my friend." The president was already at his desk, dressed in a freshly pressed battle-green suit with an open-neck collar. In front of him was the daily Communist Party newspaper, *Granma*, unopened, and his usual breakfast of half a grapefruit. "Did you drink too much Santiago rum last night?"

"I'm sorry, Comrade Presidente." Oswaldo bowed his head. "I've been awake all night, dealing with these foolish *yanqui* hostages."

The president shook his head. "I slept like a baby." Then he flashed a smile and waved his hand over his breakfast. "Come, eat!"

"No time for breakfast, Comrade Presidente. Security of the revolution never rests."

"But you must have something to eat, my friend."

Oswaldo finally conceded with a shrug. "I'll pour us coffee, Comrade Presidente. Thank you."

Oswaldo ambled over to a floral table by the window, set with a pot of strong coffee and a bowl of sugar. "Another beautiful day in our *Cubita bella*, no?" he said as he poured two cups.

"Yes, yes," the president said cheerily.

"How is El Jefe today?"

"My brother is the same. His body is alive, but his mind has died. The doctors tell me he could go on like this for years. The doctors say he could even recover."

"We have the world's best doctors," Oswaldo said, "so perhaps . . ."

"My brother will never be the same"—the president bowed his head—"I have accepted it. The nation will need to accept it. The revolution will need to accept it."

"The revolution never rests, Comrade Presidente."

"Now, tell me about these *yanquis*. What are we going to do?"

Oswaldo turned his back to the president as he dropped a spoonful of sugar in each coffee. "I've already let them go."

"They're gone?" the president gasped.

"They are already in America."

"America?"

"Gone, Comrade Presidente," he said as he slipped a white cube from his pocket into one of the coffees. He turned around to face the president, holding both cups triumphantly. "They were nothing. Just some foolish *yanqui* cowboys. I put them on a plane and sent them back to Washington."

"Washington?"

"Yes, Comrade Presidente. It's over."

"I don't understand, Oswaldo," the president said, accepting one of the coffees. "You told me this was important. These hostages were dangerous. They were *yanqui* spies sent to disturb our new friendship with Washington. That they were leverage for getting more from the Americans."

"I didn't say they weren't leverage, Comrade Presidente." Oswaldo took a sip.

"Ahhh!" The president sat back in his chair and laughed from deep down in his belly. "Of course! Of course! You are Oswaldo! You must have tricked the Americans! Or you got something valuable, didn't you?" He sat forward and slurped a healthy gulp of coffee. "Ahhh! What did we get, Oswaldo? What did we get? A prisoner exchange? Ships of wheat? Baseball? What?"

"Something much more valuable than any of those things," Oswaldo said, a smile forming on the edges of his mouth.

"What's more valuable than"—the president winced and grabbed his chest—"baseball?"

Oswaldo watched the president cough and sputter. As the old man gasped desperately for air, Oswaldo calmly took a sip of coffee before answering the question, the final words the president would ever hear. "Independence, my friend. Total independence."

81.

he! Che! Che!

Ernesto could hear the chanting in his head even before he arrived at the Plaza de la Revolución. He could imagine the people—*his people*—singing his name. As he sat in the backseat of the vintage Cadillac, waiting to be driven to the rally, he peered through his reading glasses at the speech sitting on his lap.

The Cuban Revolution is ready for the next phase! We have achieved so much, but the time for something new has arrived . . .

Ernesto hadn't slept much since landing late the night before. The woman at the airport, one of Ruben's people, had brought him to a safe house for rest and this morning had deposited him in the back of an electric-blue 1955 Cadillac Eldorado.

He was excited for the rally in the heart of Santiago, the historical epicenter of political opposition in Cuba, the site where he was to make his own history, to launch his own campaign. He was ready for the new stage of his long, strange journey.

But Ernesto was also nervous. After so many years in Africa, working in the slums, healing the sick, living close to the people, he was now venturing into wholly new waters.

The empty shelves are a potent symbol of what has gone wrong with the revolution. Corruption is eating the revolution from within, yet it is the people who cannot eat! . . .

Ruben had assured him those reasons were exactly why he was the perfect candidate. His big brother had made a convincing case that Ernesto's national service, his years in Angola, his humility, his selfless patriotism, his simple life—these truths all made Dr. Ernesto Sandoval *a man of the people.*

It was all correct, Ernesto decided. He was a simple, honest man. He could restore the country to greatness without tearing it apart. He could bridge the revolutionaries in Havana with the exiles in Miami. He was precisely what Cuba needed.

A government that cannot deliver bread, cannot deliver on the promise of the revolution . . .

His nagging anxiety was jumping from the quiet life of medicine into the shark tank of Cuban politics.

We must have free elections in Cuba! Our leaders must be chosen by the people! We must have a new government in Havana! . . .

Yes, Che Guevara had been a doctor and had famously leapt from obscurity into politics. From medicine onto the international stage. So, too, had former presidents of Chile, Malawi, Brazil, Uruguay, even the first president of Angola.

Che! Che! Che!

But what did he really know about campaigning? What did he know about rallying the masses? What did Ernesto Sandoval know about running a country?

Ruben had dismissed these questions out of hand.

"Don't worry, *mi hermanito*," his brother had assured him. "This is your time. We will help you. You just read the script. We will run the campaign. We will organize your supporters. We will bring out the people. We will win. And then we will govern."

The question that Ernesto didn't ask but was now burning in his brain this morning: *Who, exactly, is 'we'?*—

"We are not ready yet, Dr. Che," the woman said from the front seat, interrupting his thoughts.

He wrinkled his forehead. "I'm ready to give the speech," he said, waving the papers. "I'm ready to go to the Plaza de la Revolución! I'm ready to rally my people!"

"I'm sorry"—she bowed her head—"we're going to have to delay, Dr. Che."

"Delay?" he said, suddenly feeling nauseated again.

"Postpone, I mean. We will have to try again for a rally on . . . another day."

"Another day?" Ernesto was confused. The acid in his stomach flared and he was short of breath. "I flew here all the way from Africa for this. Everything was supposed to be in place."

"I'm sorry, Dr. Che, no one is in the plaza."

"It's . . . empty?"

"We had a problem."

"What kind of problem?"

"The cells were not mobilized in time."

"Cells? You spoke of these cells last night. What cells?"

"Sometimes," she shrugged, "the money doesn't arrive in time."

Ernesto cocked his head to one side. *Money?*

82.

oney! The image of all that cash swirled around inside Oswaldo's pounding head. *I've never seen so many gringo dollars,* he thought. The full duffel bag in the trunk of his car was on his mind, pounding like a bass drum, as he pulled up to the gate of the Playa Baracoa Air Base.

He had already visited the secret police headquarters, the commander of the presidential guard, the minister of the Cuban Revolutionary Armed Forces, the Party secretary, and the director of the state television studio. The air base was his last stop.

At the gate, the uniformed soldier saluted and waved him through. Oswaldo drove directly to the office of the base commander, a man he had known since they were boys in the Union of Rebel Pioneers. As he expected, the commander was waiting for him on the veranda, standing at attention.

"At ease, Commander," Oswaldo ordered, prompting the man to relax his shoulders. The two men embraced warmly.

"Are the rumors true, Comrade Oswaldo?"

"What rumors are those, Miguel?"

"El Comrade Presidente"—he lowered his voice to a whisper—"is gone."

Oswaldo bowed solemnly and nodded. He took a deep breath. "Sudden heart attack. I was with him when he passed away. Just this morning. That's why I'm here now."

"He's really dead?"

"I've just come from the state television studio, where I've cleared the official statement. They will make the public announcement at nine o'clock."

"Nine o'clock?" the commander gasped, checking his watch. "So soon? Isn't that risky? Wouldn't it be better to control the information?"

"No, Miguel. It's too late for that. The rumors are already on the streets. Already in the barracks. What kind of state secret could we keep if even you, Miguel, have already heard, no?" Oswaldo pretended to be irritated, but he knew all too well how Miguel had already known about the president's death.

"What about the Party? Has the politburo decided what to do next?"

"No. El Comrade Presidente was very clear with his final wishes. Once he was gone, he wanted Cuba . . . to hold free elections."

"Elections? Oswaldo, had he gone mad? Have you all gone mad? That is just what the imperialists want! Elections will bring chaos!"

"That's what El Comrade Presidente wished. He insisted that elections were the next phase of the glorious revolution. The will of the people must be heard. That's what I have told the politburo. That's what we are going to require of the army. To enforce the will of revolution."

"You are ordering the army to enforce free elections?"

"Yes, Miguel! That's why I'm here. And that's why I now must go!" Oswaldo said as he turned to leave.

"Where are you going now, Oswaldo?"

"To the airfield! I need a plane, Miguel!"

"Take the presidential jet. It's ready. And now—"

"No, Miguel," Oswaldo scolded, "That would be disrespectful. I need something modest for this important journey."

"I have a Cessna we captured from the terrorist traitors in Miami."

"Yes, Miguel! I will fly myself in the Cessna!"

"But to where, Oswaldo?"

"I need to inform our closest friends and to seek their continued support for the revolution!"

"Venezuela or Bolivia?"

"Yes, Miguel! I'll be back!" he said as he ran out the door.

But in his mind, Oswaldo knew he was taking the plane on a one-way journey to Costa Rica. To a secret jungle airfield in the southwest of that country. To a modest villa high in the mountains above the little village of Ojochal. For six months. To lay low, out of sight. Before he and his duffel bag full of all those American dollars could move, incognito, to Madrid or Mexico City. Or maybe even one day . . . to Florida.

83.

Jessica glared at the screen on her phone, unsure of her next move.

She and Judd had flown back from the *Granma Nueva* to the United States in silence. The only words were Judd's as they took off:

"So, you fly helicopters?"

Jessica had just nodded in response, and thrust the cyclic control stick forward, pitching the Raider's nose down and shooting them both back toward Florida, toward their children, closer to their next, unavoidable, confrontation.

Judd and Jessica were both processing what had just happened. Each was still unsure whether his or her own mission was fulfilled or not. The Rykers each stared ahead, recalling the chain of recent events, counting the lies, reliving how close they came to being killed in that floating Cuban tin can. How they nearly wound up dead and dumped in the Caribbean by the Devil of Santiago. Both still unclear what they had just accomplished. Or what was coming next.

Just as the sun peeked over the horizon, they had crossed back into American airspace and landed at Homestead Air Reserve Base. They then drove in the rented Mustang convertible north, past Miami, back to Fort Lauderdale. Again, in total silence.

Four times on the seventy-minute car journey Jessica's phone had rung. Each time, DANIEL DOLLAR flashed on her little screen. Each time, she pushed DIVERT TO VOICEMAIL. *Not yet,* she told herself.

Once back at the house, she had dismissed Aunt Lulu and put *Justice League* cartoons on the television for her children, then climbed in bed for a hard-earned nap. Judd had joined her, too, exhausted from the all-nighter, drained from the agony of their unresolved chess game.

Now, waking in crisp sheets next to her husband but still yet to face him, she glared at that tiny screen, knowing that it was better to get this first battle over. Before turning to the bigger one with Judd.

She got up without waking her husband and walked out onto the terrace, overlooking the water. She dialed a number.

"Coney Island Pizza."

Jessica took a deep breath. "I have a special order for urgent delivery."

"We're closed."

"Closed?" she asked. "What—"

The phone went dead.

Before Jessica could redial or react, she heard a loud, gruff voice calling her name from inside.

"Someone's in the house!" Judd was up.

"It's okay," she said, coming back into the bedroom.

"I definitely heard someone in the house!" he said. He threw open the closet door and grabbed a 3 iron golf club.

"Judd," she said calmly, placing her hand on his shoulder, "it's okay. I will deal with this."

"Jessica Ryker!" bellowed the voice again from downstairs.

"And when I'm done dealing with this," she said, "we'll take the boys to the beach and we can finally talk. We can sit in the sun. We can figure it all out. Okay?"

"Jessica Ryker!" boomed the voice.

"I'm going to do this now," she said. She stepped out of the bedroom and closed the door.

"It's about fucking time," the intruder said just as Jessica appeared at the bottom of the stairs.

"I was sleeping. You just walked in."

"It's my fucking house," said the Deputy Director.

She nodded.

"What did you do?" he said, shaking his head.

"Excuse me, sir?"

"You were supposed to hand over the cash to Charlie at Bacanao, but you never arrived. You fucked the whole thing up. You killed Operation Triggerfish."

"Sir, did you come all the way down here for a live after-action?"

"Tampa says you cut them off, you stole the Raider, and they think you delivered the money to someone else in Cuba. I told them, *No fucking way*. I told them there was no way that my best operative, the one I created from nothing, the one who owes me everything, would abandon my mission. There was no fucking way that my best operative kicked the living shit out of contact

Bravo. There was no fucking way that my best operative flew our most advanced secret helicopter onto a Cuban naval ship. There was no fucking way that you would kill the most important mission of my career, the one that was going to finally bring down ECP and the communists in Havana once and for all. There was no fucking way, after so many years of failure, that you would destroy our best chance to finally win Cuba back. I came all the way down here because there was no fucking way that you would betray me by taking my money and giving it to the fucking *Devil of Santiago*!"

"I didn't give them the Raider, sir."

"How did you know they wouldn't just take it? How did you know they wouldn't fly it to Caracas? That it wouldn't already be in Moscow?"

"Ricky's lucky I didn't kill him. You know he tried to kill me?"

"That's not what Bravo reported."

"You know that Bravo's real name is Ricardo Cabrera? That he's the brother of the Alejandro Cabrera. That he's working for Ruben Sandoval? And he—"

"I don't know who those people are, Jessica," he cut her off. "Don't try to lose me in irrelevant details. Remember who you're talking to. I'm not falling for it. Stop deflecting blame."

"You know Bravo blew up your boat?"

"What? My Cobalt?"

She made an explosion gesture with her hands. "Gone."

"We're talking about Triggerfish, Jessica!"

"I didn't kill Triggerfish either, sir."

"Tell me one fucking piece of the operation that you did not

kill? The whole thing has gone to shit. And wherever I see something that went wrong, all I see is . . . you."

"I didn't betray you, sir."

"You can lie to your goddamn husband, Jessica, but you can't
lie to me!"

"You're right. I gave the money to Oswaldo Guerrero. That's
true."

"I knew it!"

"Judd needed to get the hostages back."

"I don't fucking believe my ears!" he huffed. "You're conspir-
ing with your husband!" He paused and narrowed his eyes. "Are
you working for that little prick, Landon Parker?"

"No, sir. I gave the money to Guerrero in order to accomplish
the mission."

"Your mission was to deliver the cash to people who would
bring him down, not hand the money over to the enemy."

"Sir, ECP is gone. People are on the streets. Cuba's going to
hold an election. Isn't that what you wanted? Wasn't that the
objective of Triggerfish?"

"You don't have the big picture, Jessica. You never did. That's
the whole point of running an operation like this. That's the
whole point of needing everyone to just do their job. That's why
I can't have my people second-guessing me. You can't run your
own rogue operation! Not again, Jessica!"

"Cuba's having an election. How is that not mission success, sir?"

"Do you have any idea what you've unleashed?"

"No, sir."

"That's the point! No one knows. And the fucking icing on

the fucking cake is that you gave my money to Oswaldo Guer-rero? Of all people, Jessica. How am I supposed to explain this to Congress?"

"Do you mean Brenda Adelman-Zamora?" Jessica couldn't contain her smirk.

"What do you know about her?" he shot back.

"I know all about her, sir," she said.

"Why are you smiling? How do you know about Brenda? Do you have someone planted at the Willard?"

"Excuse me?"

"Are you *following* me?"

"Sir . . ." Jessica paused and pursed her lips. "I don't know . . . anything about that hotel. I . . . don't think I want to know. I'm talking about illegal campaign finance. I'm talking about her congressional campaign . . . accepting donations from secret sources. Her campaign has been secretly receiving money seized from drug traffickers during Operation Everglades."

"How do you know about that?"

"I witnessed it with my own eyes."

The Deputy Director looked Jessica up and down. "What are you going to do with that information?"

"Me?" Jessica feigned horror. "I'm not going to do anything. But if Adelman-Zamora tries to make trouble for you—I mean, trouble for *us*—about how Triggerfish went down, you could re-mind her that we know about it"—Jessica shrugged—"and that the Justice Department doesn't."

"You're just telling me this? As leverage? To blackmail a mem-ber of the United States Congress?"

"Sir, I'm simply sharing this information with you. I don't

need to know what you do with it. Consider it a present . . . In gratitude for everything you've done for me . . . And for what happened to your boat."

The Deputy Director rubbed his head and paced the foyer. Then he stopped short. "You are calculating, Jessica Ryker."

"You just said it yourself, sir. I'm your best operative."

"So, now what? You expect me to just forget everything that's happened? You want a Presidential Medal or something?"

Jessica shrugged again.

"You want me to reinstate Purple Cell? Is that it?"

"Right now, sir, the only thing I want is to take my family to the beach."

"That's all?"

"And fifteen million dollars. In untraceable cash."

"What?"

"To complete our deal with Guerrero. And I know exactly where to get it."

84.

This is a glorious day!" Brenda Adelman-Zamora tapped the microphone on the lectern twice to quiet the crowd. "We have much to celebrate today!" she crowed, bursting with excitement. The stage was tightly packed with exhausted-looking wives and children standing behind four men in golf shirts and khakis. Alejandro Cabrera, Brinkley Barrymore, Crawford Jackson, and Dennis Dobson stood awkwardly under the lights.

"Let's take a moment to applaud these brave men who have come home to their families," Adelman-Zamora said, leading the crowd in a standing ovation, punctuated with hoots and howls from the floor. Alejandro winked at the cameras while Crawford gave the crowd an embarrassed nod. Brinkley stared straight ahead, stone-faced, like a zombie.

"Their release early this morning is a victory for justice and a reminder to the world that America will not waver in the face of aggression. We held firm to our policy of never giving in to blackmail, never paying ransom for innocent civilians. We stared the Devil in the eye and we did not blink!"

Adelman-Zamora stepped in between the men, grabbed Dennis Dobson's good hand, and raised it in triumph, igniting more applause and flashbulbs. Dennis squinted and recoiled.

The congresswoman returned to the podium. "Now these courageous American heroes want to get home with their beautiful families as soon as possible. And we are so honored to have all of them with us today. I especially want to thank Pippa, Mariposa, Vanessa, and Beth for your sacrifice and your bravery. You have shown the world that strong families can help to defeat oppression. That strong women can keep us all on the path toward freedom. That love is stronger than tyranny."

The four wives nodded to the press. Pippa Barrymore took a step forward, pressed her hands together in a praying gesture of thanks to the congresswoman and then stepped back in line. Adelman-Zamora accepted the gratitude with a solemn nod and a tapping fist over her heart.

"These men have chosen not to speak to the press today. After all they have been through, we must respect that. But they have asked me, on their behalf, to thank the American people for their prayers and for their support through Twitter and Facebook. They are ecstatic to be home safe. They look forward to putting this episode behind them and to returning to their normal lives."

The congresswoman rubbed her hands together for her big finish. "Before we close, we have something else to celebrate this morning. A few minutes ago, Cuban state television confirmed that the leader of that nation has passed away. The era of the aging tyrants who have run Cuba since 1959 has finally come to an end. We are also seeing on social media that the Cuban people are now coming out onto the streets of Havana, Santiago, and every city and town across that country, to pay their respects and to call for democratic elections within ninety days. The people's yearning to be free is unwavering. The force of democracy is unstoppable.

"This is a pivotal moment for Cuba and for the United States. I have spoken this morning with the State Department and they stand ready to deliver a package of support for the elections to ensure the people's will is expressed and the transition is smooth. We expect an announcement later today from Assistant Secretary Melanie Eisenberg with more details.

"I want to stress that the United States supports the democratic process in Cuba rather than any one candidate. We should expect patriotic Cubans from within the country and those living abroad to step forward and help lead their country into a new era. We welcome their bravery and we wish them Godspeed. The days of Cuba's leaders being chosen by fraternal blood or in the back rooms of the Communist Party are over.

"If Cuba's elections are indeed free and fair and the results reflect the desire of the Cuban people, our two great nations will finally be on a path to true friendship. If the rule of law is respected and the rights of private property owners are restored, then Cuba will truly be on a path to rejoining the international community.

"Upon completion of open and democratic elections, I will introduce the Zamora Amendment in the U.S. Congress. This legislation will provide for the immediate lifting of all remaining sanctions and a generous recovery program. This is a window of opportunity that Cuba and America must seize."

Adelman-Zamora raised her fist. *"Viva Cuba Libre!"*

85.

What do you mean they aren't coming?" Ernesto Sandoval was almost in tears, nearly crying into the phone. "I've been so patient. All these years waiting, waiting. Building a life, a simple life in Africa, but it was mine. And I left it all behind to come back. I gave it all up for a promise. Your promise. And now that I'm here, you're telling me . . . no crowds?"

"*Mi hermano*, please. I didn't say no crowds. Just not yet."

"When, Ruben? How am I launching a campaign to become the next president of Cuba without the people? I don't understand. What happened to the crowds? What happened to the money?"

"The people are in the streets now."

"They aren't on the streets for me. That wasn't how it was supposed to be. You promised me, *hermano*, that you'd take care of everything."

"I will find a way, Che. We will have a campaign. I will get the money. I will get the crowds for you. For us."

"I don't know, Ruben."

"The Americans have already announced an election package. The rest I will get myself. I promise, Che. We will do it. We will fight. And we will win. *Viva Cuba Libre!*"

86.

Daddy! Daddy! Daddy! Are you just talking to *Mommy* all morning? I wanna swim!"

"In a minute, Toby," Judd said. "Give me a minute and then I'll take you in the ocean. I promise." Judd's older son hung his head and walked back over to Noah, who was digging a hole in the sand.

"Maybe we should do this *later*?" Jessica offered. "Take your son swimming. Play in the waves. We can deal with everything later. It's not going anywhere. I'll finish *Treasure Island*. I'm almost at the end, where we learn Long John Silver is the secret ringleader."

Judd considered his wife's suggestion. These conversations were always better when Judd could focus, no interruptions from his kids, no being pulled away, no distractions. And he knew he was in a position of extreme weakness. How could he possibly be mad at Jessica while she was lying next to him on a towel, a halo of understated beauty in a red bikini and a Washington Nationals baseball cap?

But after so many days of scheming, of overthinking every detail, and then nothing had gone according to plan, he felt anxious.

"Let's do it now," he said.

Jessica set the book facedown on her lap and removed her sunglasses. "Where do you want to start, sweets?"

Judd looked up the beach. Clusters of people had claimed their little patches of sand. He noticed a density pattern among the sunbathers, weighted higher near the public entrances. There must be an implicit mathematical formula for choosing your spot on the beach, he thought. Distance from the parking lot multiplied by the weight you're carrying divided by the average distance from other people . . ."

"Judd?"

He snapped out of it. "Yes, Jessica?"

"I said where do you want to start?"

Judd blinked and regathered his thoughts. "That . . . was a close call with Oswaldo Guerrero, wasn't it?"

"Yes, it was."

"Who knew a redial button could be so dangerous?" Judd offered to cut the tension.

Jessica nodded.

"I didn't know," he said. "And . . . I didn't know you were a helicopter pilot."

"A little," she shrugged.

"What else can you fly? An airplane? Can you . . . drive a tank?"

Jessica winced. "Is that really what you want to ask me?"

"I didn't want to call you," Judd said.

"I know, baby."

"Uncertainty, backchannel, cash, candidate," he said, counting out the four on his fingers, "that was my formula for Cuba. Landon Parker was on board. He just couldn't say so."

"Could be," she nodded.

"That's why the hostage negotiations were the spark. The cover he needed. The excuse to get me into the country, face-to-face with O."

"I guess so," she said.

"I nearly finished it myself."

"I know you did, sweets. I know you did."

"I didn't *want* to call you," Judd said. "I didn't need your help."

"I know," she said. "I get it."

"But I did," he said. "I needed you to find millions of dollars. To come get me."

"That's my job. You'd do it for me."

"I mean, I had no idea when I called you, how you'd get the money, much less how you'd deliver it all the way out there in the middle of the ocean. On a Cuban naval ship. But I called you and had faith. So I asked. And you did it."

Jessica blinked and wet her lips with her tongue.

"But I should have done it on my own. For Landon Parker. For S/CRU. For me. For us."

"I understand, Judd."

"Assist, avoid, admit," Judd said, "the Ryker rules of engagement. I know we agreed that we could assist each other, but—"

"Aunt Lulu isn't my aunt!" Jessica blurted out.

"What?"

"She's not my aunt."

"I figured," he said.

"And the man who burst into the house this morning and woke us up—"

"He's got nothing to do with your college friend, does he?"

"No. Sharon was a lie, too. That was my boss this morning. We're staying in his place," she said.

"Okay . . ."

"I didn't want to lie to you, Judd, but I couldn't help it. That's why I'm telling you now. Neither of us are perfect."

Judd shook his head in agreement. "What else? Any more lies you need to get off your chest?"

"Eight."

"Eight lies? You counted them?"

"Since Tuesday. Eight. How about you?"

Judd started to run through everything that had happened over the past four days and all the people in the web—the Soccer Dad Four, Landon Parker, Melanie Eisenberg, Brenda Adelman-Zamora, Oswaldo Guerrero, Jessica Ryker—his head hurt. "None."

"So you win."

"That's not the point, Jess. We aren't in a competition. We're supposed to be a team."

"We *are* a team, Judd. We just got those four Americans free. We just helped give Cuba a chance at a better future. We succeeded, Judd. Again. And we did it together."

"We did." He nodded. "But what about . . . us? What about our rules to keep it all together? To keep our family together?"

"We have to keep trying. I'll keep trying. You too."

"So . . . who were those guys on *The Big Pig*? What were they doing?"

Jessica kissed him.

"What about Ruben Sandoval?" he asked. "And Ricardo Cabrera? Who was he working for? I still don't understand how it's all connected."

She kissed him again.

"And what about you? If you were here in Florida for your boss, what were you really doing down here, Jess?"

One more kiss, this time long and deep and soft, both eyes shut.

When she finally pulled away, he cleared his throat. "So . . . now what?" he asked.

"Tomorrow"—she shrugged—"we go home. Back to work. Back to life."

"Just like that?"

"Right now," Jessica said, picking up her book, "you're going swimming."

ACKNOWLEDGMENTS

Many friends contributed in big and small ways to this book: Mike Burk, Domingo Campuzano, Francesca Contiguglia, Mvemba Dizolele, Jim Fanjoy, Amanda Glassman, Markus Goldstein, Sara Kass, Jeffrey Krilla, and BJ Pittman. Special thanks to Aida Campuzano, a real-life Peter Pan who generously shared her private memoirs with me. I also benefitted greatly from Michael Grunwald's *The Swamp*, Wayne Smith's *The Closest of Enemies*, Peter Kornbluh's *Bay of Pigs Declassified*, and the extremely timely *Back Channel to Cuba* by William Leo-Grande and Peter Kornbluh. Huge appreciation to my always wise editor Neil Nyren and the whole team at Putnam, especially Ashley Hewlett, Elena Hershey, Anna Romig, and Alexis Sattler. Hat tip and a hug to my agent, Josh Getzler. Most of all, I'm eternally grateful for the love, support, and sensible editing from Donna Moss. *Viva!*